D0173811

Ace Books by Susan Sizemore

LAWS OF THE BLOOD

THE HUNT
PARTNERS
COMPANIONS

LAWS of the BLOOD

COMPANIONS

SUSAN SIZEMORE

ACE BOOKS, NEW YORK

LAWS OF THE BLOOD: COMPANIONS

An Ace Book / published by arrangement with
the author

PRINTING HISTORY
Ace mass-market edition / October 2001

Visit our website at
www.penguinputnam.com

Check out the ACE Science Fiction & Fantasy newsletter
and much more on the Internet at Club PPI!

ISBN: 0-441-00875-5

ACE®
Ace Books are published by The Berkley Publishing Group,
a division of Penguin Putnam Inc.,
375 Hudson Street, New York, New York 10014.
ACE and the "A" design
are trademarks belonging to Penguin Putnam Inc.

PRINTED IN THE UNITED STATES OF AMERICA

10 9 8 7 6 5 4 3 2 1

For my dear Madison.
Much love, March

Chapter 1
Necessary Evil

The companion is a vampire's property. A vampire may do with a companion as he or she will. It is death to a companion who attempts to harm a vampire.

IN THE LAND BEYOND THE FOREST, 1457

He was a Roma peasant, but the boyars across the campfire were afraid of him. He was not surprised at their fear, but having a pair of nobles in their furs and jewels, with heavy swords on their belts, come humbly into the camp of his familia, did make him curious. Curious or not, he did not make it easy for the boyars by asking them what they wanted. He sat across from them, well back from the fire so that his face was shadowed, and ate roasted chicken in silence while they got up the courage to say what it was they wanted.

The rest of his familia gathered behind the boyars, staring at them. He was aware of the eyes of his people, their thoughts and feelings, always so aware that he had stopped paying much attention to them a long time ago. He knew they feared he'd brought them trouble and hoped that he'd bring them wealth. When strangers had sought him out in the past, he'd always come back with gold. But no one had ever come to him before tonight that was not one of the Roma people.

Finally, one of the boyars tugged on his thick beard and said, "Are you the *dhamphir?*"

It was his oldest uncle in the crowd standing behind the seated boyars who cackled, and answered, "He'd better be, for he doesn't look like any Roma we've seen before."

He was tall. He was blue-eyed. But *gajo* soldiers raped Roma women all the time. Who knew who his grandfathers were? His parents, though, everyone knew who his parents were.

"He is *dhamphir.*" The words came from his mother. If she said it was true, it was true.

This assertion brought the other boyar to his feet. His jaw jutted out proudly, and his hand was on his gold-chased sword hilt. "The prince has sent us to bring you to him."

While the rest of his *familia* gasped, he considered what the boyar had said. The prince was not a man to be disobeyed, not if you didn't want your hat nailed to your head or a stake stuck up your ass. The prince sending for a Roma peasant was seriously bad news for that peasant. Unless, of course, that peasant was a *dhamphir.* But if the prince had need of a *dhamphir,* that was seriously bad news for the prince.

He did not fear the prince; he feared nothing, either mortal or demon, but he was mindful that the existence of all Roma was precarious. He would not put his familia and his tribe in danger by refusing to go with the boyars. He tossed aside chicken bones and got to his feet.

"I will go with you."

He didn't go with the boyars only because of concern for his people. He went because he wanted to see what sort of trouble Vlad the Impaler had gotten himself into.

"Do you act on your feelings, *dhamphir?*"

The prince expected no answer just yet. When he did speak, the only word the man seated before him wanted to hear was *yes.* So he waited, down on one knee, gaze on the cold stone floor, head carefully uncovered, and his body as still as death, to find what it was he would be saying yes to. It would be deadly dangerous, that was certain, otherwise the man who ruled the towns and villages and great estates would not have brought a landless road rat into his own bedroom to ask for help.

He didn't think much of the prince's bedroom. A man with the power to plunder the countryside ought to surround himself with piles of gold and silver if he was going to waste his time living inside thick stone walls. This prince didn't seem to need much more than a sure awareness of his place at the top of the world. He had a bed, a chair, and a fire in the grate behind him. The prince's clothes were rich, embroidered with pearls, but his bed hangings were shabby, and there were no rugs on the floor to ease the discomfort of a kneeling Roma with bony knees.

"I trust my feelings, always," the prince went on. Prince Vlad banged a hand down on the chair arm. His back was close to the fireplace, and he wore a heavy robe lined in thick black fur. "And my feeling about Tirgoviste is not a good one. Evil dwells there."

It was good to see that the prince was warm, but a cold chill permeated the *dhamphir* from the cold stone walls and the cold night air, but mostly from the fear he read in the great man he knelt to. Silence drew out for a while, and it occurred to him that the prince was not going to name the cursed thing that so disturbed his feelings about his capital city. The word was too dirty for his lips, perhaps?

If the prince would not speak the word, he might not want to hear it. So, practicing discretion, he said, "The vermin I hunt rarely come into walled towns. They prefer drawing their victims to isolated places."

"So I had heard." Prince Vlad gestured sharply. "If it is true that it is their nature to live like wolves, what do I care if they thin the herds of the old and crippled?"

Because the herds are humans, and mostly Roma. This prince was not shepherd to his kind, but he was. He cared.

"But if, as I suspect, the vermin move into towns, perhaps into my own court, then I will destroy them."

No, he thought. *Not you. You call on the only one who can destroy them.* He cared nothing about what went on in towns, but he cared about killing *them.* He had not stopped killing them since he first found out they were flesh and blood rather than fear and rumor.

"They never dwell alone," he said. "The true ones keep secret armies around them for protection."

"I have heard that."

From where? the *dhamphir* wondered. *Did one of them whisper into the prince's ear, feeding Vlad some truth to use the prince to unknowingly stamp out a rival? It might bear looking into, but later, after the prince's wishes were carried out.* It mattered not to the *dhamphir* who died first.

"They gather secret followers, you understand," he explained carefully. "People who appear innocent in the daylight, in the churches, in the beds of their husbands and wives, but live only to serve the darkness. The slaves carry no physical mark."

Prince Vlad leaned forward. "But you recognize them? Them and their slaves?"

"I was born knowing them."

The prince pulled off a heavy gold ring and tossed it to him. "Show that, and you will be obeyed. Do whatever you must to cleanse the city. Destroy these creatures and their slaves, or I'll put everyone within the walls to the sword."

He did not try to explain to Prince Vlad that killing all the mortals within Tirgoviste would not necessarily solve the problem. Slaves could be replaced. Though he carefully kept his gaze lowered, he rose to his feet. "I will cleanse your city of the strigoi, Lord. This I promise."

The city terrified him. Not the evil that dwelled within but the size and very sight of the place itself. He'd passed through many villages. He had lived in a castle for a while when he was a boy, walled in among dozens of people. He had found it easy enough to cope with the presence of a few hundred in the stronghold of Prince Vlad. A city, though, was like nothing he'd imagined, though he knew well enough what such a place was. Tirgoviste was not even large as such places went. He remembered laughing at the unbelievable tales of a cousin who'd been to Budapest. He'd laughed even harder when that cousin made wild claims about the Hunyadi and even the Turkoman having cities that were greater still: huge walled places with thousands and hundreds of thousands dwelling within.

He wasn't laughing now.

But he wasn't showing his fear. He always claimed

never to know fear, and did not like discovering he was wrong. He was angry with himself that a *place* could make him break out in cold sweat. There were too many streets within the thick walls, too many buildings, too many churches and inns and brothels and too, too many people. Their souls pressed against him worse than the stench of unwashed *gajo* bodies and the filth in the gutters.

The thoughts that came slithering into his head were mostly filthy as well, full of all those seven sins the priests spoke of, and some things beyond even priests' imaginings. There were very few wishes hidden away in the depths of his own heart: freedom, food, a barren woman for his bed who didn't fear him. What he wanted to do in that bed with a woman who could not give him sons bore little resemblance to many of the imaginings that assaulted him as he rode through the crowds with the guards the prince had sent with him.

The soldiers had paid him little mind on the ride to the city, and they showed him even less attention now. *They* were happy to be in Tirgoviste, their thoughts on women and drink and sleeping on straw-stuffed mattresses rather than cool earth with the stars for a blanket. *Fools,* he thought, and kept his sanity through the rest of the ride up to the castle by remembering the feel of the ground beneath him as he slept alone deep in the empty forest.

By the time they reached the castle courtyard, he knew what he must do to accept the size of the place and the shape of the seething energy bottled within. Evil thoughts came to everyone, he reminded himself, a city only held more people than the countryside. More people allowed for more sin in one place, that was all. He had work to do, and as much as he wanted, he could not block his mind off from the thoughts and emotions all around him.

So, when his guards brought him to the proud boyar who demanded to know his business in Tirgoviste, he only showed the prince's ring to the boyar and made them give him a room in the highest tower overlooking the city. There he stood alone and looked out the narrow slit window and opened himself until he was so immersed in the soul of the city that there was no place in his heart for fear. He became Tirgoviste. The process caused him to spew his guts a few times, and it made his head ache, but by the time the watchmen called out the hour of midnight, he was ready to begin his work in the city.

He went out walking. The guards gave him no protest when he said he would go alone. Who cared what a Roma did, despite the prince's orders? He grew quickly lost in the twists and turns of the street. Hordes of whores and beggars and cutpurses appeared out of the shadows, wheedling and threatening. He would not let himself flinch away from the touch of their hands, though he took neither woman or boy, gave no coin, and left a thief or two bleeding out their life in the piss-filled gutter. By dawn he had found no strigoi, but he knew what he needed to know and the first thing that must be done. Then he had only to find his way back to the castle to order it.

"It is wise of Prince Vlad to finally grant the church the honor it is due."

He smirked as he overheard the words the bishop said to the boyar as they stood in the square outside the cathedral.

"This is a fine way to celebrate the feast of the Magdalene," the boyar answered. His voice was calm, but his gaze shifted around the square, resting briefly everywhere but on the bishop and the *dhamphir* standing nearby. The boyar was a creature of Prince Vlad's court, carefully schooled in blank-faced lying, but his near panic was a silent shout against the *dhamphir*'s senses.

He did not give too much attention to the men of power and their meaningless talk. He looked around cautiously, eyes narrowed. The wide space before the great open doors of the church was decorated with banners and flowers. Tables piled with food and drink filled the square, along with the city's merchant and craftsmen families in their finest clothes. Soldiers with bright tabards over polished armor looked as decorative as the banners that fluttered from the windows. Straw and wood were set in great piles to the sides of the cathedral steps in preparation for a bonfire. The merrymaking had been going on since daybreak, and wine and ale flowed as freely as the laughter. The prince had indeed granted the people of his capital a great holiday, and they made the most of it. At a signal from the bishop, the crowd parted, making way for the parade that had been heading to this spot for hours.

Sacred music played by very bad musicians sounded at the head of a procession consisting of clergy and more of the prince's soldiers herding the poor of the city, the beggars and the whores and all the scum of the street toward the church. The tables set up outside were but measly fare, compared to the feast waiting inside the church, for heralds had announced a beggars' banquet was to be the prince's gift to the most wretched of his people to commemorate the feast day of a whore turned saint.

Those who watched the procession might be a merry

lot, but many of the rabble that had been rounded up at pike and sword point had a surly, wary look about them. There were enough foolish grins at the promise of a feast among the city's poor to keep the rest calm enough. Many of them blinked like half-blind rats, once out of their alleys and exposed to the full light of day. The stench that rose up off most of those in the procession came from more than their rags and the filth crusted on their skin. To the *dhamphir,* the taint of the strigoi came off the walking dead in hot, sick waves. His inner eye saw the invisible puppet strings stretching away from the mass of bodies toward the sleeping master who claimed their service.

But he could not see where those threads led, for they were many and tangled. This told him that there was more than one strigoi for him to hunt. It would be a hard chase to hunt several of the creatures down. This morning's work was only the opening move in the game.

The bishop and many priests doused the beggars with holy water as they were made to climb the cathedral steps. The scent of fresh-baked bread and hot, roasted meat drew the beggars forward. The soldiers and a double line of black-robed monks made sure no one strayed away from the church. The *dhamphir* followed after them. When all the poor and outlaws of the city were inside the church, the *dhamphir* tossed a lit torch inside as soldiers pushed shut the heavy cathedral doors.

The bishop did not know that kindling and pitch were spread across the floor of his beloved church and piled on top of the banquet tables. The smoke and fire would spread quickly, even quicker than the screams that began even before the doors were closed. Just to make sure, the *dhamphir* gestured. Soldiers under the command of the boyar held back the stunned crowd and clergy in the

square, while the rest of the men hurried to shift
the woodpiles and start the blaze that would consume
the cathedral from the outside. Many of the soldiers
looked sick and terrified at what they did, but they all
knew what happened to any who hesitated to obey
Prince Vlad. Better to massacre worthless dregs of the
street than risk their own impalement.

*Better to kill the slaves of a strigoi quickly and under
the sight of God,* the *dhamphir* thought. *Better to free
their souls than keep the poor bastards in the living hell
forced on them by their demon master.*

He expected to be stalked. He walked the streets of Tirgoviste alone that night and the next, not really expecting the attack to come so soon, but leaving himself open
just in case. No one came after him. He watched his
back in daylight as much as he did at night. He knew
the masters would want revenge for the death of the
slaves. The only question was whether the strigoi would
take revenge personally or send mortal minions to do
the job. Why the strigoi chose to enslave the dregs of
Tirgoviste he did not understand, but he could feel no
taint in the souls of anyone else in the city. Perhaps he
would take the knowledge of what they had planned
before he killed them. Then again, probably not. He
wasn't really interested in how their minds worked.

The boyar sent word to Prince Vlad about the exe-
cutions. The bishop sent complaints about the massacre.
Citizens kept to their homes and kept their thoughts on
the matter to themselves. The soldiers complained at the
lack of whores, and a waiting stillness settled over the
capital city. On the third day, word came from the prince
that he would come to inspect the feel of his city. The
dhamphir did not like that the prince was coming. It felt,

somehow, like a trap. His loyalty was to the Roma people, and he thought it best for the Roma people, as well as for all the *gajo*, to keep the strigoi from controlling a man who was already a harsh and heavy ruler.

So, on the third night after the burning of the church, he went out of the city to seek the scent of strigoi in the countryside. It was when he went into the forest that the trap was sprung, not for the prince, but for him.

They surrounded him in a clearing, five strigoi, more than he'd ever seen together before, more than even he could hope to defeat at one time, and a handful of their special ones: companions. He took the heart out of the youngest of the strigoi before the others fell on him. He did not expect to die quickly after what he'd done to their kind, so it was no surprise when they tied him to a tree and began beating him.

"I told you he would be too curious to stay safe within the city," Rosho told the others. "I know this one." Rosho pulled his head up and backhanded him. "I tasted his blood once." He tasted it now, licking it off his fingers. "Potent. Like wine." Rosho struck again. The blow could have taken off his head.

Rosho had not been there when he was captured. The *dhamphir* was not a man who nourished many hopes, but one of them was to never see anyone from the darkest days of his boyhood ever again. Not without the means to rip their chests open.

"You . . . tasted him?"

The strigoi female who'd spoken looked shocked, sickened. All the strigoi stared at Rosho. The *dhamphir* almost laughed at how confounded the monsters were to hear of a breach of their unholy rules.

Rosho did laugh. "His mistress was weak." He

laughed again. "I was her guest. It was hospitable to share." He gestured to the companions, and the privileged slaves backed quickly out of hearing distance. Rosho then caressed the *dhamphir*'s face, making the injuries ache even more. His jaw was broken; so were many other bones. He hurt like hell, but he would mend soon if left alone. All his injuries would. That was one of the gifts passed to him from his father. His strigoi father.

"He killed his own father," Rosho said, aware of the *dhamphir*'s thoughts. "And the mistress his father bound him to for his own good."

"Never mind his sins against his nest. He lives to destroy all our kind," the female said. "Kill him for that."

"That was the plan," one of the others said. "You were right, Rosho. We only had to puzzle him a little before his vaunted defenses slipped."

"He's dangerous all right, Pyotr," Rosho said, "but not very bright. An ignorant peasant boy." He turned to face the strigoi. "A peasant you've feared for years."

"A peasant, eh?" a new voice spoke from out of the darkness. A woman's voice, but deep and commanding.

A jolt as powerful as lightning went through the gathered monsters. Fear blossomed just below the surface of their arrogant shells. Even disdainful Rosho shrank into himself, raising all the defenses in his mind, but still terror leaked from him. From all of them. And all this from the sound of a woman's voice. Despite the pain, the *dhamphir* looked curiously into the night, wanting to see this monster's monster, willing Rosho to get out of his line of sight.

"Move away, boy," she spoke to Rosho. "Let me have a look at this prey you've taken without permission."

"Olympias, we thought—!"

"Did I give you permission to think?" the one called Olympias cut the other female off. "Did I call a hunt?"

"But he's . . . the *dhamphir!*"

"I've heard of him," Olympias answered.

"His crimes—"

"Despite what you might have heard," Olympias said coldly, "the hunters still rule the night. Stand aside, Rosho."

The strigoi moved, and he finally saw the woman they so feared. She was the tallest woman he'd ever seen, as tall as he was. She was thin, of course, but all lean gristle and muscle, with a sharply boned face and square, stubborn jaw. She was beautiful in the way a fine knife is beautiful. And her eyes—

He wished to God the moment their gazes met that he'd never looked into her eyes.

Her eyes were the night, with all the stars in it and all the flames of every fire that had ever burned.

He had never feared fire. He had never feared the strigoi. And he didn't fear her.

It was much worse than that.

The hell of it was, he knew it was the same with her. She stepped up to him, where he hung from the tree like trussed meat, and put her hands on him. She caressed him as Rosho had, but from her—

"You need to die, *dhamphir,*" she said and smiled to show her beautiful, glittering fangs. "I need to kill you." Her mouth came down on his, and her voice came into his mind, *But I won't.*

Chapter 2

"So. Who's next?"

Selena carefully avoided her mother's gaze and the implication in the oh-so-innocent question that was ostensibly about cake. She was well aware of slyly amused looks directed her way from other parts of the room and had the good grace to offer a wan smile all around. A wedding shower was dangerous ground for a single woman in her early thirties to tread, and Selena couldn't just get up and leave. She was the hostess.

Doing her bit for the family cause, she'd made the pretty lemon and coconut cake her mother was dishing out to aunts, cousins, friends, and future in-laws of the bride to be. Her austere apartment was decorated with fresh flowers, silver bells, colored balloons, white lace, and pastel ribbons. There was a crystal bowl full of rum-laced pink punch nestled between cheese and veggie

trays on the kitchen table. Presents were piled on the
china cabinet. Thirty women, dressed to impress each
other in soft summer dresses, crowed Selena's small Evanston apartment. Amid all the teasing, giggling, and
female bonding, Selena had gradually relaxed until she
was almost taken by surprise by her mother's attempt at
sly innuendo.

"It's the rum, isn't it?" she murmured to herself.

"I heard that."

Mothers had the most amazing hearing, at least hers
did. Downright preternatural.

Selena took her cake and sidled closer to the cousin
who was the object of all these mysterious Midwestern
female tribal nuptial rites. The wedding was scheduled
for the Church of the Sacred Heart, the reception for one
of the luxurious tour boats that sailed Lake Michigan
out of Navy Pier. This shower was the first of many
celebrations leading up to the Bride's Big Day. Selena
had been reluctant to get involved with wedding plans
at first, but after good long talks from both her cousin
and her godmother, she took a deep breath, plunged in
with both feet, and found that she was enjoying the
whole family-bonding thing immensely. She guessed she
had been too aloof from her roots as well as the ordinary
world in the last couple of years.

"So, Karen?" she asked the bride to be. "Did I get it
right?"

"Pretty good for an amateur," the bride acknowledged
with a sweeping look around.

Okay, so she had not been the most social member of
the clan in recent years. "At least you didn't say *old
maid*."

"Detective Crawford, I know you have guns in the
house." Karen's blue eyes returned to Selena's with a

teasing twinkle. "We are playing party games, right?"

"I keep guns in the house."

"I want games."

Selena winced. "Not the toilet paper wedding dress thing. Please say you don't want to do that."

"It's traditional."

"I don't have any extra toilet paper."

"I brought a bag."

"Fiend."

Karen giggled. "It's my party."

"And I'll cry if I want to," Selena muttered around a forkful of cake.

"Don't talk with your mouth full," her mother admonished from the other side of the table.

How did she *do* that?

Her mother gave Selena a quick once-over look, and Selena knew exactly what she was thinking: that she'd rather see her daughter dressed as a bride than as a bridesmaid.

"I'm so glad you chose green for your attendants," Selena's mom said to Karen. "They all have the coloring for it. Especially Selena."

Karen Bailey was Uncle Mike's only child: bright, pretty, just out of college, and engaged to Kevin Crawford, one of Selena's cousins on her dad's side of the family. The two families were thick as thieves, and this was not the first time a pragmatic Crawford had wed a whimsical Bailey. Selena had a decade on her cousin, but they were close. There was a strong family resemblance, Karen being a shorter, thinner, more fashionable version of the Bailey fair-skinned, red-haired, tall Celtic genes. Selena was six feet to Karen's five foot five, athletic being a kind description of Selena's large-bosomed figure. She was pleased to have been picked as a bridesmaid, and the green dress wasn't *too* ugly.

"Are you having a shoulder holster made to match?"

There was a moment's tense silence after the question was asked by one of the other bridesmaids. This young woman was a college friend of Karen's and a stranger to Selena, so the girl was unaware that her words had been annoying rather than a lame attempt at humor.

Selena had the temper to go with her flame-red hair and was well aware of the nervous looks turned on her by her relatives. *Her* relatives knew not to discuss her job. They all knew she was a Chicago cop, and some were aware she worked mostly as a homicide detective with the violent crimes unit, but they'd learned long ago that cops did not like to talk business with civilians. And cops *really* hated having their profession used for entertainment value.

Karen could get away with a joke about her having guns in the house, but for this stranger, the most polite thing Selena could manage was a stiff smile and a shake of her head. Then she gave her relatives a quick glare for worrying that she'd go off on someone who didn't know she was being rude. *You raised me to be a proper hostess, Mom,* she thought and got an amused look from her mother. Mom had not been one of the family who'd tensed up.

Selena turned to the punch bowl, only to have her hand stop in middip when her mother said, "What I'm wondering is who you're bringing as a date to the wedding, Selena."

What Selena wanted to know was why her mother was in the mood for throwing bombs at her this afternoon.

"It probably has something to do with grandchildren."

Selena spun to face the woman who'd spoken.

Aunt Catie continued without bothering to look up, "You're an only child, and you're not getting any younger."

There was a folding table set up in a corner of the living room, draped in a paisley shawl. Caetlyn Bailey sat behind it with her back to the wall, with her favorite deck of cards spread out before her. Aunt Catie was Mom's sister, and she was as colorful as Mom was prosaic. Catie was Selena's godmother, had chosen her name, and was the closest thing to a confidante Selena had among her huge family. Aunt Catie'd volunteered to do tarot readings for the shower guests and had been too busy telling fortunes to join in the conversation until now.

"The urge to mate and reproduce is an irresistible one," she went on placidly, flipping out cards in a cross pattern. "It seems your mother feels it's high time it caught up with you."

"What about that young man you were seeing a couple years ago?" her mom asked. "Catie told me all about him."

"Not all," Catie said, still turning cards and not looking at her sister.

"Catie says you've kept in touch."

He's not that young, Selena thought. *And no, we haven't.*

"He certainly understands about mating urges," Catie said. "Doesn't he, Selena?"

Selena put down the punch ladle and her empty cup to the sound of snickering female laughter. Holding her temper was getting harder by the second, but for Karen's sake, she was going to do it. Or die trying.

She turned to face the room, a big smile on her face, and rubbed her hands together briskly. "Game time!" she announced. "We're going to divide up into teams and see which team comes up with the best toilet paper wedding dress."

It was after ten o'clock when Selena finally closed the door on the last of the shower guests. Her mother and Aunt Catie had lingered to help with the cleanup, but the conversation over the dishpan had turned to recent movies and favorite television shows rather than men, mates, and babies. If the success of a party could be gauged in how long it took people to leave, Selena decided she could call the wedding shower a success. Overall, she was pleased to have played hostess but was delighted to finally be alone after a few hours in company. She'd done her bit for the wedding cause, proved that she wasn't a complete recluse, showed off her cooking skills, there were lots of leftovers in the fridge, and her apartment was the cleanest it had been in years.

The flowers and other decorations had been taken away as gifts to the other guests, so she had her place back the way she was used to, simple furniture, pale hardwood floors, uncluttered and uncomplicated. Her mother had once made the comment that she'd seen better decorated convent cells, but Selena had never had much use for possessions. The only artwork on the beige painted walls were framed reproductions of pages from the Book of Kells, gifts from Aunt Catie, reflecting the Irish side of her ancestry. Selena's television was old and mostly unused, but the stereo system that took up much of one living room wall was high-end, and high-tech.

Selena put a selection of Clapton CDs on the carousel, checked the time, and settled on the couch with a book until it was eleven o'clock on the West Coast. When the time was right, she considered going to bed instead, but she got up and turned on the computer on the desk in her bedroom. She logged on to the Internet via an anonymizer browser account rather than her regular ISP account. The chat room ran on Pacific time, which was inconvenient for someone like herself who was not a night person, but she found herself drawn to the sessions just the same. She went by the screen name Layla.

Selena hadn't exactly found this very tentative on-line community by accident, but she had found it because of some web searching while she was involved in an investigation Homicide worked with the cyber crime child porn unit. She'd discovered a talent for working on the Internet, was taking classes to improve her skills, and was seriously considering transferring to the cyber crime unit. Then again, getting off the street could fight burnout but contribute even more to the tendency toward isolation from the rest of humanity that she'd tried to combat ever since Aunt Catie commented about how weird she was getting a few months ago. Even though it was a bit incongruous, even getting involved with this Internet group was a response to turning into a hermit.

She *would not* let the bastard win!

Is it always going to be this way?

Her fingers typed and sent the words before she even knew she was thinking them. Selena stared at the screen, appalled at seeing her vulnerability and fear laid out in block-lettered black and white. The way she burned sometimes, the letters ought to be scorched into the screen with a branding iron.

The only other person in the room was Fyrstartr, who typed, What way is that?

Longing. Waiting. Wanting. Obsessed.

How long since you've been together?

Two years since I've seen my monster.

Selena didn't want to see him. If her mom and aunt hadn't brought up the subject this afternoon, if she wasn't alone with the de facto leader of this elite little group, she doubted she'd have mentioned the frustration that built without her conscious awareness that it was there. Bitterness seeped out of the place where she hid it and leaked out her fingertips.

When does it end?

Two years!? Fyrstartr responded. Selena could feel the other person's consternation in the words on the screen. **My *friend* drove me crazy with lack of attention for a year once—for my own good. Trying to save me from my fate.**

Good for your *friend*.

I LIKE my fate! Nearly drove me insane. But what was decided was for my good wasn't something I had a say in. You know how that goes.

They used a lot of euphemisms in this group. Selena didn't like all the nonsense with asterisks and code terms and veiled allusions, but she went along with it for security's sake. They weren't supposed to be talking to each other like this. They weren't even supposed to be aware of each other's existence, without permission from their "friends." Where they were and who they were was something they kept as secret as possible, from the society they lived in and from each other. *The society some of them lived in,* Selena corrected herself. Even having found them, she was still an outsider.

She typed, **My friend and I aren't friends. We have a unique relationship.**

Don't we all? The response was from DesertDog, the third person to enter the chat room. **Finally fessing up to having a jerk boyfriend, sweetheart?**

DesertDog always came off as aggressively male, despite the rules about never being gender specific in the group. Selena worried about calling herself Layla—it sounded so feminine—but she'd explained early on about being a Clapton fan and told them that was all the aka meant. She suspected that Fyrstartr was a woman, and that she lived in California. Then again, Fyrstartr might be a bearded, potbellied biker in North Dakota that ran the chat room on Pacific time to add another layer of security. You needed security when going against the rules. They were a small band of nervous rebels lost in the land of the weird. The ones currently in the chat room, which now included Ghost and Carmlaskid, were the ones who showed up on a regular basis. Then there were Moscowknight, Canuk, and Sandswimmer, whose participation was less frequent. In fact, it had been weeks since Sandswimmer'd put in a virtual appearance. What they had in common was a resentment of the way things were. There were those who proclaimed how, when they were in power, things would be different, and those like herself and DesertDog, who wanted things to be different *now!*

In Selena's case, the truth was that she wanted her involvement, however tentative, with this underneath world that she still knew so little about to simply be a bad dream. One of the things that drove her nuts about the whole situation, besides the loneliness and the sicko, perverted cravings, was how little information she'd been given by the one who'd made her a part of this unnatural lifestyle. The jerk.

They're all jerks, Selena typed. **We ought to do something permanent about them.**

The gasp wasn't audible, but Selena felt it coming

from Fyrstartr, who quickly typed, How can you say that?

'Cause Layla isn't as brainwashed as some of us, DesertDog typed back.

We're all entitled to our opinions, Ghost contributed. Or should be. Right, Layla? Free speech for all!

Don't care about making speeches, Selena typed.

Maybe what you need is to get laid, Ghost typed back.

Maybe.

Me, too.

Will you two cut it out? DesertDog wrote. We're here to plot the overthrow of the master race, right?

I want a different way of doing things, Fyrstartr wrote. What do you want?

Not to get caught being naughty, Carmlaskid chimed in. Sorry I'm late. Has the revolution started? Why don't we do this in the daytime? It'd be safer, you know. We're gonna get in trouble for this.

Speaking of which, DesertDog wrote. I heard a rumor of trouble in Denver.

What kind of trouble? Fyrstartr asked.

Somebody got

Selena began to type a question of her own, but before she could finish and press the Enter key, her ISP decided she'd had enough excitement for one evening and the connection was broken, knocking her off-line before all of DesertDog's post appeared. Selena swore. After ten minutes of trying to get back on-line, she shut off the computer.

Her curiosity was aroused, but a glance at the clock and the knowledge that she had to work the next day kept her from trying to make technology cooperate any longer. She'd already surprised herself and said too much with only Fyrstartr around. No need to risk opening up even more with the others present. She'd wait for another chat session, maybe next week. By then she'd be over feeling sorry for herself because there was never going to be a white wedding—or possibly even a proper funeral—in her future.

Chapter 3

"I didn't expect to die like this."

Not in the center of a nightmare.

The woman with the blue-diamond eyes cupped Selena's cheek. "No one ever expects this."

The gentleness of the woman's caressing touch was more revolting than a slap. Selena would have pulled away, but she was held fast by those eyes.

"She didn't say she doesn't want to die, I noticed," one of the others said. A ripple of laughter spread around the circle of monsters.

"No one wants to die," the diamond woman replied. She took her hard gaze away from Selena long enough to stab a look at the one who'd spoken. "Don't be in such haste to take life, Lawrence. Savor it. Always savor the moment." She turned back to Selena.

"I didn't say I wanted her to die," Lawrence said.

"I do," several of the others spoke as one.

"This is all a mistake," Selena told the woman. This one was obviously the leader.

Selena tried to ignore the others, especially the feral glitter of their eyes; eyes that glowed like animals out of the darkness. The eyes of animals intent on devouring her. It was a large storeroom, poorly lit, full of human-shaped creatures. Shelves and boxes disappeared in the blackness beyond the fluorescent bulb over her head. There were plenty of hiding places for more monsters out there.

Selena knelt at the leader's feet, on cold concrete in the center of a pool of pitiless white light. She was trapped in the center of the crowd. She was sure she wouldn't survive the flight even if she could break away from this group. She also knew she'd run the moment she got the chance.

The woman touched her cheek with only the needle tips of her long, painted nails. "But we want you to run." Her eyes gleamed with anticipation. Her smile gleamed with long, sharp teeth. "The more desperate the quarry, the more determined the victim to escape, the happier it makes us. If you want to live, don't run."

Selena gulped down a scream, one that was as much of anger as it was alarm. The woman's words sent images of fresh terror through her, but they didn't change her resolve.

Selena's mind was her own. The diamond woman wanted it. Selena could feel the leader of the monsters as she tried to force her way into her thoughts. There were claws trying to pry her head open from the inside. A horrible power pushed at her will.

And Selena pushed back. She felt like she was going to be engulfed by a firestorm at any moment, but she resisted. She couldn't see anything but the woman's glittering eyes. Even those narrowed down to white-hot pinpoints of flame. She heard a whispered voice in her head. *The voice commanded.* Selena ignored it. She stared at the flames and made herself think of birthday candles. *Maybe, if she could find air somewhere in this stifling dark place, she could blow those candles out.*

The diamond-eyed monster bent close to whisper in Selena's ear. *"Open to me willingly, child, and live."* She ran a finger down Selena's throat and rested it against the pounding pulse. *"I'll take your memory and let you go free."*

"No one's taking my memory." *The diamond woman was worried. It was as though Selena could read her with a sense she'd only just discovered. Or maybe it was just the sixth sense any cop acquired on the streets that kicked in over the fear she fought so hard not to show.* Selena decided to play for time. "I'm Detective Selena Crawford. I'm a police officer."

There was a collective gasp from the gathered monsters. *The air went colder, more dense with danger, as a murmuring that reminded her of the swift scuttling of rats' feet raced around the room. The diamond woman's grasp tightened.*

"Tell me more," *the woman suggested as some of the others moved into a tight circle around them.*

Selena wondered how much time she had before she died. *Maybe the truth was the last thing these creatures wanted. She sensed they were disturbed by her words, but that it only made her situation worse. Maybe they weren't afraid of the consequences that came with cop killing. She didn't suppose they had anything to be afraid of. She only wished she hadn't opened the wrong door at the wrong time and overheard too much of their unholy meeting.*

Selena took a deep breath before she went on. *She was glad that her voice didn't shake when she said,* "I was

checking out a lead in a murder investigation. I found—"
  Vampires.
  The voice that uttered the word in her mind was not her own or the woman's. It had been spoken in a deep, masculine growl. The word had been an explanation, but the texture of it had been pure command.
  Selena looked up, freed from the diamond woman's stare, and found herself instantly snared by a gaze as deep as blue velvet night, as wild as an alpha wolf's. A moment before, she'd been freezing, cold with fear and fury and stubborn determination. Fire ran through her veins as she looked deep into the newcomer's eyes. Fire ran between them that had nothing to do with fear and that made desire *a tame word.*
  She didn't know whether the need was her own or his, but for the first time in her life, she suddenly knew what it felt like to be truly hungry. It took more will to break eye contact with him than it had with her captor, but Selena managed it. Not that she looked away; instead, she studied the sharply drawn features that were clear to her despite the shadows around him. Shadows that were somehow of his making and not just an absence of light.
  He was tall and lean. All the creatures were slender, but this one had the presence of a wolf among rangy alley cats. His face was long, sharp, narrow but for the width of high cheekbones and the sensual slash of mouth. It was an ascetic face, cold, hard, but for the mouth. His mouth promised all the pleasure in the world.
  His eyes, however, promised nothing. They were ice blue, sharp as volcanic glass, colder than space. And yet, a moment before . . .
  "Vampire."

Unfortunately.

"You aren't paying attention to me, darling," the diamond woman said. *Nails dug into Selena's shoulders, bringing her attention abruptly back to the immediate danger. "Why is that?"*

"Because you're not the most interesting thing in the room."

Selena didn't know why she said it; this was not a woman to cross; but the words were snapped out as an almost triumphant snarl. Then it struck her that she had said vampire *about the newcomer without a flicker of disbelief. Of course all these monsters were vampires. What else could they be? She'd been told that magic was real often enough, but—*

When they hunt you down and sink their teeth in you, it will be real enough.

Do you mind? *she demanded of the intruding voice.* Did I invite you to walk into my head and try to scare the living shit out of me?

Try?

Why did he have to sound so amused? I'm scared, *she acknowledged.* So?

Her captor shifted her hold and sank her claws deep into the soft flesh of Selena's bare arms. Selena's cry of pain blended with the gasp of desire that came from the vampires as blood scented the air.

"Pay attention, child. I am Maria, the mistress here. It is up to me to decide your fate." A few drops of blood from the deep punctures trickled over the diamond woman's fingertips. She stretched a hand out. *"Lawrence."*

"You spoil me, Maria."

"It's because you're so pretty."

He bent over Maria's hand and swiftly licked the

blood from her fingers. Then he planted a soft kiss on her palm in gratitude. "She's delicious."

From her kneeling position, Selena had a close view of the male vampire and the erection that bulged beneath his tight jeans. The bastard had a hard-on from tasting her blood! Vampires were dead! This guy obviously wasn't.

"You people have some kind of kinky blood fetish, right?"

"Exactly," Maria answered. She waved Lawrence off. He took one reluctant step. "Do you want her?"

He drew his lips back over extended fangs.

"I see you do."

A ripple of laughter spread around the room. Selena suppressed a whimper as a hand twisted in her hair and she was pulled to her feet. Maria ripped open Selena's sleeveless white shirt. The popped buttons scattered like seeds on the concrete floor. Lawrence's gaze settled on her breasts.

"Will you take her as a companion?" Maria asked him.

Lawrence's head came up sharply. "What?"

"That's your choice, boy. What else can we do? Her will cannot be subverted in the usual way. We all know that some mortals resist chaste mind control."

"Those are the best kind," a woman said from the back of the crowd.

"Entertaining," one of the others declared. "Chastity is so boring."

Selena tried to pry her hands away while Maria shook her like she was an annoying rat. "Take her, Lawrence. You could use a companion."

Lawrence shook his head. "No way."

She was pushed toward the male vampire. "But you want her."

"But not permanently!"

"Why not?"

Lawrence looked around wildly. "Take an unwilling companion? I'd rather slaughter her."

"They're never unwilling for long," someone said to the accompaniment of shrill laughter.

"She's beautiful, Lawrence." Maria ran her hands over Selena.

Lawrence looked her up and down. He bared his teeth. "I'm tempted."

"Indulge," Maria urged.

Selena didn't know if they were planning to rape her or kill her or both. The diamond woman's touch had been obscene; her voice, as she urged the man on, was worse. Selena knew she had to get out before she could be used to entertain the troops.

"Help me!" she called to the man in the shadows.

There was no answer but the laughter of the others. Maybe he was laughing, too. Maybe he wasn't even there. He certainly didn't care. There was no one to depend on but herself.

Alone she might be, but years of training and years on the street counted for a lot. She was on her feet; that helped. The bitch only had one hand on her, and her attention was elsewhere. Selena saw her opportunity and used it to pull away. She left a lot of hair behind, but a stinging scalp was worth the price of getting out of the diamond woman's clutches. She was still surrounded by the crowd.

There was nowhere to run, but there was room to spin and kick as hard as she could. Her foot landed squarely in Lawrence's abdomen and again in his face as he bent *forward. The vampire went down. Selena leapt over his prone body, through the gap he'd left. She ran into the darkness. They followed, howling like a gleeful pack of hyenas at her heels.*

She remembered the staircase, and the door to the outside on the landing above. Heart pounding, the monsters' screams freezing her blood, Selena ran for the stairs.

He didn't step out of the shadows, they parted to let him through. One moment the stairway was clear before her. The next he was there, solid and dangerous and waiting for her.

He opened his arms.

Hell was behind her. What waited before her radiated fury and contempt and a strange promise of shelter. She couldn't have turned back to face the others if she'd tried. So she kept going in the hope that she could somehow get around the lone wolf on the staircase.

"Let me go." She said the words quite calmly, under the circumstances.

"Or you will do what? Arrest me?" He took her in his arms. "You shouldn't have run."

"I didn't have any other choice. Let go of me." She spoke through gritted teeth.

"It's him! He's here!" Lawrence shouted out the warning.

Selena heard them behind her. She also heard the edge of terror in the monsters' voices as a name was repeated, passing like a wave through the crowd. The one holding her scared them nearly to death. If they scared her, and he scared them, just how bad was he? What was the monsters' monster going to do to her?

I might do a great many things.

His voice was a silken caress in her mind. And how

come he could read her thoughts when the other ones couldn't?

Stop that!

You started it, his thought answered hers.

He turned her so that her back was pressed against his chest. He put one arm tightly around her waist. The stair tread was narrow, so they were of necessity very close. Necessary or not, the press of her hot flesh against his sent a shiver of desire through him. The warmth of his flesh sent a shiver through her.

The leader of the vampires made her way to the front of the crowd. She put her hands on her hips and looked up, past Selena to the vampire holding her. "You're late, old friend."

His breath brushed Selena's ear when he spoke. "Caught in traffic."

"Caught the mouse we were chasing, as well." She held out a hand. "Now, if you'll just hand her back."

"She's keeping me warm."

Maria's smile didn't waver, though annoyance radiated from her. "But I'm giving her to Lawrence, my dear."

Lawrence didn't look happy, but he nodded rather than contradict his leader.

"You always were a matchmaker, Maria." He had one arm around Selena's waist; his hand hovered just beneath her breast. The touch, even the hint of a touch, was disturbingly intimate. "She's not Lawrence's type."

"I'm Type O-negative, to be precise," Selena whispered angrily.

"Universal donor," he whispered back, amused by her grim humor. "Slut." She banged her head back hard against his shoulder.

"She's no innocent we abducted for the hunt," Maria

explained. "We didn't bring her here. The situation is of her own making. We caught her spying on us. She won't respond to persuasion."

"She's a cop," Lawrence added with a bitter sneer.

"That is a problem."

"So we can either take her or kill her," Maria went on. "What other choice do we have, my dear?"

"This has nothing to do with why you're here," Lawrence insisted. He looked around at the rest of the nest. "None of us is involved in that."

"A cop would make a dangerous companion." His hand had settled over her breast. Selena was aware that he was aware that her nipple was hard and hot against his palm. "So I think I'll take you for myself."

"Shit! Shit! Shit!"

Selena scrubbed her hands over her tear-streaked face and swore some more.

The worst part about this recurring nightmare wasn't waking up covered in sweat, scared out of her mind and with a racing heart. Selena almost didn't mind the terror. It was the unbearable arousal that drove her up the wall, at least out of her bed to stumble across the dark bedroom into the bathroom.

She washed the sweat off her face, which woke her up further. That really wasn't what she wanted. What she wanted here, alone, in the dead of night, was black oblivion. No dreams, no memories. She sure as hell didn't want to think, and being awake meant thinking. She was trembling, her body aching and alive, and she hated it, wanted to divorce her mind from singed, singing nerve endings and the siren call that was never answered. That she never wanted answered, but still, she couldn't help but radiate—

She stepped into the shower still wearing the T-shirt she slept in and stood in a cascade of cold water that did nothing for her body but get it wet. The burning didn't go away; it never did. Masturbation didn't help, so she didn't bother. She stood with her hands braced against the tiles and tried to get over it.

Instead, as her senses gradually grew sharper, she began to realize that the longing was more than inside her. It was in the air around her, the water washing over her. When she closed her eyes, it was a presence she felt on her skin rather than icy needles of water. The scent she breathed in was the musk of sex rather than the aroma of soap or shampoo. This wasn't all her doing, and it wasn't a dream. Her imagination was not of the vivid sort. She'd found out she had some gifts—curses—she didn't know she had, but Selena Crawford never imagined things.

When she turned off the water, she knew. She wasn't alone. She wasn't the only one *consumed* with this vivid need.

She jerked back the shower curtain. The bedroom was darker than it should be beyond the open bathroom door. She pulled off the soaked shirt and dropped it on the floor. "Steve?" she said, walking naked through the doorway. "What the hell are you doing here?"

Chapter 4

SHE ALWAYS CALLED him Steve.

She didn't pretend she was happy to see him. That didn't stop her from being all over him the moment he stepped out of the shadows. It didn't stop him pulling her down on the bed. He thought that maybe he could stop himself if he wanted to, but if that was true, he'd have an answer for her question. What the hell he was doing here was all too evident, especially since he wasn't wearing any more clothes than she was. He'd shed them as soon as he'd come in the window, while she was still in the shower, while they were both still in the clutches of a dream that was no dream at all.

There were no words between them as they made love and no thoughts, either. But for the low, urgent sounds of passion, they moved in isolated silence. Neither wanted the act; both needed it.

And the taste of her! Sweet wine that almost made him believe this curse was the gift of a goddess. He was blood drunk the moment he pierced the skin of her breast. In that moment, she found the strength to dig her short nails deep into his shoulders. It was not possible for a mortal to wound him, but Selena wasn't one to pay attention to limitations set by god, man, or monster.

You belong to me.

I've heard it before.

Her answering thought made him laugh. Selena was the only person in the world who could make him laugh. Laughter drove out some of the beast, enough so that he lifted his head reluctantly from the puncture wounds he'd been suckling. He'd taken no more than a few drops, and he'd given back nothing. *Not this time,* he swore.

The actual swearing came from Selena, even as she made the vow he was bound to eventually break. "Goddamn, it! You want to fuck, or do you want to think?"

He realized he'd risen to kneel between her widespread thighs. For a moment, he looked down on her as if from a mile away. Her skin was white as milk against the dark covers, and there was so very much of it. She was a wide-hipped woman with large breasts and long, long legs. She had hard muscle rather than feminine softness, and the lines of scars from old wounds were beauty marks to him. She looked up at him with blue eyes, electric with hate and passion, and held up a hand. The gesture was more demand than pleading. Any moment now she was going to grab him by the hair and pull him down on top of her.

He was breathing hard, but he managed to draw in enough breath for irony. "I don't suppose you could manage terror or gratitude."

He got a sharp punch in the gut for his trouble. Laughing once more, he sank down on top of her, into her,

both her body and her mind, and she opened both to
him.

"You need a haircut."

It was a ludicrous thing to say. Worse, it sounded so
domestic. They did not have a domestic relationship nor
any relationship at all. She should be asking him what
he was doing in town, or, more importantly, when he
was leaving.

"A man's strength is in his hair."

His hair was shoulder length, and her fingers couldn't
seem to stop stroking through it. When they'd met, his
hair had been short, combed back off his high forehead.
If he wasn't a vampire, he'd be bald. "Don't give me
that Samson and Delilah crap."

He lifted his head to look at her. "I was quoting Ozzy
Osbourne."

"Isn't he dead or at least bald by now?"

He shrugged. "Don't know."

They were being talkative. Selena wondered if he
found that as worrisome as she did.

Yes.

Telling him to stay out of her head at this point was
as futile as telling oxygen to stay out of her lungs.
They'd made love for a long time, and she ached all
over, partly from lack of practice, partly because making
love with a vampire is not a gentle thing.

*You've had a lot of experience with vampires, have
you?*

This time she said, "Get out of my head."

He yawned. "I noticed you didn't say to get out of
your bed."

Selena pushed him all the way off her and sat up. She
looked at the clock. She glanced out the window, where

night was beginning to fade. "Tell me you're not staying."

A moment later, he was on his feet without her having seen him move. "I'm not staying."

That was something to be thankful for. She wanted him out of her life as much as she'd longed for him to return to her a few hours before. He'd explained to her long ago how the craving was because he'd made her drink his blood on that first wild night together. It was what bound her to him. There was no emotional entanglement, despite what they'd been through two years before. Some lives had ended, some had gotten saved, all in a day's—night's—work for a pair of cops, never mind which side of the divide between mortal and monster each was on.

What they were left with was a craving worse than any drug. It was an addiction without a cure or treatment programs. Selena almost laughed at the notion of getting up at some twelve-step meeting and announcing that she was addicted to sex with a five-hundred-year-old creature of the night. One that she was currently thinking about asking if he wanted a snack, a cup of coffee, to move in, let her wait on him hand and foot.

Yeah. Right.

That was the bloodbond talking. *She* didn't want him to stay. It was her cop's curiosity that made her ask, "What are you doing in town? Does Ariel know you're—"

"How do you know about Ariel?" His blue eyes narrowed to slits. "Does Ariel know about you?"

She wasn't sure what Ariel thought she was, some strig's girl, she supposed. The Enforcer of the City knew she was a homicide cop. She knew about the homicides Ariel sometimes allowed. They had a certain uneasy understanding. "We've had some professional contact," she admitted.

His wide mouth narrowed to match his eyes, but he didn't pursue the subject. "How's your aunt?"

Selena used the adrenaline from the stab of fear to roll off the bed and stand on the opposite side from him. "Why?"

His lips quirked up just a little, in something resembling a smile. "She keeps putting love spells on me."

"Oh." After a moment, curiosity got the better of her. "Are they working?"

"I'm here."

He continued to dress slowly, like a strip in reverse, watching her without saying anything else. She didn't know if he was deliberately teasing her or if the heat that still glowed through her was making her hallucinate. He had wide shoulders, but the rest of him was all long limbs and wiry muscle. She'd always had a thing for arms and hands, and found Steve's particularly attractive.

Watching him move was pure pleasure, until Selena reminded herself of the times she'd seen him still as stone, his skin as pale as blue-veined marble. Maybe he wasn't exactly dead—no one could fuck like that and be dead—but he wasn't human. And what was between them was—

"I could just as easily enjoy your pain." She remembered him saying that when they first met. *"You'd love me while I tortured you, if that's what I wanted from you."*

At least he'd never made a secret that he could be an utter and complete bastard.

Steve smirked, letting her know that he knew what she was thinking. Selena pulled herself away from watching him and put on some underwear. Standing around naked in the presence of her lord and master didn't interest her at the moment.

She couldn't help but wonder if Aunt Catie did have something to do with Steve's late-night visit. Aunt Catie was a very good witch indeed. Of course, good witches weren't supposed to provide their goddaughters with their own private incubus, Selena amended. Okay, Catie was a talented witch, if not exactly a candidate for sainthood. Her aunt should not know about the existence of the strigoi, either, but she did, and as far as Selena knew, no Enforcer had ever come after her.

"I pity anyone who'd try." Istvan couldn't help but tease her about the strong women in her family. Selena's aunt reminded him of his own mother, who'd also made her living telling fortunes. "A fine woman. It's a wonder no one's taken her for a companion yet. All the women in your family have the—"

"Don't say it! Don't you *dare!*"

"Not I. I have—"

"Leave them alone!"

Her fury blazed around her, so much that the fiery color of her hair gave the impression of a crown of flames. He loved her deep emotions, absorbed them like a drug, but he truly hadn't meant to anger her. He decided not to mention the wedding invitation, though he did wonder where Aunt Catie had gotten his post office box address.

He held up a hand. "Peace."

He'd been joking; Selena saw that now. Damn, but he could set her off. "Fine," she said, embarrassed at her temper. She hated when she let herself go. She'd worked for years to find a certain amount of emotional equilibrium, only to have every defense blown out of the water the moment this joker showed up and sank his teeth into her. She felt the aching spot just above her left nipple. "Why can't you just bite me on the neck like a normal vampire?"

He cocked an eyebrow in answer. No need for him to tell *her* that he wasn't normal. He pulled on a black shirt. "You say the oddest things."

She returned to an earlier question. "What are you doing in town?"

He considered telling her. That was her blood inside him, urging him to trust, confide, cherish, and share himself with what was his. They were alike, or they wouldn't be mated. She was tough. She knew the streets of her town. They'd partnered once before, reluctantly, after Maria set him up for the fall he'd spent five hundred years avoiding, and things had happened that shouldn't have. It was the second time in his lives he'd been trapped.

Selena's presence among the nest of vampires had been no accident. Maria Ventanova had searched long and hard to find him the perfect mate, had Selena waiting there, blood pumped full of adrenaline, a sacrificial diversion Maria hoped would save her own life. Maria knew he had never taken a companion, never wanted one, and that no strigoi, even Istvan the *dhamphir,* could go forever without eventually being struck by the overwhelming psychic bonding. It had worked, and it hadn't. Maria still died, and how he wished he'd been the one to take Maria Ventanova's heart.

He also noticed that Selena was carefully not glancing toward the desk across the room, carefully keeping her mind blank about anything to do with computers. He might be a bit long in the tooth, but he was almost as high tech as the West Coast vampires that prided themselves on being thoroughly modern monsters. He kept up, even had his own private hacker for research purposes. He owned a laptop that he'd been using at a truck stop earlier in the evening. But if Selena wanted to keep a medieval image of him, he wasn't going to enlighten her. The point of their relationship was that they didn't have a relationship. He wasn't going to ask about what she didn't want him to know. What he didn't know couldn't hurt her.

He decided that since the trouble he was currently investigating wasn't in Detective Crawford's town but much farther to the west, it was best not to involve her. He said, "Maybe I came to see you."

"I may be crazed, but I'm not crazy. Why? What's going on that the local Enforcer can't handle?"

Even those who had the right to ask him questions generally didn't. Her attitude toward him was quite refreshing. "Just passing through," he told her. "Your streets are safe from me."

"But not my bedroom."

"You wanted me here." He grinned. "Briefly."

Her indignant surprise pleased him, because her indignation was for him, for once. She kept to business when she spoke. "If there's someone who needs eliminating in my city, I'd rather have you on them than anyone else."

Her nontraditional attitude toward him was always so . . . tempting.

The more time he spent with her, the more time he wanted to spend with her. That was the curse of companionship. Because the more time they spent together, the sooner she'd become a vampire. And there was nothing he hated more than vampires.

Despite a temptation to stay, with the excuse that he

could check out any local rumors, he really had been just passing through, heading west. The last thing he'd planned on was turning onto a tollway from the interstate after he left the last truck stop and driving from the tollway to the north side of Chicago. He'd left his vehicle a long way away from Selena's neighborhood. He had a long way to get back to it now before dawn. He had no intention of being seen or sensed by any of the city's strigoi inhabitants anywhere near her. He protected his companion in his own way, which was mostly by staying away from her.

Of course, recent research had indicated that—

He tried not thinking about the warnings he'd gotten from Lady Valentia about recent events in Los Angeles and a too-long E-mail with too many big words from Char out in Arizona on the same subject. This was the bloodbond's insidious way of exerting a hold on him. He wasn't any ordinary strigoi. He was *dhamphir,* son of a vampire, reborn into the strigoi life, already the strongest of the Nighthawks, the enforcers of the laws. He was the Enforcer every other Enforcer feared; he would fight the bond. Of course, if he was going to keep control of the situation, he was going to have to stop biting Selena on the boob, even on a biannual basis.

Maybe next time he would go for the throat.

"Later."

Steve turned into smoke and was gone before she could ask what he meant. "How do you do that?" she demanded of the empty room. "And don't come back!" she added, just in case he was messing with her mind and was really still standing across the room from her.

Turn into smoke indeed! Real vampires couldn't do that, or so delicate inquiries had led her to believe. They couldn't fly. They couldn't shape-shift. They didn't need to drink blood to live, but they did need to hunt. Vampires hunted mortals, Nighthawks hunted vampires, and the magic of immortality was drawn from the sacrament of consuming living flesh and fear. They did need to exchange blood for reproduction, which was where the legends of the caped dude sucking the blood of innocent virgins came from. Only the capes and the virgin parts were all wrong. Vampires craved sex as they craved all intense sensation.

What made them monsters was the driving, insatiable need to hunt. They ate emotions as much as they did human flesh. They craved the emotions of the ones they took as lovers as much as the ones they hunted to kill. Sometimes Selena didn't know if it was worse to be one of the victims vampires killed or one of the victims chosen to be a lover. From her point of view as one of those designated lovers, it wasn't a pretty place to be, even with a master as indifferent as Steve.

"Bloodsucking parasite," she muttered. "And that's just your good points."

They were stronger than mortals, very hard to kill, incredibly fast, and had amazing psychic powers. Sunlight didn't destroy them, but they did sink into a near-death state between dawn and dusk. Even Steve needed to do that. But Steve . . . Steve wasn't like the others in so many ways.

Selena looked at her alarm clock. Too late to go back to bed now. She glanced down at the rumpled sheets. She almost smiled at what was not an unpleasant memory. *Insatiable bastard.* "And I like him that way."

Definitely too late.

Chapter 5

"THE POINT IS, there aren't many ways it could have gone down," Olympias told him. "We *can't* harm our own kind, but that doesn't stop one of our own from making arrangements with outsiders."

Istvan liked using his cellular telephone while he drove. It was better than telepathy, and the looks of stinging annoyance he received from drivers who noticed him made for nice sensory snack food while on the road. Even on city side streets at four thirty in the morning, there were enough annoyed people around to give him a buzz. But it was only empty calories after a night spent with Selena.

"It's possible for a strigoi to kill a strigoi without hiring a hit man," he answered the Enforcer who'd called him from her home in Washington just as he was looking for a place to sleep through the day. "It's even quite pleasant."

"Watch your tongue."

He laughed. "And my teeth? Admit that it's possible."

"You were a gifted child. You've always been different. You only made threats when we were together. You didn't try it with me."

Olympias wanted to hear that she was special, even after all this time. She did it just to annoy him. "It's late," he told her instead. "Even later where you are. Go to bed. I'll find the killer for you. Don't I always?"

"*Harm* is a more circumspect word, you know. Not that you were ever circumspect."

He knew she didn't like him talking so openly over the telephone. That was one of the reasons he did it. Never give a vampire any measure of comfort. That was one of the rules he lived by. Another was to find as inconspicuous a place as possible to wait out the daylight. He saw a parking ramp next to a shopping mall and turned in while he enjoyed Olympias's growing impatience with his silence.

"All right, what if it isn't one of us?" she finally asked. "What if it's a complete outsider?"

A mortal vampire hunter, she meant. There had been threats of that sort of thing in the past, but the threats had always been contained before any harm was done.

The parking ramp had three levels. He pulled into a spot on the second floor. It would be a nice, shady place to spend the day. He had no interest in mortals. "Hope not. I like to eat what I kill," he answered and switched off the phone.

He was still closer to Selena than he wanted to be, but it was also too late to do anything about it, other than try to keep his mind away from her as he slept. *This close? After the night?* "Fat chance," he muttered. He might as well have stayed in her comfortable bed rather than returning to his usual resting place.

He felt Selena deep inside him as he moved from the

driver's seat into the back of the vehicle. He even caught himself smiling, remembering her first reaction on seeing his wheels.

"A Suburban?" She had sneered, her gaze raking the considerable length of the Chevy he called home. She turned the sneer on him. "You a vampire or a soccer dad?"

"It's black," he had offered.

She shook her head. "Uh-uh. You want to bite my neck, you better get yourself some new wheels. Show up in a black Jaguar, and we'll talk."

"I don't do necks."

Nor had he gotten a cool car. Though he had, to his chagrin, thought about it. The point of having a companion was that they were supposed to unconditionally adore their strigoi lover, no matter what they drove or looked like or did. Selena wasn't unconditional about anything. Or maybe he was just a wimp.

The box in the back of the Suburban was camouflaged to look like a pair of storage containers; it was not a coffin. He settled into his bed an instant before the paralysis that came with daylight overtook him. He was tired enough to actually sleep, at least for a while. Sleeping, he knew he would dream.

He was not surprised when the first thing he heard in his dreaming, was,

"I have to go to the bathroom."

It wasn't the first thing he'd thought he'd hear upon waking up. The woman's words were too prosaic not to be real. It was a humiliating thing for her to have to admit, and probably not the first thing she'd planned to

say when the vampire in her bed awoke, but it was no doubt the most pressing thing on her mind.

Istvan had half hoped the woman was part of a long, erotic dream. Half, because too much of any emotion was a dangerous thing. Of course she, and the dangerous situation, were very real. It would have been easier to let her die at the hands of Maria's nest, but he had tasted her instead of having the others hunt her, and now she was·his. He did not know what had come over him when he arrived at Maria Ventanova's nest, but here they were, tied together by the bloodbond he'd always rejected. He had responsibilities. She had needs. She looked at him with anger and defiance, but she still needed something from him.

He knew he should make her ask. Defiance should not be permitted, dependence should be fostered. That was the safe, traditional way to start with a companion.

He moved his arm and let her up. When she bolted out of the room, he followed her.

The bathroom was across a hall from the bedroom. Istvan took a few moments to check out the other rooms. There was a second bedroom that looked to be used as an office/guest room. The room held bookcases, a pillow-strewn daybed, and pots of orchids on a long table under grow lights. He found the exotic blooms pleasant to the eye and smiled to find that the woman cultivated such an interesting hobby.

He turned back to deal with the woman. When he entered the bathroom, he noticed that she'd put on a short green bathrobe and that she was holding a large gun in a two-handed grip.

If you keep a gun in the bathroom, where do you keep the handcuffs?

He enjoyed her blush at the erotic overtones of his thought.

"Stop that!" She carefully aimed at his heart. She refused to look him in the face, though she knew he wanted her to. He knew that she still knew he was smirking. "Stay out of my mind."

I can't do that. He took a step forward.

He knew she'd never shot anyone before, but she was trained to do it. She had plenty of motivation. Her memories flooded him, of him pressing her back on the bed, his hands on her, of his mouth, the sharp prick of teeth, of him on top of her, inside her, of the hot intoxication when his blood poured into her mouth. It hadn't felt like rape. She hated that she couldn't feel like she'd been raped, no matter what she could objectively tell herself.

It had been rape all right. In a way, they'd both been raped.

He took another step.

She fired the gun.

The little room echoed with the roar of the shot. She'd been braced for the recoil, but it still took her back a half step.

Istvan yawned. He stretched. He scratched the spot where the bullet had entered his chest. He didn't bleed, fall down, and die.

"I need a shower," he said.

He should have at least been writhing in agony. He almost reacted to the pain that shot through her head and back to him with such sudden intensity that it forced her to her knees. She didn't drop the gun, though. Istvan plucked it out of her hands.

The trick was not to let her see how much it hurt. If he hadn't been prepared for it, he'd be bleeding all over her white-tiled floor right now. Strong, stubborn will kept him going.

First, he carefully placed the gun in the cabinet beneath the sink. Then he grasped Selena's wrists and pulled her up. Her expression reflected the pain they both felt. His fingers were numb, but he managed to untie the belt of her robe without fumbling too badly. He gave himself points for style and was just glad the bullet had made a fiery exit through his flesh instead of lodging in the rib it had shattered. Thank God for high-caliber projectiles, *he thought, as he dragged Selena into the shower stall with him.*

Hot water helped. It usually did. He'd discovered that sometime in the fifteenth century, when he'd been dragged into a castle to entertain—

Istvan cut the memory off before the loathing and anger could fully surface. The boyar had died long ago, and Istvan had made the discovery that he liked being clean.

Even hell had a few amenities.

He didn't mind remembering what happened in the shower after Selena shot him, but thinking about the first vampire he'd ever killed was not a daymare he wanted to relive. Then again, centuries-old memories didn't surface among his kind without a reason. Istvan lay in his box, fully awake but completely immobile. He considered what he knew of his current assignment and what he remembered of the mortal boy who'd ripped out the heart of a—

The *first* vampire who'd made him a companion.

He'd been young, eleven, maybe twelve; it had been a very long time ago. The noblewoman who kept him in her castle was of an ancient, haughty line that had ruled in the mountainous forest from time out of mind. *She* had ruled from time out of mind. He was hardly the first Roma she'd taken to her bed, to her heart. Her kisses drew blood. She taught him bed play deep into the nights, though his young body had had no such male stirrings before she touched him. She gave him her blood, only a little, saying she wanted him to grow into a fine, big man. That she wanted him as her bed slave for decades. That's all companions were to her, slaves worthy of a bit more time and torture.

The taste of her pure, noble blood sickened him, disgusted him. He had felt no devotion, but he had pretended, and she had believed. Her pride had killed her as surely as the knife he smuggled into her bed. He had known enough to take her heart and burn it. He had taken her head as well, just in case, and burned her beautiful body and scattered the ashes in the sunlight.

He chuckled silently now at the boy's thoroughness. The heart had been enough, but he hadn't known that then. Still, he'd enjoyed destroying the body that had used him and used him and destroyed everything that was left of his childhood.

He'd been a companion who could do the impossible and kill the vampire who bled him. Selena had tried to kill him with his blood singing fresh in her veins. But he was *dhamphir,* she was the *dhamphir*'s companion. He didn't think it was possible for him to have taken a bonded lover that wasn't as strong-willed and ruthless as he was. What would be the point?

The Enforcer in Denver had reported the death of a local vampire to Olympias. The body had been found by mortal authorities in a public park. The remaining members of the victim's household had disappeared. The Enforcer of the City was concentrating on keeping the mortal police and media from finding any information about the victim or any clues to the killings. Istvan's job was to find and stop the killer, which was the height of irony, since he'd never seen how killing vampires was a bad thing. Still, he'd agreed to live by the Laws of the Blood.

Since strigoi claimed to be instinctually unable to kill each other, Olympias had listened to the Denver Enforcer's report and suggested to Istvan that a strigoi had used a mortal to destroy an enemy. This sort of killing used to happen in the days when nests fought Mafia-style wars with each other. Olympias was a bright female, but she was an old broad who didn't get out of town much. There were two or three other possibilities Istvan could think of that Olympias hated to consider. He was surprised at her reluctance to think out of the box on this one, but even the thought of mortals acting on their own made strigoi nervous. Sometimes she showed her old-line sensibilities at the oddest times, but she was anything but a fool.

Once upon a time, before the founding of the Council, before the oral code of Laws had been written in blood, legend said there had been a city full of vampires. The legend was one of the things the oldest vampires, the *surviving* vampires, kept very quiet. Because they didn't want anyone to know how that city had been destroyed. But Istvan knew.

That was why his past bubbled up to remind him of what he'd done when he was still close to being a normal human being. That was why the memory of Selena's defiance when she'd barely been bitten filled his dreams. It was not a strigoi he needed to look for or a mortal vampire hunter who'd put his trophies on display as a warning to the world. His instincts told him the killer he was looking for was a companion.

A few suspects came readily to mind. One of them was Selena.

Chapter 6

"THERE ARE SOME things man was not meant to know." Don Raleigh held up a hand. "I am not listening to any of it, Crawford."

It frustrated Selena that her partner didn't want to hear about her cousin's wedding shower after his telling her that she looked like something the cat dragged in. How else was she supposed to explain her obvious tiredness? She couldn't very well tell him that the bags under her eyes had more to do with being up all night satisfying the insatiable sexual needs of a vampire than it did with bridal registries, pink punch, and party games. She was disgusted that the man was easily scared off by the slightest mention of Karen's bridal shower.

"What about women?" she asked him.

"What about them?"

Raleigh was a big man, with amber eyes, skin like satiny dark coffee, James Earl Jones's voice, and a diamond stud earring she'd given him for Christmas two years ago that he's started wearing when they worked tactical out of narcotics. His wife did not approve of the earring. That he wore it now told Selena that Raleigh and the missus had been fighting again.

Being a cop was very hard on marriages.

Raleigh told her communication was the key, especially after a couple had a disagreement.

Of course, the last time she'd had a fight with Steve, he'd threatened to not only break her neck but to have her for lunch. She'd laughed in his face—and bitten him that time. Hadn't heard from him for a long time after that, except for all those hang-ups on her answering machine. Calls she'd had traced to pay phones all over the country. He never bothered answering his cellular phone when she called. Damn caller ID, anyway. They'd both been fighting playing this stupid noncommunication communication game with each other for two years.

"What about women?" Raleigh asked again, pulling Selena out of a brief fantasy about what marriage must be like for vampire cops who bothered dealing with their mates at all.

Since she didn't want her thoughts to go in that direction, she went back to teasing Raleigh. "If there are things men aren't meant to know, how about women? What are women not meant to know?"

"Women are goddesses. Women know everything."

"Hmm." Selena tilted her head to get a better look at him over the top of her computer screen. Their desks in the Area Three squad room were set back to back, so piled with shared work and possessions it was hard to tell where one ended and the other began. "Goddesses, eh?"

He nodded.

"Sounds like your diversity training took."

Raleigh tugged on his earring. "I have it from a higher

authority." He grinned. The look in his eyes made Selena reconsider her earlier thoughts. Maybe Raleigh and Sharifa had come to some sort of amicable compromise over his choice of jewelry. She'd been told that there was a certain amount of give and take to a successful marriage. A proper marriage was supposed to be a win-win situation, right?

And she wished she'd get her mind off marriage. And Steve. And the unfinished conversation in the companions' chat room last night.

Since the morning briefing, she and Raleigh had settled down to catch up on paperwork. She looked around the room now, restless, pinned in by the solid walls and the everyday duties of her not-all-that-normal daylight world. "Too quiet," she murmured. She glanced at the clock on her computer screen. She yawned and stretched aching muscles. "Hasn't anybody gotten murdered yet this morning?"

A few seconds later the call came in, and she had her answer.

"This is interesting."

The beat cop who was the first person on the scene had the usual understated, unimpressed attitude of a street veteran. There were a lot of ways to define *interesting*. Considering the blank face and lack of emotion in the voice of the patrol woman, Selena assumed that *interesting* in this case meant grisly and disgusting.

They were standing at the entrance of an alley in a nice neighborhood of row houses not too far from Oak Street Beach. The midmorning sun shone down from a clear sky on red brick buildings with blue painted moldings, and on the bright blooms in a row of first-floor flower boxes. But for the police on scene, the squad cars,

coroner's wagon, and the gathering of curious bystanders being kept well back from the alley, this was a peaceful, quiet place. Selena took out her pen and notebook,
ready to start her crime scene log.

Raleigh gestured beyond the yellow tape strung up by
the crime scene unit. "Let's go have a look."

Selena tried to clear her mind of all suppositions before seeing the body. A dead body found in an alley did
not automatically constitute murder. Her job right now
was to look at the body and physical evidence and to
interview witnesses, not to make assumptions. Despite
the beat cop's oblique warning that what was waiting
ahead of them could be a suicide, it might be a death
caused by accident or natural causes. Her training told
her to be objective. She smiled slightly, cynically. Ob-
jectivity was for rookies. Her instincts knew it was a
murder.

While it was a fact that anyone could get killed anywhere at any time, there tended to be a pattern for the
types of bodies found in different settings. This was not
the sort of neighborhood where Selena expected to find
a dead hooker or crack addict, though maybe one had
been dumped in the alley. It could happen, but most
murders were easy to solve. People murdered people
they knew and got caught. Most murders really were
crimes of passion, or of at least immense stupidity
brought on by overwhelming emotion.

She was only a few feet into the alley before she
smelled burnt flesh. Then she saw the head, a pale visage
sitting in a puddle of congealed blood. The mutilated
torso was a few feet farther back, propped up against a
brick wall. There was a lot of blood and flies. The victim
certainly didn't belong in this part of town. At least not
at this time of day.

"Definitely interesting," Raleigh said.

And certainly a crime of passion, Selena decided. You had to really be pissed off at someone to do that much damage to them. And you knew how hard they were to kill.

"Nice clean cuts," the beat officer said. "What do you think? Chainsaw?"

DesertDog had mentioned using chainsaws once, in explicit detail, in one of the companion cabal's more heated discussions. Shit.

Raleigh made a noncommittal noise. Selena noted that the photographer was finished with pictures and approached a forensics technician. She bummed a pair of plastic booties and once her shoes were covered, she gingerly stepped up to the unattached head.

Raleigh was there before her, not as fastidious with his footgear as she was. "Male," he said. "That the whitest white guy you've ever seen?"

"No." She took a careful look at the pavement and the surrounding buildings. "Not dumped here. Too much blood."

The beat cop said, "So far, nobody we've talked to heard a thing."

No, Selena thought. *Most wouldn't, if the killer didn't want them to.* The Force had a strong influence over the weak minded, and all that crap. She had a certain skill at it, but—

"How fresh is he?" Raleigh inquired.

"Rigor's set in," the forensic tech said. "From that and the flies, I'd give a rough guess of four to twelve hours."

Selena put away her notebook. She checked her watch and glanced at the position of the sun in the sky. It was her guess that somebody dragged the body outside soon after dawn. She didn't think any vampires lived in this neighborhood, but there could be a safe house around here somewhere. "Any neighbors recognize him?" She didn't.

"Everybody that's had a look so far has tossed their cookies."

"Wimps." She stepped up to the torso propped against the wall. "Heart missing?" she asked.

The tech looked up in surprise. "How'd you know?"

"Lucky guess." That explained the burned meat smell. The killer had destroyed the heart. Wise move.

"You've seen something like this before, Crawford?" Raleigh asked.

She grinned at him. "Oh, yeah." She pointed at the victim's several severed pieces. "There's this game chicks play at wedding showers, called Maenads, where we run around ripping guys to shreds. You should have been at my place yesterday."

Raleigh shook a finger at her. "You know I don't want to hear about that girly stuff." He grew serious. "You know something I don't about this case?"

Sort of. Maybe. Well, she knew who—what—the victim was, at any rate. "Nothing," she said to her partner and friend, looking deeply into his eyes. "Nothing at all."

He believed her because, of course, she wanted him to believe her. She hated that she was able to do that to him. She could deal with Raleigh on this investigation, but he was the least of her problems. She looked around. There were people everywhere. How was she supposed to control a situation involving a vampire's murder when so many mortals had already seen the thing? It was only going to get worse. Wait until the coroner had a look at the corpse. This was not her job. She should just leave it alone. She was not the goddamned Enforcer of the City.

She wanted to spit on the damned corpse. She was not going to get involved in Enforcer business. She said, "I'll take over interviewing the neighbors."

• • •

"Get in the car."

Ariel bridled exactly as she'd expected him to when she pulled over to the curb and spoke. It was past ten, and traffic on this street off Lake Shore Drive was sparse. Nobody, not even the building's doorman, was anywhere near the vampire on the sidewalk. Ariel brushed pale hair off his shoulders as his head went up proudly. He stared through her with eyes pale as ice cubes. A sneer curled his beautiful mouth. The Enforcer of the City was not accustomed to being addressed with anything less than groveling respect. Selena couldn't recall ever having groveled for anyone. Showing respect to a *mere* Enforcer was out of the question.

Ariel was the most beautiful creature she'd ever seen. Tall and elegant, he reminded her of silver and mercury, and—What was that stuff?—mithril. Not only did his name sound like it belonged to an elf, he looked like one. Very Tolkienesque was Ariel.

She'd left a message on his answering machine during the day. They were both surprised that he'd met her on the sidewalk outside his high-rise condo building. He hesitated long enough to give her a disdainful sneer, then slid into the passenger seat and slammed the door. The first thing he said as she pulled into the street was, "I should kill you for this, mortal."

She'd expected him to ask how she'd gotten his phone number. "You and what army of darkness, Tinkerbell?" she answered as she turned a corner.

She was terrified but had long ago learned not to let
it show in her attitude or her surface emotions. Bad guys
could sense fear. Vampires ranked high on the empathic
scale, but she dealt on a daily basis with mortals every
bit as nasty and sensitive to vulnerability as any blood-
sucker. Her own lord and master was the only one she'd
encountered since that first run-in with a nest that she
let faze her. In fact—and she hated to admit it—not all
vampires were bad people. Most obeyed their laws and
kept out of mortals' way. Some of the things they did,
when properly regulated, even helped to bring a certain
rough, peremptory justice to a dark and ugly world. She
just didn't want to be one.

And no way was she letting them step over the line
in her town.

"What do you want with me?" Ariel asked. "Officer."

"That's Detective Sergeant."

"Detective Sergeant."

He looked straight ahead out the front of the windshield, not deigning to glance her way. He did give her
her due with a slight nod. "Detective."

"Hunter," she reciprocated. "I want you to identify a
corpse," she told him.

He swiveled his head slowly to look at her. He lifted
a pale eyebrow and drawled, "Is this an official investigation, Detective?"

"That'll be up to you."

That got his attention. "Who owns you, companion?
Who dares to let you interfere with my—"

"Indignation doesn't become you. Stick to business,
and I'll get out of your way."

Jerk, she thought. *Ought to be thanking me instead of
bringing up the little matter of—*

She cut off the thought before Ariel could goad her

into an emotional slip that would let him into her mind. Screw the strigoi and their dominance games.

Selena pulled into the alley she'd been looking for. It was a quiet, private place, at least since she'd rousted some gangbanger drug dealers out of it earlier in the evening. They wouldn't be back for a while, and the regular beat patrol car wouldn't be likely to come this way for another half hour at least.

She killed the engine and lights, popped the trunk, and took a flashlight with her when she got out of the car. Ariel followed her. He stood quietly back, hidden in the shadows, while she unzipped the body bag inside the trunk.

He moved to stand by her shoulder when she shone the light on the corpse. Neither spoke for a few seconds. Finally, he said, "Where did you get that?"

"Stole it from the morgue."

"I . . . see."

Selena wasn't sure what he saw but didn't ask.

He made a slight gesture toward the head and torso. "How many people know about . . . him?"

"Quite a few. I can take care of some of the paper trail associated with your boy, here, but I can't put the whammy on that many people."

"That is my job," he conceded with one of his slight nods.

"Fine," she said. "Good." Selena played the light over the dead face. "Who is he?"

Ariel looked at her with his cool, pale eyes. "I have no idea."

Chapter 7

"He's not a local boy?"

"He is not from any nest in the city."

Not a local boy. Shit. Selena *knew* she shouldn't have gotten involved. It was none of her business—except that it was a homicide, and that was her department. And now it looked like it was more complicated than she'd thought. The plan had been to take the body to the Enforcer of the City and leave the trouble for him to deal with. A simple plan. She'd figured it for a simple crime of passion. Signs indicated that somebody who knew and hated the victim took out their rage in a nasty, thorough way. Vampires claimed they couldn't kill each other, but Selena knew anyone could kill anyone if sufficient motive, means, and opportunity were present. She hoped this was a vampire-killing-vampire case. She wasn't going to let herself think about the other possibility while Ariel was around. The other way was too complicated.

Complicated crimes among the strigoi tended to call

for a specialist. *The* specialist: Istvan. Meanest Mother in the Valley. Her Steve.

Shit.

"Local strig?" she asked hopefully. "Territorial war between some new boys in town?" The strigs were technically loners, living outside the protection and laws of vampire society, but that didn't mean the local Enforcer wasn't aware of most strig activity in his town. Any good cop would know potential troublemakers.

"Possibly."

"Any nest have a safe house off Oak Street?"

She didn't blame him when he didn't answer. He reached past her and closed the body bag, his long white fingers elegantly graceful against the shiny black plastic. He took the body out of the car trunk as if it weighed nothing and put it over his shoulder, then turned a very frightening, stern glance on her. "This is my case from now on, Detective. Thank you for your help." Then he disappeared, leaving a momentary white blur in the corner of her eye as he moved with the swiftness of his kind.

It was not, she noticed after a moment's reflection, anywhere near as fast as her boy Steve could move. She wondered why that was and pulled out of the quiet neighborhood to drive through heavy traffic on the way home to Evanston. She knew Enforcers were different than regular vampires, almost a breed apart, and that Istvan was different even than regular Enforcers. What she didn't know, and he'd certainly never bothered telling her, was why and how. It had become habit to try not to think about anything to do with the monster in her life. Cop's instincts told her that might not be wise right now, not when she'd just risked her own career to clean up a mess that had spilled over from the world she pretended didn't exist.

"It's not pretense, it's a survival tool," she muttered as a driver using a cell phone cut her off. She hated using her own car, and she hated people who used those things while they drove! "Idiots. Where was I?" Oh, yeah, telling herself she didn't pretend vampires didn't exist. It was only Istvan, her boy Steve, she tried to pretend didn't exist. Tried and failed utterly.

She hated admitting that, not because she loathed personal failure but because she dealt with people who lied to themselves all the time, and they were stupid. Murderers were especially good at mental gymnastics that convinced them that they had a right to take life, that it was the victim's fault they'd been killed. And sex offenders: God, sex offenders were the worst at finding anyone to blame but themselves for the sick lives they led. And what was a vampire but an immortal rapist-murderer?

And she was one of them.

"Now there's a chilling little admission." Selena glanced in the rearview mirror to look herself in the eye. Somehow that ritual helped reassure her of her current humanity. At least she could see herself in the mirror. She remembered how she used to check her teeth to see if they were getting pointy and brushed and flossed five or six times a day after she was first bitten. She supposed she'd nursed some crazy hope that good dental hygiene would save her from the fate that awaited her.

A largely unknown fate, she admitted, after two years of lurking around the outside edge of strigoi life. She didn't know what it was like to be a vampire, and she had only a warped and fragmented notion of what it was like to be a companion—from fellow dissatisfied companions, at that. She sometimes suspected that her aunt knew more about vampires than she did. And Steve—Istvan, the Meanest Mother in the Valley—what did she really know about him?

Did it matter for a murder investigation she'd just turned over to the vampire police department? Her instincts told her it did. Her instincts, she pointed out to herself, were screwed up by hormones, or pheromones, or blood loss from last night's little romp with Fangboy the Magnificent. And was he really hung like a stallion, or was it some sort of vampire hypnotism that made her think he was? And did it matter, considering the force and frequency of the orgasms the illusion—or possibly reality—induced in her?

"Yes, damn it!"

Reality mattered. Controlling her life mattered. And why the hell had she turned over the case to the Enforcer in the first place? She banged a fist against the steering wheel. She and Raleigh had taken the call. It was their crime scene, their case. For some reason, she'd reacted like a vampire's pet blood donor instead of Detective Sergeant Crawford. The tendency to want to please and obey the master race that was built into the relationships the biters had with the bitees was really sick and disgusting and so damn hard to fight. Hard to even notice unless you worked very diligently at it. All the time.

Selena sighed. Now that it was done, she didn't know whether taking the body to Ariel was the right thing to do or not. What she hated was that her reaction had been a knee-jerk protection of a community she wanted no part of, and that she had not understood her response until it was too late. They'd gotten her again, and she'd done it to herself. For better or worse, she'd let the initiative go. She tried not to think about it anymore on the rest of the drive home.

Okay, I'll bite. Selena typed the E-mail message to DesertDog's ICQ. She was thankful she'd found him online this early in the evening and glad she'd exchanged instant messaging information with at least some of the chat group. DesertDog was just the person she wanted to talk to after a day spent making sure the corpse missing from the morgue wasn't traced back to her. She typed, **What happened in Denver?**

Was there a chainsaw involved? she wondered. *Were you?* She considered asking but restrained herself and sent the message with only the one question.

After a considerable wait, the other companion responded, **One of Them was found dead in a downtown park. Sloppy job.**

How do you know about this?

She'd checked with Denver Homicide, but there'd been no reports of heartless, headless corpses. She wondered if Steve knew about this. He'd said he was heading west. Again, there was a lot of lag time before DesertDog sent a reply.

A friend told me.

Your friend?

Wait.

Yes.

Nighthawk clan?

The loop members avoided direct questions about their own personal demons, but Selena was sick of generalities. Oddly enough, DesertDog answered immediately.

Yes.

So she wasn't the only pet person of an Enforcer in

the dissident group. She was not surprised. Bet you're happy to get that off your chest, she wrote.

Yours? Was DesertDog's answer.

My chest?

Be happy to talk about your chest, but I asked about your lover. Got a Nighthawk sucking on you?

Maybe he—or she—wasn't telling the truth. Maybe DesertDog was boasting about who his vampire was, or he was lying about a dead vampire in Denver. There were lots of maybes and plenty of reasons to hide facts in their tightly guarded little world. Their world. Not hers. Just because she didn't want to be a vampire and was ignored by her master didn't mean she didn't want to know what was going on. Curiosity made her a good detective.

And killed cats.

I'm a dog person, she told herself, remembering the time Steve had turned into a wolf, or at least made her think he'd turned into one. Selena typed, I'm not sure what mine is.

How can a companion not be sure?

Long story.

I bet.

Let's return to the sloppily killed vampire. You know details?

Head and heart cut out. Method was sound, but other stuff was stupid.

Method?

The critter was killed in a way I would have done it, but I didn't. I wouldn't have left the body out for anybody to find.

Think some mortal's trying to expose the underneath world?

Maybe.

Or maybe it's one of them.

Maybe.

What do you think? Selena asked.

Why do you want to know?

She was glad he'd denied involvement in the crime—
Was killing a vampire a crime?—before she asked. She
didn't question his claim, not just yet. Should she tell
DesertDog about the dead one she'd delivered to Ariel?
Should she make an attempt to spread the word around
the vampire community through the companions? It was
Ariel's business, right? It was not a companion's place
to—

While she continued to debate in her head, her fingers
typed, There's a headless, heartless vampire in Chicago.

Good. The fewer bloodsuckers we're going to have to
nail when our time comes, the better.

You really believe that? Bring on the revolution? That
things will be different when we take over?

Don't you?

I'm asking the questions.

You sound like a cop.

I take that as a compliment.

Selena knew, even as she sent the words, that they
were a mistake, but she couldn't call them back once
the Enter key was pressed. DesertDog was off-line the
moment he read the message. Apparently he didn't like
cops. She swore and turned off the computer. She'd been
stupid, but at least she had some information from the
other companion. What was she going to do with it?
Merely asking the question gave her a headache.

She took aspirin, poured herself a tall glass of iced
coffee, put some CDs in the stereo carousel, picked up
a yellow legal pad and pen, and did what she always did
when a case was giving her trouble: She let her mind

wander and began to doodle. It was one of those *Trust the Force* things she'd learned to do when she accepted the fact that she really was psychic.

The last thing she expected to see when she came out of her trancelike state was that she'd written her Aunt Catie's phone number over and over and over. She didn't know what it meant, but she supposed it was better than drawing little hearts with her and Steve's names in them.

"Let's have a look."

The Enforcer of the City sneered. He did it very well, Istvan thought, especially after being grabbed by the hair and dragged down here from his lover's bed. "You have no right to—"

Istvan slammed him back against the basement wall with a casual swat. The impact left a spiderweb pattern of cracks in the brick foundation of the Victorian-era building that Ariel's companion ran as a trendy northside restaurant. "I'm not here to steal your lunch, fairy boy."

"Elf," Ariel corrected, with a toss of his pretty white hair.

"Whatever." Istvan rather liked Ariel, he respected his abilities, but it was Istvan's policy never to cut any of the undead any slack. He didn't blame Chicago's Enforcer for resenting the wicked *dhamphir*'s walking into his private storage crib and making arrogant demands. *If I were anyone but me, I'd hate me, too.* He grinned and made it an insult by showing mating fangs like a total alpha jerk. He pointed toward the row of meat lockers. "You want to pay for the repairs when I rip the doors off?"

Ariel ignored his smile and didn't bother answering Istvan's question. He went to a door and worked the

combination lock. A moment after Ariel opened the
locker, Istvan grabbed him by the back of the neck and
took the Enforcer inside it. It was very cold within the
shallow walk-in freezer, with barely enough room for
two living vampires to stand side by side and look upon
the remains of the dead one. The corpse did not look as
though a Nighthawk had been at it. One sniff told Istvan
that the corpse was fairly fresh, two nights old at most.
So, the mortal killer *was* here. It was nice to see that his
guess that there was something rotten in the county of
Cook had paid off. He almost wished he hadn't turned
around somewhere in the middle of Iowa and headed
back, but if you didn't trust your instincts, what was the
use of having them?

Istvan picked up the head by its long, silky brown
hair. "Who?"

"I haven't the faintest idea."

Istvan felt how Ariel hated making the admission.
"Local strig?"

"You're not the first one to ask that." Ariel took in a
sharp breath, as though trying to draw the words back.

Istvan tasted raw fear as he turned a very fierce stare
on Chicago's Enforcer. Ariel fought meeting his gaze
and failed. Ariel's eyes became suddenly very dark and
very wide, and his strongly shielded mind opened to
Istvan like warm butter yielding to a knife. *Who brought
you the body?*

Did he really have to ask?

Flashes of a face appeared in Ariel's mind, though he
tried to hide it. A conversation over an open car trunk
spilled into Istvan's head. Ariel's thoughts managed at
last to form into coherent words. *How did you know?*

It's a dhamphir *thing,* was all he'd reply to the Enforcer. "Who is she?" he asked out loud, just to see what Ariel would answer.

"She's a Homicide detective." Ariel knew that wasn't what Istvan meant. Istvan had only to quirk an eyebrow to start Ariel babbling. "I don't know *who* she belongs to! All I know is that she's from a witch family. She knows every nest in the city but doesn't bother us."

"And you don't bother her?" Istvan smiled a thin, dangerous smile. "Why haven't you killed her, Enforcer of the City? What would the Council say?"

"I enforce the Laws! How can I kill her without knowing who her master is? She's not mine to punish or hunt. Strigoi are my rightful prey, not mortal property. When I find her master, I'll make him deal with her."

Good, honest answers. Points to Chicago's righteous, law-abiding Enforcer. Istvan noticed that his claws had grown quite a bit while he listened to Ariel, and hot rage bubbled very close to the surface at anyone daring to threaten *his* companion. He battled down the anger, reminding himself that it only stemmed from the link forged in blood and sex by the ridiculous reproductive drive that had finally caught him. The truth was, it would be better for him and Selena if someone did kill her. Only that someone wasn't going to be Ariel the Elf!

He retracted his claws and said quite calmly, "I'll deal with the woman."

"You mean you'll deal with her—"

"Did I say you could contradict me?" He looked deeply once more into Ariel's eyes and spoke to his soul. *You . . . you will forget you've ever heard of her, have ever seen her, ever thought of her.* He stepped back and bounced the dead vampire head from hand to hand while he gave Ariel a moment to come to himself. When the Enforcer was fully in control of himself once more, Istvan tossed him the head. "The case is mine," Istvan informed him. "You can keep the meat."

Chapter 8

CAETLYN BAILEY WAS not the black sheep of the family, it was Selena's mother who was the despair of the Bailey clan, having rebelliously run off to become an accountant and marry a cop. The Baileys were, to put it mildly, eccentrics in the middle-class American landscape in which Selena's mom had tried to disappear for a while. She had settled into the prosaic world of the Crawford family and been happy to be wife, mother, and career woman for awhile. But by the time Selena was born, she'd mellowed to the point of taking the old broom and wand out of the closet and called Aunt Catie in to instruct her kid in at least *some* of the Baileys' way of life. There were a lot of things Mom had drawn the line at, and many things Dad was never going to know about Mom's side of the family. Not that he was Darren to Mom's Samantha, but, all in all, relations between the Crawfords and the Baileys were kindly and close.

Selena thought it was fortunate that Mom had reconciled with her past and her family, especially now that

Selena was an adult, and Mom no longer tried to shield
her from anything remotely weird. There were *lots* of
things Mom didn't know and didn't want to know. "I'm
with Mom on that," Selena muttered as she approached
the door of Aunt Catie's shop. She didn't have a choice,
of course, and that was what always pissed her off the
most about all this magic, supernatural, paranormal crap.

Her cousin Paloma was behind the counter in the public part of the shop. This was the part that sold the New
Age books and gifts, jewelry, scented oils, and other
innocuous stuff. The second floor was used for psychic
readings and classes. Aunt Catie lived on the third floor.
The basement was where every real magical practitioner
in town came for their supplies. Aunt Catie actually had
a catalog she sent out to these special customers. As far
as Selena knew, her aunt didn't yet have a web site, but
that was inevitable, wasn't it?

"Why don't people believe there are monsters under
the bed?" was the first thing Selena said when she saw
that Paloma was alone in the shop.

"Not to mention in the bed," Paloma answered with
a twinkle in her eyes that was all too knowing. "If we're
lucky."

Selena didn't blush; she knew Paloma wasn't talking
about vampires. "You're still studying sex magic, aren't
you?"

"Tantra." Paloma gestured toward the stairs and held
a finger to her lips. "Aunt Catie does not approve.
Wait'll she sees the Hindu god I'm bringing to Karen's
wedding."

For a moment, Selena considered asking if Paloma
was being literal or metaphorical, then remembered that

her cousin was dating a physician from Bangladesh, and left it alone.

"You have a date for the wedding yet?" Paloma asked. "Want me to set you up with someone?"

"No. No." Selena glanced at the stairs. "Aunt Catie working?"

Paloma nodded. She looked at her watch. "Late appointment. I'm getting ready to close up and go practice some Tantra."

"You go. I'll close."

Paloma grinned, grabbed her purse, and was out the door a moment later. Selena came around the counter and opened the cash register. All the Bailey cousins worked for Aunt Catie at one time or another. She knew the drill for closing up the shop. That included the warding spells that were the very last duty to be performed at the end of the business day. Aunt Catie was always very concerned about burglars.

Her concern was that anyone who broke in wouldn't have their soul sucked out by some grimoire or magical tool stored in the basement. When Selena had commended her for such compassion, Aunt Catie had replied that she didn't give a damn about any would-be thieves, she simply didn't want to spoil the spirits that dwelled in the basement. "Next thing you know, they'll be expecting human sacrifices, and *we* don't do that sort of thing."

Selena had been a teenager and a thorough nonbeliever when she and her aunt had that conversation. She'd been shocked, amused, and certain her aunt was joking. Selena Crawford did as she was told, but to her, Caetlyn Bailey's profession was some sort of profitable scam. Working in the shop had been a fun part-time job, much better than slaving at a fast food place. How she wished now she'd paid more attention.

As if on cue, her aunt's client came downstairs as Selena finished all but the last part of the ritual. The woman was distracted and thoughtful. She didn't notice that Selena wasn't the same woman who'd been in the shop when she arrived. Selena gave her a bright smile, ushered her out, then waved a smoking stick of incense in the prescribed pattern, rushed through the ritual words, and headed upstairs, trailing a cloud of sandalwood behind her.

The room at the end of the short hall where Aunt Catie did her readings did not have a particularly otherworldly look to it. It was comfortably furnished with a couch and chairs, bookcases, Tiffany-style lamps, and low tables. About the only thing that looked mystical was a beautifully done piece of calligraphy in an intricately carved frame on one blue-painted wall. The calligraphy read, in Gaelic, *"I see dead people—all major credit cards accepted."* And, oh, yeah, there was an Irish harp in one corner, and an old photo of an Irish traveling cart on top of one of the bookcases. For Aunt Catie, these touches were to remind her of her roots and keep her honest.

Aunt Catie didn't glance up when Selena came in. Her head was bent over a tarot spread. She said, "Put that thing out, Selena."

Selena backed out of the room long enough to douse water over the incense stick in the second floor's small washroom, then strode back in to confront her aunt. "So," she said as her aunt scooped up the cards, "what am I doing here?"

Catie Bailey gave a dramatic little cough and waved a hand in front of her nose. "Stinking up my inner sanc-

tum, for one thing." She stood. "I take it Paloma is off
to practice sexual gymnastics." She smirked. "If only
there was an Olympic event for it, the girl'd bring home
the gold. You'd do well to follow her example," she
added before Selena could contribute so much as a
snicker.

"But—"

"Never mind that, now. Come on." Aunt Catie led
Selena from the reading room and up the stairs to her
apartment.

Selena became aware of the vampire just before she
stepped through the arched doorway to the living room.
Selena was furious with herself for not detecting its presence sooner, but this was Aunt Catie's place, where the
magical vibes were strong and contradictory enough to
blend and conceal and cancel each other out.

"Besides," Aunt Catie said, "No one knows what's
going on in my house until I want them to. Put that thing
away," she added as she moved past Selena to lead the
way into the room.

"I should have known," Selena grumbled to herself,
and put away the Glock she hadn't been aware of drawing. She quelled the useless impulse to ask her aunt what
a vampire was doing in her house and followed Catie
inside to find out for herself.

The vampire lying on the couch did not look well at
all. Pale from vampires she was used to, sickly, she was
not. Selena studied the emaciated male who looked back
at her with fever-bright eyes and almost didn't recognize
him through the expression of pain on his face. "Larry?"
she asked finally. "What the hell happened to you?"

"He was attacked," Aunt Catie answered for him and
spread another comforter on the pile that already covered
him. She touched his forehead with the back of her hand.

"The poor dear." She turned back to Selena, who was just managing not to gape. "You two talk. I'll make some coffee."

Larry sat up with a great deal of difficulty as Selena came closer, and he made an effort to throw off the cocoon of blankets. She was amazed to see him so weak but didn't offer to help him. Once he was finally free of the confining coverings and sitting upright, she saw what his problem was. Somebody had cut off his left arm.

"Ouch," she murmured, almost sympathetic. "That had to hurt."

"No, shit." His voice was rough and weak.

Selena took a seat in the chair on the other side of the couch. There were quite a few questions she wanted to ask the injured vampire, many of them quite personal. Of course, she could guess the answers to many of the personal ones, and the one about just how close her aunt and Lawrence were she didn't really want to know.

"He hasn't bitten me, if that's what you're wondering," Aunt Catie said, coming back into the room.

Of course not, Selena told herself, almost embarrassed at her own relief. She'd have recognized the difference in her aunt if there were some psychic thread binding her to a vampire lover. The bonds between the strigoi and the mortals they put the bite on were easily detectable by anyone else involved in the life. Weren't they?

Selena eyed her aunt critically. Glenda the Good Witch here *might* be able to mask her private life from prying vampire hunters. Larry was a strig, after all, a loner who was technically rightful prey to the Enforcer of the City, should Ariel decide he was in the mood for a nosh some evening. Rightful prey or not, the Enforcers usually left strigs alone as long as the vampires who lived outside the system kept their heads low and noses

clean. Larry was a law-abiding sort of guy, in his own
way. She'd been there when he'd gotten disillusioned.
His nest leader, Maria, the Enforcer of the City at the
time, went bad and had very nearly gotten every vampire
in Chicago killed for her own mad, selfish reasons. Larry
had helped Selena and Steve take out Maria, but then,
in disgust, he walked away from the life as much as he
could. Selena didn't hold with bad cops, either, and ap-
plauded Larry's decision to leave a system he thought
was corrupt.

Which was more than Larry could do right now.

"What are you smiling about?"

Selena wiped the smile off her face and answered her
aunt, "Bad joke."

"I can guess." Aunt Catie's look was reproving.

Selena squared her shoulders and forced herself to
take the matter of an injured vampire seriously. She *liked*
Larry, who had once refused to make her his companion
because he didn't bite people who didn't want to be
bitten. He was no vampire rapist. A lot of them were.
They deserved to be cut up, slowly, but not Lawrence.
"You going to be all right?" she asked first. "What happened to you? Do you know who?"

In the kitchen, the coffeemaker buzzed. Aunt Catie
left the room.

Larry held up his hand, blinked a few times, and focused his attention on Selena. "I'm left-handed . . . I *was*
left-handed. This is going to take some getting used to."

"It'll grow back, right?"

"I hope so. Your aunt says I can stay in her basement
while I'm waiting to see if the regeneration stuff is a
legend or not." He eyed Selena nervously. "That okay
with you?"

At first, she wondered why he was asking her, then

Selena remembered that he was the only vampire in the world who knew about her and Steve. Steve didn't want anyone to know and neither did she, but they owed Larry. Apparently, Larry was also her aunt's friend. "It's Catie's basement," she told him. "Who she keeps there is no business of mine . . . or anyone else." She wasn't going to promise that she wasn't going to let Steve eat him, or mess with Larry's head if he took a mind to. She only made promises she knew she could keep, but if Steve hadn't messed with Larry by now, she doubted he was likely to. "You probably picked the safest spot in town."

"You have a good heart." His eyes took on a twinkle more of humor than fever. "Sorry, bad joke."

"Mind reader," she accused, with something that sounded disgustingly like affection.

"Goes with the territory. But never yours," he added. He glanced at his left shoulder. "What is the sound of one vampire hand clapping?"

Catie came back with steaming mugs and handed one to each of them.

Larry looked into his and made a face. "Chicken soup?"

"Broth." Catie left again. Selena sipped her own coffee. Larry sipped the broth. Catie came back with a mug for herself and sat down on the couch near the vampire. After a few oddly cozy moments, Catie said, "Tell Selena what happened, Lawrence."

"Somebody cut my arm off."

"Lawrence."

He took a deep breath. Vampires hated telling anyone anything. "I was asleep. It was daylight. I was out, but I was sleeping, not dreamriding or doing any out-of-body stuff. Then I felt somebody in my house. I couldn't move, and I never came fully awake enough to focus. I heard a noise . . . roaring. Felt this overwhelming fury. And then it *hurt*. It hurt like hell, and that was all I knew for hours." He glanced at his shoulder again, and the dangling sleeve of the plaid bathrobe he wore.

"He brought his arm to me," Aunt Catie said. "It's on ice in the basement. It wasn't a hack job like with a knife or an ax. Not that precise, either, but a pretty clean slice."

Larry looked like he was going to throw up at the description of his wound. He focused on Selena. "She could have killed me."

"Aunt Catie?"

"Of course not! What are you talking about?"

"You said *she.*"

He blinked. "I did?"

"Yes."

"Yeah. She. I think." He closed his eyes, thinking with great effort. He looked weak and weary. "The anger that hit me . . . yeah . . . it had a female feel to it. I didn't see anything. I don't know who did it."

He wasn't telling her everything. "Where were you?" Selena put her mug on the coffee table and leaned forward. "Were you alone?"

"That's not—"

"You live near Oak Street Beach, off Goethe. And you had company." She had not known it was possible for a vampire who had lost a lot of blood to blanch, but Larry did. She didn't let him know her knowledge came from working homicide and not from having special powers as Steve's girlfriend. "Who was he?" she asked as Larry slowly nodded.

"He?"

"I need to know. Better me than Ariel, or—"

"I don't want any trouble!"

It was so annoying that she didn't even have to say the *dhamphir*'s name to get that reaction. Of course, if she didn't want to scare Larry into full cooperation, she shouldn't allude to the thing that scared him the most. *Only using a cop's trick,* she told herself, *getting co-operation from the suspect the easiest way.* Larry wasn't officially a suspect in anything yet. Right now, he was a victim of attempted murder, but he was trying to hide facts. Detective Crawford didn't put up with that.

"Then tell me who the murdered vampire was." *And why am I having this conversation? It's not my job!* Neither Ariel nor Steve would appreciate her interference. That made her smile and gave her all the reason she needed to go on. Annoying the lords of the under-neath world was much more fun than giving in to the compulsion to serve at their command. "I need to know everything, Larry."

"And she won't go away and let you rest until you tell her," Aunt Catie added. She patted him on the knee. "Finish your broth first, then tell her."

He gave her a piteous look. "I could use a drink."

"I've got a call out for a volunteer."

"Talk to me," Selena interrupted.

Larry gulped down his chicken broth and told her. "His name was Peter. I barely knew him. He was a friend of the vampire who made me. I keep in touch with the old crowd."

"The old crowd where?" Selena prompted.

"Why?"

She gave him her steeliest look.

"Colorado."

"Could you be a bit more specific?" He was trying to protect his home nest, she supposed. Commendable.

"You're a strig now," she reminded him. "They wouldn't protect you."

"In theory."

"Yeah." Friendships and loyalties often went beyond the letter of the law, in mortal and immortal worlds. "So why was this guy running from Denver?"

He shrugged with his one good shoulder, winced, and showed not a twinge of reaction to her naming a city. "He told me he needed a place to stay."

"To lie low?"

"We usually do that."

"He was on the run from someone. They found him."

"Peter's an ancient one, an Old Country strigoi."

"Was."

"If a strigoi doesn't want to be found . . ." He trailed off in a low, pained laugh. "Sorry about the bravado, Hunter. Habit. Yes, I guess they found him. Found us."

He didn't notice using a title Selena had no right to, and she didn't correct him. "But the murderer didn't kill you." She bit her lip and rubbed her chin. "Why? Chainsaw ran out of fuel? Left you as a warning?"

"About what?" Aunt Catie asked.

"I've no idea. I'm just throwing out ideas here." She looked back at Larry. His head was thrown back, eyes closed. About at the end of his strength. Odd to think of one of *them* sick and vulnerable. Selena didn't think she was going to get any more help from Larry tonight. She stood. "Want me to help you get him downstairs?" she asked her aunt.

Her aunt got to her feet. "I'd appreciate that. Then you'd better get home, yourself. Oh, and Selena," she added. "I did a reading for you today. Be careful."

Chapter 9

"LUCY, I'M HOME!" Selena would have jumped out of her skin if she hadn't known that was exactly the sort of reaction Steve wanted. She considered whirling around in the small kitchen and demanding to know what he was doing back in Chicago, back at her place, specifically. She considered throwing her soapy arms around him and kissing him silly, but that wasn't what *she* really wanted to do. She firmly did not think about having left Aunt Catie's place an hour ago. Instead of following any impulse, she didn't bother turning away from the kitchen sink where she was doing dishes, and said, "Don't you mean, Mina?"

Istvan studied Selena appreciatively for a moment. She was wearing a gray sports bra and biking shorts. Her workout clothing showed off pale skin over well-toned muscles. Very well-toned muscles had his amazon princess cop. She knew he was studying her, and her scent changed in subtle, inviting reaction. They both hated that the girl couldn't help it. To keep his mind off what both their bodies contemplated, he said, "I was quoting an old television show you're too young to remember."

She laughed. "Honey, they're quoting *I Love Lucy* on Alpha Centauri by now. *Everybody* knows what you were talking about."

"Oh." He reached out and put a hand on her bare shoulder, drinking in the mortal warmth. He couldn't help it. "Then what were you—"

"Dracula," she said.

He jumped back. "What did you say?"

"You know, Mina, Lucy, Jonathan, Count Dracula, ruler of the land beyond the forest."

"How did you know—?"

Steve sounded shocked out of his wits. Rather than feeling as if she'd won some sort of victory from him, Selena turned in surprise. There was an expression in her vampire's blue eyes that was almost painful and not quite here. It made her heart ache. He backed away from her. She failed to fight the urge to take a step toward him. "What's the matter? You've never heard of Dracula?"

"Heard of him?" He laughed, a sound so caustic it must have burned coming out. "Honey, I used to work for him."

She crossed her arms under her breasts. Bubbles of dishwashing soap dripped from her fingers.

She laughed, and if it wasn't caustic, at least it was sarcastic. "Yeah, right."

"No, really. I did. For a while. Couple weeks back in the fifteenth century. He never paid me. Of course, I quit kind of suddenly." Why was he telling her this? Istvan didn't want to think about that time, what had happened. The urge to pour out the whole story was simply there on the tip of his tongue, drawn there by the intensely curious look on her face, the sympathetic interest she didn't realize she was projecting. What was wrong here? Confiding in his companion? How very . . . typical.

Olympias used to tell him private things about her past, share her sadness and the mortal memories of her abusive husband and the mad son that had died in a faraway land. He'd soothed her, held her, made stupid, comforting noises and gentle, passionate love to help take her pain away. And he'd genuinely *cared*. All because he was her companion and his mistress wanted him to care. He would not inflict that sort of false devotion on anyone.

Selena tried to fight off her consuming curiosity, but she'd never been any good at not being nosy. She eyed the vampire the other vampires were scared of suspiciously. "Dracula's real?"

"Real. Deadly. Cunning. Cruel. I liked him."

"Definitely your kind of guy." She found his affirming the existence of Dracula hard to believe. Not that he'd ever lied to her. Not that he'd had much chance; they didn't talk much. He had a perverse sense of humor; it was hard to take any comment seriously. His body spoke to her, though, with a wired tenseness in his muscles that got her attention. She'd learned to read intent from body language as a beat cop, and still as he held himself, she read that this was no joke. "You worked for the king of vampires?"

"No. That would be me."

"Your modesty—"

"Underwhelms you, I know."

There was an expression on his long, thin face all of a sudden, something in Steve's eyes that amazed her. There was eagerness there where his emotions were usually so closely guarded, and she saw hunger, too. She was used to seeing a predatory gleam in his narrow blue eyes, but this was different and not directed at her. At least not in a way she was used to. There were memories there, opinions, and a longing to share them.

She reminded herself that she hadn't had enough experience with this being she was bound to, to really know what to expect from him. She didn't know him. What she knew about Istvan was rumor, legend, whispered hearsay, and all she'd learned centered around his killing abilities. She didn't need anyone to tell her how dangerous he was or how much he hated his own kind. He was a force of nature, like a hurricane. Did a hurricane need reasons? Have a past?

Did the hurricane have to show up in her apartment just before midnight on a work night? She wasn't surprised to see him back in town, not after she'd found the body. Not when she'd already figured out that he meant Denver when he mentioned heading west. The action had moved away from the west, and he'd trailed the murderer back to Chicago. Good for him. Bad for the killer. She didn't know quite what to think of that yet. For the moment, she let speculation go and allowed her curiosity get the better of her with the matter at hand.

"There really was a Dracula?"

"The Romanian tourist attraction version, yes. I knew him." Steve stepped back to lean against the kitchen doorframe. "Met him. Who was I to know a prince? Or want to."

Who indeed? She did not have to speak the words to receive a dark, warning glare from him. She pointed a finger at him. "I didn't start this. But if you're going to do the revelation thing, I'm going to do follow-up."

"Why?"

The combination of genuine annoyance and surprise made her laugh. She waved in the general direction of the bedroom. "I'm not in the habit of going to bed with strangers."

"Until you met me."

The most terrifying creature on the planet looked at her with such open vulnerability it made her toes curl. Selena knew he didn't know he'd completely dropped his hard façade. She couldn't completely let herself be glad that he had. It was unwise to dive beneath the surface here, but she took a deep breath and went on.

"Meeting you was—"

"Unfortunate."

"Don't interrupt."

The king of vampires ducked his head. "Yes, ma'am."

"Unfortunate," she agreed. "It wasn't fatal."

He smiled a little at that. "You won't recover."

She put her hands on her hips. "Yeah. From what I hear, neither will you. We're stuck with each other. You run. I cope."

He took a dangerous step closer to her. "Do you?" His voice was soft, menacing, the words alone might have struck dead with terror anyone but her.

Selena snorted. "You want some coffee?"

Istvan looked at the kitchen clock. "Isn't it a little late for you?"

"I asked if *you* wanted some. I'm being a good hostess."

So she was, he realized. *Simply being polite and not behaving as a devoted slave.* His tendency to underestimate her annoyed him. He ran a hand through his hair. "What were we talking about?"

"Bad books and old television shows."

Or old books and bad television shows. He shrugged.

What did it matter? They had been talking. No, he'd been talking. That was stupid. "You won't even call me by my real name. Don't pretend you want to get to know me." He'd done it again! He slapped himself on the forehead. He would have put a fist through a wall, but she would have yelled at him for damaging her property.

"Oh, for God's sake," she responded to his childishness. "Do you really want to be introduced to people as Istvan? That is *so* fifteenth century."

"It's a perfectly good name."

"If you live in Romania."

"What's wrong with living in Romania?"

"Nothing. But you don't. Steve's a good American name."

"Why must Americans change things? Simplify them?"

"Because we're good at it."

"What about diversity? Multiculturalism?"

"What about it?"

He was babbling. He didn't babble. He was the strong, silent type. Ask anyone who knew him who didn't flinch or faint at the sight of him. Which was about three people in the world. Three people too many. "I'm going to have to work on my numbers."

Selena wasn't the flinching or fainting type. And she knew exactly what he was talking about. "It only cuts down your Christmas list."

He couldn't stop himself. "What does?"

"Making everyone scared of you."

"It keeps me alive."

She knew what he meant this time, too. "Revenge isn't what keeps you alive. It's only what keeps you going."

But how did she know? And why did she care? Not

because she was a companion and she must care, he was certain of that. It shook him down to the soul. "You make me crazy."

She grinned. "Good."

The next thing he knew, she was on the floor beneath him, with her shorts pulled down and her bra hiked up. They were both breathing very hard. It tickled when her nails scraped across his back with all her strength. "Sex is no substitute . . . for co . . . munication."

"And it's hard on the knees," he acknowledged. "This floor is *hard*." That said, he hauled her up and over his shoulder.

On the way to the bedroom, she said, "I'm not impressed."

He laughed. "Give it a few minutes."

At no point over the next several hours did he bite her.

Selena didn't know which was worse, having him in or out of her bed. No. The in bed part was fun, it was living in suspended animation the rest of the time that sucked. For that, she hit him on the shoulder once she finally recovered her breath and her senses after a particularly prolonged and intense orgasm. "Okay," she admitted. "I'm impressed."

She expected and received a smirk. Then he rolled over and lay on his back, his long body stretched out beside her, and groaned. "That wasn't supposed to happen."

She wasn't sure if she was amused or annoyed at his sounding so chagrined. "Pleasure before business?"

"Turned out that way."

"I didn't figure you came back because you were horny."

"You should be offended."

"Cut the old-world gentleman crap. I'd rather know what you're doing here."

They spoke while staring up at the ceiling. Selena glanced sideways at the alarm clock on the nightstand. It was very late at night or very early in the morning, depending on how you looked at it. Either way, Steve got to sleep all day; she didn't.

He turned toward her and lay a hand flat on her bare stomach. "You know what I'm doing here. I've had a talk with Ariel. I've seen the body you brought him."

"And . . . ?" she prompted.

"Ariel no longer remembers you," he told her. "But, knowing you—"

"You don't know me."

"I doubt he'll forget you for long. You should keep your nose out of strigoi business."

"Not when they kill people in my town."

"It is not a companion's place to keep the nests honest. Ariel's a good Nighthawk."

"So was Maria, you told me once. Until she decided not to be anymore."

"Point taken." He flopped back onto his back, not touching her at all. She made no attempt to cuddle or cling to his warmth.

They'd never discussed Maria after her execution, any more than they discussed anything else. He'd come to town two years before, done his job, and left. During the proceedings, there had been a brief sexual interlude that utterly changed her life, ripped away all her psychic barriers, introduced her to the underneath world, and he left her to cope on her own. Steve didn't hang around for the aftermath. Two years she'd waited, wanted, and dreaded his return. Of course, he'd only returned because there was more trouble in town. Selena did not take kindly to this intrusion into her affairs.

"Who are you to tell me what a companion should do?"

Istvan didn't have to look at a clock to know the time. Nor was this a discussion he could afford to get into, even if there were plenty of hours left in the night. "I also told Ariel to forget about the case." His chest rose and fell in a deep, disgusted sigh. "I spoke too soon. Now I actually have to do some work."

"Which is where I come in."

"Which is where you come in."

Selena carefully schooled her thoughts and emotions. She'd been practicing shielding herself, with a lot of help from her aunt. Aunt Catie said Selena was good at mind tricks. It was because of worry for Aunt Catie that she didn't immediately mention anything about Lawrence being attacked in his sleep to Steve. Maybe the Enforcers' Enforcer was in charge of the case, but Larry was in Aunt Catie's basement. Selena wasn't setting her aunt in Steve's way. Even though he knew, and so far tolerated, Catie Bailey's being aware of the strigoi community, there was no guarantee he wouldn't kill her if he found out how deeply she was into the life. Besides, it was habit and professional pride that made Detective Sergeant Crawford still disgruntled with turning over a case to another law enforcement agency.

"Where do I come in?" she asked.

"The vampire's remains were seen and examined by mortals. All records of that have to be wiped."

"Well, duh. As if I haven't already thought of that. The paper trail is growing more confused all the time."

He reached over and patted her, his big hand cupping her breast when he did it. "You're clever. I'm thorough. I'm going to have to have a little talk with everyone who dealt with the body."

She sat up and looked down on him in a whirling mixture of terror, skepticism, and outrage. "You want me to bring all of them to you? What are you going to do to them?"

"Talk to them. Make them forget."

"Magic doesn't work like that! You can't make *everybody* forget."

He propped his hands behind his head. "I can."

Maybe he could. "Promise me you won't kill anyone you can't hypnotize."

He didn't argue. He yawned and closed his eyes. "I promise. It's dawn," he added.

Which didn't give her time to tell him she didn't believe his promise. It was just as well, as he might have gotten all outraged with wounded honor. Selena dragged herself out of bed and headed for the bathroom. All he wanted was a list. Fine. She'd get him a list, then maybe he'd get out of town. Out of her life again. She closed her eyes and leaned against the wall as hot water poured down over her. Another sleepless night spent arguing and in the arms of Steve left her shaking with reaction. Her fingers found the starred hole that had been left in the tile when she'd shot him a couple years ago. She almost smiled at the memory, except it reminded her that a companion with a weak bond or sufficient motivation was capable of killing a strigoi.

Steve would remember that as well. It made her wonder if she was his main suspect and if that was the real reason he was back in town. Maybe he was playing cat and mouse with her and would pounce once the mortal witnesses were disposed of. Maybe he wanted to see if she had accomplices. Her on-line companions' support group came to mind, and the thought was blocked as quickly as her tired mind would allow. She figured she was safe from Steve's mind walking intrusion for the moment. Even he had to experience a time lag between passing out at dawn and being able to project his thoughts while his body was frozen. Still, she was grateful she didn't know any of the other companions' real identities, so she couldn't be forced to rat them out, even if Steve found out about them.

When she got out of the shower, she got dressed and escaped the apartment as quickly as possible, without once glancing toward the bed. She rushed down the building's back stairs as the sun lit up a beautiful morning. The cool breeze helped revive her a little. She told herself she'd stop for coffee on the way to work. Frequently, she took public transportation, and she and Raleigh used a pool car to work cases. Today, impulse told her to take her own car. Her car was parked in the alley behind the old brick apartment building. She approached it with an odd sense of foreboding and wasn't surprised to find an envelope tucked under the windshield wiper on the driver's side. Somebody, it seemed, had left her a message.

She plucked the envelope from under the wiper. It was heavy in her hand. There was a small piece of folded paper inside, and something else. When she tipped the object out of the envelope, a gold coin fell into her palm.

The gold coin bore the incised image of an owl on one side. There was writing in a language she couldn't read but did recognize on the obverse side. She knew exactly what this was and was pretty sure where it came from. What was it doing here? And why had it been given to her?

Selena got in the car and drove. She didn't unfold the piece of paper that came with the Enforcer's coin until she was seated at her desk in the precinct office.

Chapter 10

"RALEIGH, HONEY. IT'S not like we don't have a lot of
other open homicides on our book."

"Yeah, but this one really—"

Selena watched guiltily as her partner shook his head.
The confused look in his eyes hurt her, but she carefully
did not urge him to continue. He was trying to remember
the details of the decapitated corpse case. She didn't
have time or energy or the stomach this morning to try
to refresh his forgetfulness. Raleigh was her friend and
partner. Messing with his mind went deeply against her
conscience. Besides, she wasn't a vampire. No one but
a vampire—and an enforcer, at that—was good at permanent psychic mind wiping. She could suggest, but the
suggestions wore off quickly. *It's safer for him not to
remember,* she reminded herself, *or at least not to care.
Safer for everybody involved.*

Aching conscience or no, Selena looked him in the
eye, sucked in a breath between her teeth, and said, "It's
a dead-end case. We've got no witnesses, and what

physical evidence we had was corrupted by the lab. Didn't I mention the forensic problem before?"

He stared into her eyes for a while, long enough for his eyes to glaze, and a blazing headache to start burning white hot between her eyes. Finally, Raleigh shook his head again. "No. No, you didn't."

"Sorry." She fought painful weariness but managed to keep her movement casual as she gestured toward her computer screen. "I've been exchanging E-mails on the lab screwup with Forensics. Thought I told you."

"I haven't seen the autopsy report."

"Body's been misplaced."

He looked more cynical than disbelieving. "You're kidding."

"The whole thing's a screwup, Raleigh." She tapped a stack of file folders piled on her desk. "Plenty here with a chance of solving. We're a lot closer to bringing in a suspect on the Herrera, for one."

"Yeah."

She felt like a rag, an aching one, but she managed a smile. "Want some coffee?"

He wasn't too fooled. "You look beat."

"Couldn't sleep. Came in early."

He glanced at his watch. "Eight-thirty now. How early is early?"

"I don't know. When's dawn this time of year?"

"Early. I'll get the coffee."

Summer, she remembered, had short nights. Which physically kept Steve out of the picture, or out of her hair, depending on what she was doing, for long hours yet. Once Raleigh was away from her desk, she picked up the envelope again and spilled the coin into her palm. God, but her head hurt, so badly that the lights in the room—from her computer screen, even the glinting gold of the coin—sent excruciating stabs of pain through her.

"I'm a cop," she muttered. "Not an Enfo—" Selena closed her hand on the coin. Hidden away in her tight grasp, the gold was warm and heavy and all too real. She had a moment's panicky thought that maybe even a mortal's holding the coin was a blasphemy that would bring a terrible retribution. Like maybe the owl image on the coin would burn into her hand the way the Eye of Ra thing had burned into the Nazi's palm when he grabbed the amulet in the Indiana Jones movie.

Far from frightening her, this image made her laugh at the ludicrous comparison. But then there was an echo of laughter inside her head, and she felt the brush of a presence inside her mind. She pushed at it. It pushed back. She stumbled, tumbled, grabbed hold, and they fell.

Selena's eyes flew open, and—

The golden wings fluttered, the talons reached out to grasp—

If anything in the world could have made Selena scream, that would have done it. Instead, she dropped it as though she had been burned.

Another hand snatched it out of the air, and she found herself looking into laughing blue eyes. "It's only a trick of the firelight."

Those eyes she knew, though he looked so much different. Darker. Younger. "The mustache is not you," she said, referring to the drooping mustache that framed his wide mouth.

"It's a fashion statement."

He wasn't wearing black, either. He was dressed in a wide-sleeved brown shirt decorated with red and yellow embroidery and baggy pants tucked into worn, flat boots. She had to admit that the mustache did go with this Eastern European outfit. He looked like an Istvan for once. And the place . . . She looked around. They were standing near a campfire in a forest clearing. Primitive tents and carts, dogs, and people populated the shadows. The stars were infinite overhead, and close. The air was full of the scents of pine, woodsmoke, and horse droppings, but oh, so clean and delicious to breathe.

She looked back at Istvan, utterly relaxed and smiling, tossing the coin in the air and catching it over and over in the flickering firelight. He didn't look any less dangerous in his peasant garb. There was a long knife sheathed on the belt that cinched his narrow waist. She'd doubted he'd ever be mistaken for a nice guy, no matter where he was.

And just where—

"Ah," she said, understanding with a swift clarity that burst on her like one of those stars above going nova. "This is where you live."

"You walked inside my head," he agreed.

"You started it."

Even as she spoke, the usual urge to argue left her. Inside his head, he was human still. He hadn't invited her in, but here they were. He wasn't trying to push her out or close her off, not yet. Curiosity and a wary pleasure in being with him like this kept her from complaining that he shouldn't have come dream walking into her thoughts in the first place.

She concentrated on the coin as it flashed up into the air, then down into his palm. "Why owls?" she asked him. "Why coins?"

"Did you know that the Enforcer of Los Angeles is a

dealer in rare coins?" he asked. "No. Of course you
don't. Do you?"

"Maybe."

He didn't ask how "Been over to his web site, have
you?"

"Even Enforcers have to make a living."

"So they do."

She drew closer to him and to the warmth and light
of the fire. "What is it you do?"

He gestured. It took in the camp and all the world
that encompassed it. "I kill vampires."

"Why?" It was an odd question to ask, she supposed.
And how odd to find anything odd, considering the situation.

"Family business," he answered.

She could feel a change around them, in him. He drew
back, she held on fiercely, refusing to be left behind as
his mind shifted back through time, deeper into the reality of some long-ago time and place. Perhaps he could
have tossed her out, if there hadn't been that cord of
connection between them. For a moment, everything
went black around her, suspending her between her life,
his, and the tangible world. Fear of the dark emptiness
almost drove her away. Then she realized what it was
and deliberately spread herself out into the void and
through the loneliness he wore like a cloak . . . No, a
black leather coat, she thought with a smile.

"We're going to have to work on this fifteenth-century
mind-set of yours . . . Steve."

She heard him sigh. Felt him give in.

And suddenly they were seated before the fire. His
arm was around her shoulders, her body relaxed against
his. He held the owl coin up to the light, tilting it to left
and right. The bird of prey stamped into the pure metal

*did seem to move on the surface of the gold. "There's
no magic in it," he said.*

*"I see. It is a trick of the light. Where do they come
from?"*

"The coins? Or the vampires?"

"Either. Both."

*"The coins traveled from a land far to the east, where
the Silk Roads run. So did my people, I'm told. The
Roma. They say the Roma fought wars against the strigoi in ancient times and followed after when the strigoi
fled, but I think that's a lie. We're not a warrior people.
Our blood's entwined with theirs somehow, and we're
the best at killing them. That much I know is true."*

*Silk Roads? She vaguely remembered a travel show
she'd seen on television. "The Silk Road's a trade route
that crossed central Asia from China, isn't it? Vampires
are from central Asia?"*

*"Where they came from I don't know. I only know
that they built a great city there once. The city is gone
now, in ruins for hundreds of years, that much my father
learned and he passed on to me before he died."*

*He did not sound like he regretted his father's pass-
ing. She didn't offer condolences. "What happened to
the city?" She was pretty sure she knew what happened
to the father.*

*He shrugged, and she felt the movement all through
her body. "Destroyed."*

*"How?" She held her breath. The answer was im-
portant; she knew it. She felt his sudden reluctance. He
hadn't held back yet.*

*He didn't this time. "There are many stories, all of
them whispered, none confirmed by the oldest ones. But
there's a deep fear in the old ones . . . about what happened in the city. It's the reason, I think, that they treat*

the ones they take to change so harshly. The city was not destroyed from without. That much I've learned."

And who living within would want to destroy a vampire city? It was a question she wasn't going to ask or even think about. Even though she was in his head right now, she knew how easily he could turn the tables and strip every bit of information he wanted from her. She would put up a fight, maybe prolong the agony, but how much of a match was she for a pissed-off dhamphir, really?

"What the hell is a dhamphir, anyway?" she asked. She knew what her aunt had told her. She'd heard whispered rumors. *Might as well ask the source.* "And why are they all so freaking oblique whenever your name comes up? It's like they've got this Beetlejuice superstition going that if they say your name three times, you'll appear."

"Beetlejuice, Beetlejuice—"

"Don't you dare."

"It was only a movie."

"And I don't believe in vampires, either. Let's not push our luck."

He chuckled.

She said, "What are you?"

"You are too inquisitive. It will always get you into trouble."

"Or a promotion to detective lieutenant. We're talking about you right now."

"What I don't understand is why."

"You kill vampires. I nag them."

"My parents were married for ten years before the vampire took him. The strigoi was a great lady, a boyar with a castle and many soldiers to protect her. Even if she had not been a vampire, she could have had anyone

she wanted brought to her bed. My father was a musi-
cian. When he played at her castle, she kept him, a new
companion to do whatever she wanted with." He spoke
in a bitter rush, getting it over with before she badgered
him any more, she guessed. "It's not the hunting I hate,"
he went on, staring grimly into the fire, his muscles tight
with tension. "It's the stealing of lives."

How well she agreed with that, she who'd had her
life stolen by him.

After a while, he went on. "My parents had three
children that lived already. My mother was left to raise
them without a man, though there were brothers and
uncles to help. She was the best fortune-teller in our
familia, valuable to the tribe, but she couldn't even re-
marry as her man wasn't dead . . . and wasn't going to
be, since he was being turned into a vampire. After a
few years, the boyar drained him and turned him, and
had no more use for him. So the fledgling vampire wan-
dered back to his familia, back to his wife, and she took
him back to her bed. There are some who can slake the
craving for mating blood without it ever changing them.
My mother was such a one, but she wasn't immune from
making a child with the vampire: me."

"That's what I'd heard, that your father was a vam-
pire. But it sounded like an insult to me, like calling
someone a son of a bitch."

"My mother was a good woman, but I am a son of a
bitch."

"No argument there."

"I was born able to sense them, think like them, to
hunt vampires with their own abilities," he said. "That's
what a dhamphir *is, a vampire hunter fathered by a vam-*
pire. We protect the Roma, and our people are proud of
us."

After a moment of considering a couple of recent en-
counters, she began, "Could we . . . could you father a—"

"It only happens between Roma and strigoi. Very
rarely."

He probably thought he was being reassuring. She
didn't pursue the point. "You were born a vampire?"

"No. That came later." He put his fingers under her
chin and tilted her face up to look at her.

"When one of them stole your life from you." No
question.

"Yes." A simple answer.

"But they got more than they bargained for, didn't
they?"

He made no attempt at modesty. "Much more.
They've made a law since, that no dhamphir is ever to
be turned. But the horse was already out of the barn, as
you would say."

"I wouldn't say that. I'm a city girl."

"I . . . dislike cities."

"You live in a Suburban." He still thought of himself
as a traveling gypsy peasant, didn't he? Always restless,
always on the move, wanted nowhere. "You should try
settling down. You might like it."

"With you?"

"On the other hand, the gypsy life probably suits you
better."

"One of the things I like about you is how much you
dislike me."

"At least we have that in common."

"But enough about me."

He moved his hand, no more than a gentle flick of a
finger. The campfire rose up on a great gust of wind,
swirled around her, and Selena was suddenly trapped
inside a threatening circle of flame. Selena looked past

the ring of fire and saw only a pair of penetrating ice-blue eyes. "A little melodramatic, but nice work," she acknowledged.

"Couldn't you, just once, be terrified of me?"

"It would only spoil you. Besides, I make it a point to be terrified of you at least once a year. On our anniversary."

"Remind me to be there for it sometime."

"Only if you promise to bring flowers."

The fire surrounding her turned into a ring of lilies, orchids, and lilacs. Her favorite flowers, damn his hide. She wondered if he thought this was endearing enough to get her to tell him everything he wanted to know. "What do you want to know?" She put her hands on her hips. "What do you mean, sneaking into a woman's head in the middle of a workday?"

"You weren't supposed to notice. Besides, my motives were pure."

She knew then what he wanted and breathed a sigh of relief. She did not know when her hands had come to rest on his shoulders or his on her waist. This closeness was no less disturbing and distracting for all that it was an illusion. This was all a dream, or possibly a dream on his part, and a hallucination on hers. She was technically awake, sitting at her desk, doing her job. "I can't do it all."

This reaction brought a cocked eyebrow from him, and a mildly sarcastic, "You mean you don't think you can do everything on your own?"

"I can't do your job. I'm not psychic enough to wipe all the evidence from every mind involved." She hated everything she'd already done to cover up the vampire's death by destroying physical evidence. "I'm a clean cop."

"I know."

When had his arms come around her? When did her head sink onto his shoulder? This was all too comforting and cozy. "You're laying it on a little thick," she told him, but she rubbed her forehead against his shoulder as she spoke. "You don't need to seduce me into helping with this."

"When have I ever seduced you?"

She didn't answer him. She conjured up the memories and information she'd caught him looking for when he entered her mind. She gave him faces, names, facts, and impressions that would help him make psychic connections with the people who all needed to forget an encounter with a dead vampire. When it was done, she felt a last brush of energy from him, something that was almost sweet, almost gentle.

When Selena came back into her physical surroundings, the first thing she did was touch the spot in the center of her forehead that felt as though lips had brushed across it in a lingering kiss.

"Hmmph," she muttered, blinked, and looked swiftly around the squad room to see how much time had passed in her mental absence and if anyone had noticed. No one was doing CPR on her, or even staring worriedly her way. Good. There was a cup of coffee by her hand. It was cold. The gold coin had dropped from her hand to the floor beside her chair. She scooped it up quickly and rose to her feet.

Raleigh was seated at the desk across from her. His hands were folded in his lap. There was a peaceful, vacant expression on his face. Steve was inside Raleigh's head, she supposed, doing the work she couldn't. A jolt of fear for her friend and partner went through her, but she had to grudgingly admit that this was something that needed to be done, and that a vampire was infinitely more qualified to do it than she was.

Besides, better to keep Steve occupied. She squeezed the coin tightly in her fist, studied the paper that came with the coin again, and checked the time. She had an appointment to keep.

Chapter 11

THE AUTHOR OF the note had not put the message into anything so incriminating as words, but Selena recognized it as a rendezvous point all the same. The slip of paper contained a drawing, a silhouette of a high-heeled woman's shoe centered underneath the rayed circle of the sun. It had taken Selena a while to make a guess at what the cryptic drawing meant, but at high noon she showed up at the sculpture garden at the entrance to Navy Pier. There was a statue here of a huge silver high-heeled pump constructed out of high-heeled women's shoes. A shoe made out of shoes that made quite a memorable impression. At least it had on Selena, who loved buying shoes, even though she wore a size eleven, spent her workdays in sensible flats and athletic shoes, and had to battle limited supply and transvestite shoppers in the hunt for sexy footwear.

The statue seemed like a logical place, and high noon seemed a logical time. Selena didn't base her assumption on the sun having been drawn on top of the shoe, but because what better time was there for mortals to meet to talk about vampires than in the middle of the day?

Selena was a veteran of too many stakeouts to stand in front of the statue and look like she was actually waiting for someone. Instead, she settled on a nearby bench with a bag of fast food like any officer worker enjoying a quick lunch by the lakefront. She fed pigeons French fries and appeared to look anywhere but at the big silver shoe. Her roving glance took in the sparkling water of Lake Michigan in the distance, the huge Ferris wheel that towered fifteen stories high over the other Navy Pier buildings, and the huge flood of tourists enjoying the attractions on this lovely day.

Selena didn't seem to pay attention to anything in particular, but it didn't take her long to spot her quarry, detecting a shift in energy even before turning her head to get a look at the source. The woman by the statue was slender, dark-haired, beautiful, and sunburned. She wore black leggings and an oversized white men's shirt. People subconsciously moved to get well out of her way, leaving her alone in front of the statue despite the crowds on the sidewalk. She paced the length of the silver shoe and back again with an intense nervous energy that Selena would have put down to drugs once upon a time.

It was a psychic drug the woman was on, Selena knew, and the stranger's aura gave off a bad reaction of some sort. She paced up and down in front of the statue while Selena stayed on the bench, waiting for the stranger to notice her. "Something not normal about that girl," Selena finally muttered. She rose from her seat, crumpled her empty food bag, tossed it in a trash bin next to the bench, and walked through a rising mass of disgruntled pigeons to face the other companion.

"What do you want with me?" Selena asked, coming up as the stranger turned in her pacing to face away from her.

The stranger spun around almost vampire fast. Selena took an automatic step back, and her eyes met the other woman's wild gaze. The scariest part was the look of worshipful recognition in the stranger's dark blue eyes.

"Who the hell are you?" Selena asked. She opened her fist for a moment, to show a glimpse of the coin. "Why me? What the hell am I supposed to do with this?"

Selena almost bit her tongue to keep from going on. This was not how she'd planned to start the conversation. There was the matter of two dead vampires and one seriously injured one, and this woman was a link to all of it. Selena should be dealing with the facts of the case and developing information. Instead, she had a hysterical urge to grab the woman and shake her while shouting that she wasn't—

"I'm *not* an Enforcer," she said with a calm she wasn't feeling. "Who are you, and why have you come to me?"

"Where's your master?" the other companion asked. She looked around as though expecting to have vampires leap out from behind the bushes and statuary. "Did his slaves follow you?"

She put a thin hand on Selena's arm. Selena noticed the bruises on the woman's arm and at her throat. The woman was suffering from more than sunburn. And the energy that came off her: dark, confused, and in deep psychic pain.

Selena looked around, aware of what their conversation would sound like if they were overheard. She found herself falling into the sort of code used in the companions' chat room when she answered, "My friend and I don't have that sort of relationship."

"Are we alone?" The stranger tapped the center of her forehead. "In here?"

"He's busy working a case," Selena answered, fairly confident that Steve's psychic attention was concentrated on dream walking through the heads of the witness list she'd given him. "I'm free to talk. Let's do it somewhere else."

Selena turned and walked away. The other companion raced to catch up with her, and Selena led her to her car in the depths of the Navy Pier parking garage. Once they were seated inside the car, Selena turned to the other woman and was disconcerted by that worshipful gaze once more. She flinched under its intensity. "Don't do that."

"You're her, aren't you? You are Layla." She sighed. "I could feel your strength from the beginning. Knew you were the one."

The one what? Selena wondered. She didn't want to ask. People who got labeled The One ended up having people trying to lob their heads off with swords, or going on quests, or finding out Darth Vader was their daddy. "Or all of the above," she muttered. The woman's words and tone sent a nasty, warning jolt through her that made her want to push the companion out of the car and drive away very fast. She kept a rein on the impulse and said, "You're one of the chat group."

"I'm Sandy. Cassandra." She gave a hard shudder and had to gag before she went on. "*He* always called me Cassandra. *He* said it was the name *he* liked. *He* never asked me. Donavan wasn't like *him*. Donavan loved me, but then *he*—"

"Sandy." Selena spoke with gentle firmness. "Let's talk about you right now. Who are you? What name do I know you by?"

"Sandswimmer, of course." She giggled, and took a while to stop.

Selena's nerves grated at the sound, but she gripped the steering wheel tightly and waited quietly for the other woman to go on.

"I'm Sandy Schwimmer. I couldn't come up with a clever screen name, like you or DesertDog or the others. All I could think of was something short for my own name. That wasn't very smart, was it?"

"It's a good name," Selena answered. "Should I call you Sandy?"

"I like Sandy. Donavan called me Sandy. Poor Donavan."

Sandy's pain whenever she spoke Donavan's name was so sharp it was tangible against Selena's psychic senses. "You're Donavan's companion?" she asked, and was hit with a chaotic blast of anguish and fury that nearly knocked her out.

"Not anymore! Not since *he* came!" Tears streamed down her cheeks as Sandy beat her fists against the dashboard. "*He's* in me and Donavan and the others, and it *hurts!*"

Selena's head hurt so much from being near the woman that she wanted to scream. She stared straight ahead and saw not a concrete wall but a dark kaleidoscope pattern made up of fragments of unrecognizable faces, hard, grasping hands, red, wet mouths . . . and sharp, glittering fangs. Her stomach heaved.

Selena forced the chaos away. She had to remain calm, couldn't let herself get upset. Steve might take notice. Whatever was going on with Sandy Schwimmer, this was no time to draw the Enforcer of Enforcers' attention.

"Sandy." She put a hand out, almost, but not quite,

touching the other woman's shoulder. Selena couldn't bear the thought of contact. She kept her voice steady and reassuring. "Sandy, calm down. We have to talk calmly. Emotion draws attention, remember?"

"They won't find me. They can't." Sandy laughed, soft and bitter, with the hysteria drained out of it. "Not yet. There's too many of them inside me. They'll unravel me . . . but not yet."

Selena put her hands back on the steering wheel. She needed information as quickly as she could get it. For all her experience at interviewing witnesses and suspects, she was at a loss at where to start, what angle to take with the woman. The ground here was shaky, as shaky as Sandswimmer's sanity. Selena decided to go back to the point they had in common and take it from there.

"You haven't been on-line for a while, Sandy," Selena said. "We've missed you." *How did you find me,* she wondered. *How the hell did you find me?*

"I . . . the group . . . yes." Sandy nodded so hard Selena was worried she'd break her neck. Then she took a pink plastic diskette out of her purse. "For you."

"What is that?"

"Everything I could find." Sandy opened the glove compartment and tucked the diskette inside the crowded space.

Curious as she was about whatever was on the diskette, Selena didn't have a computer handy. She concentrated on extracting information from the distraught person beside her. "Tell me everything, Sandy."

"*He* doesn't know about you. I swear. I'm strong. Kept my secrets. Wiped the hard drive." She laughed. "Not that *he* went looking. We are dolls to him. Toys don't have lives of their own. Him and his kind. The evil must die." Sandy clutched Selena's arm with bruising force. Selena gasped and shook her off. "You'll help me," Sandy went on. "You all will! You have to do what you can, any way you can. Fyrstartr is good at organization, but you . . . you, me, and DesertDog, we're the tough ones. The strong ones that won't put up with any shit from *them*."

"We all put up with shit from them, honey." *Some more than others,* Selena thought, observing the distraught woman. DesertDog did talk tough, but Selena didn't recall ever sounding particularly militant on the board. She thought of herself more of a whining complainer than an activist of any sort.

"But we don't have to! I agreed with Fyrstartr at first, that we should plan now for how we'd behave when we're changed, to put together a charter for companions' rights that we'd all lobby for from within the system. Fuck the system! Bring it down now."

"And what is it that changed your mind?" Selena injected quietly into the other woman's fierce tirade.

"*He* did, of course. Him and his sick friends. They invaded our nest. Destroyed our home, our lives. Donavan's his now, and all that belongs to Donavan. Me! I belonged to Donavan." Sandy was shaking, tears streaming down her face. She didn't look tough or dangerous at the moment, but scared and hurt.

Selena couldn't help but put her arm around Sandy and draw her head down on her shoulder. Sympathy overcame all professional detachment. "Jesus, girl, what did he do to you?"

Sandy pressed her face against Selena's shoulder and sobbed. "In here," she said after a while, the words muffled. "They're all in me. I'm in them. Pieces of me everywhere. Have to get the pieces back."

Selena didn't understand exactly what the woman meant, but she saw clearly what Sandy had been doing. Serial killers always had a reason for what they did, even if it only made sense in their very sick minds. "You're killing them to get yourself back."

Sandy drew away from Selena's embrace. "Yes! Of course! How else can I survive?"

"And leaving the bodies where they'll be found by mortals."

Starting the revolution by dragging the vampires out into the light? This part made sense to Selena, though ritually displaying victims' bodies was another behavior pattern exhibited by some serial killers. And why was it easier to think of this woman as a typical serial killer than as a revolutionary vampire slayer? Maybe she thought too much like a cop sometimes. Maybe because she'd had so much more experience thinking as a cop than thinking as a vampire's companion. And whose fault was that? No, no, this was no time to be thinking about her *him*.

Speaking of which . . . "Who are you talking about, Sandy, if not Donavan?"

"Donavan loves me!"

A fresh blast of pain shot through Selena's head at Sandy's shout. Dizziness erupted around her again, along with the dark, ugly images. By the time Selena pushed it all out of her head, Sandy had the car door open and was getting out.

Selena dived after her. "Oh no you don't!"

She grabbed Sandy and pulled her back inside. Selena held the other woman down with an arm across her chest and took a quick look around the garage. All she saw was parked cars, no people around to witness any odd behavior. Satisfied that they still had privacy, she turned a glare on Sandy. "You came to me," Selena reminded her. "You killed a vampire in my town. That makes trouble for me, and I don't like trouble."

Sandy looked down like a contrite child. "I'm sorry. But I had to kill him. He ran, and I followed him. When he came to Chicago, it was a sign. I knew you'd help me. Then, when I saw you standing over the bastard's corpse, I felt your mind, and I knew it was you. You were sent to help me." She lifted her gaze and smiled at Selena. "The magic's working for us this time."

From a family of witches, Selena was uncomfortable with amateurs' definitions. "Magic is a form of energy. It doesn't choose sides."

"It brought me to you," Sandy said with an unnervingly serene smile. "That, and some high-level hacking. That's a form of magic, too, isn't it?"

Was messing around with intent in cyberspace a way of manipulating energy? Was magic a place where art, intuition, and science collided? "Maybe," Selena conceded dubiously. "You're a hacker?"

"I'm a computer security specialist. I catch the hackers." A tear rolled down her sunburned cheek. "I did." She closed her eyes for a long moment. "It's so hard to concentrate for very long now. This hurts. Trying to stay me hurts."

"Uh-huh." Selena fished in her pants pocket and drew out the coin. "Where'd you get this? Which nest does it belong to? Why give it to me?"

"It's to acknowledge you. You're our Nighthawk. The companion's Enforcer."

Oh, shit. Well, she'd wanted an answer; she didn't have to like it. That kind of presumption on Sandy's part could get both of them killed if the Enforcers ever found out. She resisted the urge to press it back into Sandy's hand. The habits of being a cop were too ingrained in Selena to let her lose a piece of evidence, even one that could get her killed.

"That covers the why of the coin," she said. "Now answer the other questions."

"It was Donavan's, but *he* took it from him. He said he collects them, but I took it back before I left. Not the others in that black velvet bag he carries, just Donavan's. But Donavan's nest doesn't exist anymore. Donavan wouldn't have taken it back, even if I'd dared try to give it to him. Donavan answers to *him* now. I couldn't bear to watch him groveling anymore. I couldn't stay."

"Stay where?"

"Denver."

It was the answer Selena expected, but she hadn't been going to prompt her suspect—the mentally impaired companion—in any way. "You killed a vampire in Denver."

"Simona . . . the bitch! It wasn't easy. I thought it would be easy. I did it the way DesertDog said would work, and it did."

"What did you use?"

"A chainsaw, of course. But I had to use a knife to cut out her heart. That was messy. There was blood everywhere. They bleed just like us. I don't know why I didn't think there'd be much blood. I didn't find me inside her, but she didn't take much of me. That's why I picked her, to see if it would hurt any. I thought that she wouldn't hurt as much 'cause I wasn't in her much. It hurt a lot." Sandy smiled proudly. "But I still did it. I only had to kill one of them, and they ran like rabbits. I followed one of them." She laughed. "Pretty Euro-trash Pyotr. Pretty Pete went right where I wanted him to go.

To Chicago. To you. I think it was me in him that gave him the idea to come to you."

"He didn't know anything about me."

"He came to our Nighthawk's town."

"Don't call me that. He went to his friend Larry's place."

"To another vampire, yes. All I had to do was wait for daylight." She smiled. Selena didn't see a shred of sanity in Sandy's eyes. "The other vampire was a mistake."

"You cut off his arm."

"I didn't mean to hurt him. I dropped the chainsaw."

"You dropped the — " Selena closed her eyes. This was all way too strange.

Closing her eyes was a big mistake. The moment she did, the fractured, terrifying, painful images erupted inside her head again. She might have screamed; she certainly heard the echo of screaming. It reverberated through her like the tolling of a great and horrible bell. The sound overwhelmed all her other senses, and the pain rose and the hellish kaleidoscope faded to impenetrable black.

When the world came back, the first thing Selena noticed was that Sandy was long gone.

Chapter 12

"How did she do that?"

Magic, of course. Sandy had somehow managed to throw a spell past her defenses. Or had both their mental defenses slipped, and Selena had gotten a dose of what went on inside Sandy's screwed-up head? Selena sincerely hoped not, for Sandy's sake. Better to believe in bad magic than to think the woman was suffering that much.

Selena checked her watch again. Yep. Hours had passed since she'd met Sandy at high noon. Sunset wasn't that far off. Selena swore and slapped a hand in frustration against the steering wheel and sternly ignored the pounding headache. She deserved the pounding headache.

"How did I let her do that? I had a confessed murderer in custody, and I let her slip away." She considered pounding her head against the steering wheel next, but why abuse the car when there was a nice, solid concrete wall not five feet away that she could use? "What kind of an Enforcer lets the bad guy get away? Not Enforcer . . . cop. I'm a cop." A mortal, human police officer, she reminded herself.

What is the matter with that woman? she thought. *More importantly, what was done to her to make her like that? Was anything done to her? Was the woman's mental state induced by some sort of abuse committed by a vampire, or was there some other explanation for her condition?* Selena tried for a moment to be objective about Cassandra Schwimmer's state of mind. It was a very short moment. Of course a vampire had messed with her head. Several vampires, maybe, though this made no sense to Selena. Vampires didn't play nicely together, and they didn't share.

"And they run with scissors," she muttered as she started the car.

What a day, she thought, as she negotiated heavy traffic away from the tourist delights of Navy Pier. As near as she could recall, it had started with a night of passion in her vampire lover's arms. A sleepless night, and she'd much rather have the vampire whose touch she craved well out of town right now. They'd gone from passion to her holding an interior dialogue with the *dhamphir* while her body sat at her desk, and she'd capped the daylight hours off with an encounter with a lunatic rogue vampire hunter she knew from on-line.

And that was only the daylight hours. Who knew what the night would bring? Selena certainly didn't look forward to finding out. Her first impulse was to run home and confess all to her vampire master.

"Fuck that," she informed the impulse.

Telling Steve about Cassandra Schwimmer would lead to his finding out about Sandswimmer and all the other on-line radical companions. Sandy's actions would get them all killed if an Enforcer found out about them. And there was still Aunt Catie and Larry's possibly forbidden relationship to consider. Nope. No way Steve was getting involved in this if she could help it.

She thought about going back to work but settled for calling in to check for messages. She wasn't surprised when there weren't any. Steve was busy making people forget about the case. He'd probably put in a few suggestions to make people ignore her erratic behavior and presence for a while. Normally, this would piss her off, but right now, she thought it was just fine. With vampires to deal with, she didn't need to be handling her regular caseload as well. Or, God forbid, answering official questions about her performance, behavior, and state of mind.

She didn't need to go in to the precinct. She wasn't ready to go home. Even with Steve lying still as death at this time of day, she wasn't ready to calmly face him as though nothing at all was wrong. As well as disgusted with herself, Selena was nauseated and had a horrific headache. Besides, there were a few other things she needed. So she drove to the nearest pharmacy and did some shopping.

"What's all the stuff in the other bedroom?"

Selena nearly screamed in surprise at the sound of Steve's voice. She settled for slamming the door behind her and demanding, "What are you doing out of bed?"

He was standing in the middle of the living room, naked and with damp hair. He looked like he'd just gotten out of the shower. He gestured vaguely toward the living room window. "Sun's down."

"Just barely." She caught the scent of brewing coffee coming from the kitchen. He *was* an early riser. She could have sworn she'd had a few minutes to spare before he came out of the daylight trance state to complicate her life once more. "What do you mean, what's in the spare room?"

"It's full of exercise equipment and boxes now. What happened to the orchids you used to grow? I liked them."

She put a lid on the rush of pleasure from hearing him say he was pleased with something she did. She refused to take even a clinical interest in his unclothed state. She put the plastic bag from the pharmacy down on the coffee table. "What are you doing snooping around my apartment?"

He smiled. "Testy this evening, aren't we?"

He was *not* cute when he teased. He was Istvan the Enforcer, for God's and Goddess's sake. She would *not* smile back. "Having you around gets on a girl's nerves."

"You have nerves of adamantium." He scratched his bare chest and looked at the bag. "Whatcha bring me? Groceries, I hope. A day of head hopping makes a man hungry. Mission accomplished; the mortal world has forgotten all about headless strigoi."

"What about the media coverage?"

"There's always another gruesome crime to cover. I already finished eating the leftover party trays in the fridge," he added with a hopeful look.

"Just what I need to have around the house, a chatty vampire."

"A chatty, hungry, naked vampire," he amended. "Do you think that's a good name for a rock band?"

She grunted. "Which reminds me." She dug into the pharmacy bag and tossed him a small box. "I did bring you a present."

He stared at the box for a few moments before he said, "Condoms?"

"If you're going to hang around my house naked, and it hangs quite nicely, then you—"

"Condoms? What do I need condoms for?" His teasing good mood was past now.

"We need to talk."

The sound of a key turning in the lock canceled any further conversation. They looked at each other, sharing surprise that neither of them had noticed any psychic trace of someone's approach. Then Selena whirled around and said, "Mom! Aunt Catie!" as the door opened and her relatives stepped in.

"Oh, you're home. We forgot the boxes of party stuff for Karen's next wedding shower and—"

Her mother's rushed explanation trailed off into stunned silence as her relatives stared past Selena's shoulder. The temperature in the room dropped like a stone. For a moment, the lights seemed to dim, but Selena figured that was a trick of oxygen trying to flee her brain and let her faint from the shame. In the farcical pause while Selena forgot to breathe and every other crisis paled compared to her mother confronting a naked man in her living room, the only sound for an infinitely long moment was the soft thud of the condom packet hitting the hardwood floor.

That was worse.

Selena did notice that neither of the staring elder generation had the decency to blush. She, on the other hand, felt the heat rushing to her face like a wave of solid flame. She made a strangled noise and a feeble gesture. A part of her wanted to round on Steve and shout at him that this was all his fault. A terrified part of her recalled that she was the only thing that stood between her beloved mother and aunt and the most dangerous vampire in the world. She would give her life to protect them, but what good would that do?

Finally, it was Aunt Catie who said, "What a handsome animal."

"He's huge," her mother responded.

"Mother!"

She looked at Selena. "Does he bite?"

"I'm sure he doesn't," Aunt Catie said, coming forward with a hand stretched out before her.

Selena's impulse to tackle her aunt and shove her out of the way was arrested by her mother asking, "When did you get a dog, Selena?"

Selena whirled around. To see her aunt scratching the ears of a big, black—

"Looks more like a wolf," her mother went on.

"Oh, no," Aunt Catie said as the big, black—dog—butted his head against her palm when she paused in petting him. "I know this breed. He's a Romany shepherd, isn't he, Selena? A very rare dog." Aunt Catie took a seat on the couch and the big, black—dog—jumped up to lie beside her. Selena noticed when Catie shoved the condoms under the couch with her foot. "Dog-sitting for a friend, Selena? Or is this big boy a member of the family now?" The Romany shepherd licked her sloppily on the face for this. She laughed and shoved his head down. He put it in her lap. "Fresh."

"A Roma dog?" her mom said. "How delightful. Does that make him kin? What's his name?"

Selena almost said Steve, but a warning look from both her aunt, and the dog—who had blue eyes—stopped her. "Gypsy," she answered. Selena's heart was pounding at this wild turn of events, but she'd had enough supernatural surprises in the last few years to act with as much aplomb as her aunt. "And he's not here permanently."

"That's almost too bad," her mom said. "You could use a companion." Selena choked on a gasp, and her mom only made it worse by adding. "Of course, I'd rather have grandchildren."

Aunt Catie took this as her cue and pushed Steve's head aside far enough so that she could get up. "We don't have time to stay," she told Selena as she dusted fur off her slacks. "We'll get the boxes out of your back room and go."

"I'll help," Selena said and followed the women into her spare bedroom. The cartons were quickly gathered up, and she escorted her aunt and mother to the front door. As she opened it for them, Selena said, "You still want me to come by your place later tonight and help with those New Age party favor things you're making?"

Aunt Catie didn't miss a beat. "I'd appreciate it. See you whenever you can make it. You know I'm always up late."

Selena nodded to her aunt and kissed her mother on the cheek. As she closed the door on their departure, she turned to the blue-eyed wolf stretched out on the couch with his head on his paws. "Off the furniture."

The change was so sudden, she didn't see it, though the room wavered and spun a bit as he moved. One instant a black wolf bunched his muscles and leapt toward her, muzzle bared. The next instant a naked man grabbed her by the shoulders and shook her hard.

"What was that about? What did she mean by kin? How did she know about the Roma?"

"You turned into a wolf," Selena countered. She barely noticed that his grip hurt her. "Vampires can't do that."

"I can."

"But—" She'd seen him changed into a wolf once before . . . or thought she had. If it was an illusion this time, it was a damn good one. "How did you do that? Why?"

"Answer me," he countered, his eyes taking on that compelling vampire glow she found so irritating in others but rather fetching on him.

She let out a nervous giggle. "Fetching." The giggle escalated into a hysterical laugh. "Fetching. Oh, God." Suddenly she couldn't stop laughing.

She *wanted* to tell him, she really did. Any companion couldn't help but want to obey their lord and master's demands, but the stress of the day and the absurdity of the situation took away every last shred of self-control she had. Tears sprang to her eyes, and all she could do was laugh.

He was the most dangerous man in the world. Istvan knew this for a fact. He'd held the title for half a millennium. He had gotten used to a certain amount of respect. To be precise, what he was used to was groveling terror. Never before in a very long life had anyone ever reacted to his bullying by cracking up. He found it rather appealing.

He helped her to sit on the couch. He got her a glass of water. He went into the bedroom and put on his clothes with the sound of her laughter ringing in his ears. It wasn't an altogether unpleasant sound, and he could see the absurdity of it all. "All right," he admitted, coming back into the living room. "Maybe I shouldn't have morphed like that."

Selena looked up at him, eyes red-rimmed. She wasn't laughing now. "You always avoid meeting your girlfriends' mothers like that?"

"No. I avoid having girlfriends."

"Wise choice."

He took a seat across from her. The natural tendency was to seek mental, physical, and spiritual closeness with a companion. Unnatural tendency, rather. He'd been giving in to that tendency an alarming amount recently.

"I'm not a bad man," he said. "I'm just a very good vampire."

"You're a terrible vampire."

He had no idea why he said it, or what she meant by her answer. They had a more important matter to discuss. "What did your mother mean about Roma being kin?"

"We are Roma."

"You don't look—"

"And you do?"

He'd heard about his less-than-gypsy appearance often enough not to argue further with this pale-skinned, red-haired amazon. "What tribe?"

"We're a Traveler familia. The Baileys are Irish Roma, though we don't exactly advertise it to the world. You know how gypsies are treated."

Nothing to argue about there, either. He should have known what was special about her. "Maria Ventanova must have known."

Her blue eyes flashed hatred. "I didn't get a chance to ask her."

"I might have asked her how she chose you for me if you'd hadn't shot her head off with an AK-47."

"It was an Uzi."

"My mistake." And it had been quite an impressive display of firepower by his companion, he recalled fondly, though he'd been very annoyed at the time.

"Companions aren't supposed to be able to kill vampires," he reminded her. He didn't point out that the penalty for a companion harming a strigoi was death. She knew that already, and he'd let her get away with it, under the circumstances.

No one knew better than he that the belief that companions and slaves were unable to harm vampires was complete fiction. It wasn't easy for a bonded mortal to do anything but happily obey, but it was certainly possible. Companions were force-fed the idea that their master owned them, body and soul, and there was nothing they could do about it, with their first taste of blood. He'd even tried it on Selena and gotten shot in the chest for his arrogance.

He could have broken her. Many strigoi took great pleasure in doing just that with their so-called lovers. Many companions lived in abject terror of what would happen if they raised a hand to their master. Companions were already primed to believe in their invulnerability to blooded mortals when they made the change, and it was their turn to be in charge. The ones who'd been mistreated tended to go on to become sadists themselves.

But some people didn't put up with shit from anyone, no matter how much blood magic was forced on them. "We both know how pig-headed you are. It must be the Roma blood."

"Must be."

"Do you enjoy killing vampires?"

Her surface emotions remained quite calm, though he was aware of the ripples beneath. She folded her hands in her lap. "This conversation has strayed a bit," she said. "I was going to tell you about being Roma before my family showed up. I didn't realize it might be relevant until today."

"Answer my question."

"How long have I been your prime suspect?" she questioned him. "Recalling, I hope, that I was the one who turned the corpse over to Ariel."

"That action could have been a diversion."

"Why?"

"Because you are very clever."

She gave a faint laugh. "Not that clever."

He stood. "I agree."

"Thanks."

"I didn't believe you'd killed the vampire. Belief is not the same as proof." He walked to the door. With his back to her, he said, "My business with you is finished. I won't be coming back. Not to a Roma woman." The words were harder to say than he'd thought they'd be.

Why was he telling her at all? Because she was Roma, and one of the People deserved consideration? Because talking to her was a habit he'd developed with terrifying speed? Companions were like drugs. He'd watched strigoi caught in the addiction to their bloodbonded lovers for hundreds of years but never understood the devastating need until ending up an emotional crackhead himself.

He heard her rise. He felt the changes in her, physical and emotional, as she tried not to react or show a reaction. "Not coming back? You've said that before." That her voice was tight with pain did not mean that the part of her that was free wasn't glad.

"I meant it then, too." He shrugged.

He was gone an instant later. Selena stared after him, empty without him, heartbroken, tears rolling down her eyes. The separation wrenched at her gut, at her heart, at her soul. She sank down on the couch and buried her shaking sobs in the cushions. She hated the weakness but gave herself up to it simply to get through it.

After an awful while, she sat up and wiped the tears away. She even managed something like a small, triumphant smile. *Well,* she thought, *who knew the truth would prove to be such an excellent diversion?* Steve was gone, never intending to return.

Good. Never mind that thinking about the loss tore her to shreds. She simply wouldn't think about it.

There was a murderer out there she had to apprehend before the Enforcers did if she didn't want an entire conspiracy of companions to be discovered. Steve had superpowers, but she had a witness. Time for her to talk to Larry.

Chapter 13

"How do you feel?"

Lawrence was a handsome guy, big and broad-shouldered, with a strong jaw, thick black hair, a sculpted mouth, and a strong beak of a nose. Selena remembered her first impression of him, on the terrifying night they'd met, as fey and beautiful in an otherworldly sort of way. That had been vampire magic, a glamorous projection brought on by the lure of sex and the hunt. She preferred him the way he really was, good looking in an ordinary way. She didn't like thinking that her aunt and he might—no, she wasn't going to think it. She was here to talk to Lawrence because of a case. She was going to keep her mind on a murder investigation.

He looked better than the last time she'd seen him. Not much, admittedly, but enough to quell her conscience's complaining about questions adversely affecting an injured witness's recovery. He was still swathed in bandages. A dark green satin robe was draped over his shoulders. She couldn't tell from looking at him whether his arm was showing any evidence of regenerating, and she was reluctant to inquire, more out of polite reticence than anything else.

"He has the best witch in the Midwest looking after him," Aunt Catie said, reading Selena's concern. "Which is much the same as being in the ICU unit of the University of Chicago Hospital, only with magic."

They were seated in Catie's reading room on the shop's second floor, Lawrence propped up on the couch, with Aunt Catie seated on the other end. There were cards set out in a circular pattern on the table before her. "You told Steve about the family history," she said after a moment's study. She tapped a major arcana card with a frosted pink polished fingernail. "Didn't like it one bit, did he?"

"Who's Steve?" Larry asked.

"He's not important right now," Selena said, desperate to keep personal relationships out of this, hers at any rate. Istvan the Enforcer was what she had to worry about, not her . . . boyfriend, for want of a better ter—

"Husband," Aunt Catie interjected.

"Hardly."

"Who's Steve?" Larry repeated.

Aunt Catie patted him on the knee. "You know him by another name."

Larry considered for a moment, then blanched even paler than blood loss and vampire night dwelling warranted, and said, "I definitely don't want to know about *his* private life. And may he stay out of mine."

"He is family, Lawrence."

Selena ignored one implication but said, "Steve is not family."

"You two would make quite the power couple if

you'd accept the inevitable," Catie went on, her gaze on the cards again.

Larry chuckled weakly, his gaze on Selena. "Terminator and Terminator Two, you mean."

Selena tried not to be either amused or flattered by this description, but she was a bit of both. She bent forward in her chair and poured a cup of tea from the rose floral pot next to her aunt's tarot spread. The tea was some pale green herb stuff, probably medicinal rather than caffeinated, but Selena was thirsty and took a quick gulp before she continued talking. "This is good." Her aunt smirked at her surprise. Selena drained the cup, hoped she hadn't ingested some sort of love spell or something, and concentrated on Larry. "Who is Pyotr? Why did someone want him dead?" She knew who, which she was not going to tell Larry. She wanted to know why. All her senses, cop and psychic, told her it was important to know why. She didn't think she was going to find out from deeply disturbed Sandy Schwimmer.

Larry's dark, arched eyebrows lifted. "Pyotr. I haven't heard him called that for a long time. How did you know—"

"It's a gift."

"It's a terminator thing," Aunt Catie added. "Or should I say Enfor—"

"No, you don't want to say that." She cast a quick glare at her witchy aunt. "And just how much do you know about Roma and strigoi relations?" Selena waved her own question away. "Never mind. That's another discussion. Pyotr, Lawrence. Tell me everything you know about him."

"I didn't like him," Lawrence said and looked surprised at his words. He gave a silent, mirthless laugh. "I admired him, the way I once admired Maria: age, wisdom, ruthlessness, beauty, traditional values . . . all that crap you suck in with your first blood in the nest."

"He was one of the old dudes?" Selena asked. "Thousands of years old?"

"Nobody's that old. At least nobody I ever met. Hundreds, though. Five, six hundred years old to hear him and some of his friends talk about the old days." He gave another mirthless laugh. "I used to love hearing about the old days. I majored in history in college, you know? That's how I got involved with a vampire." He gave an almost furtive look toward Catie, who was frowning, ostensibly at the tarot cards. "But you don't want to hear about my old girlfriends."

"No, Selena doesn't," Catie answered.

"Peter," Larry went on. "When he was on his own, he went by Peter."

"On his own. You mean he was a strig?"

Larry shrugged and looked like he was going to faint for a moment afterward. He took in a long, whistling breath and said, "I shouldn't have done that. Kind of a strig, part of the time, I guess, but not really." He went on, "There's an old custom. . . ." He shook his head. "It's hard to explain."

"Try."

"A long, long time ago, Peter was part of a nest back in Central Europe someplace. He beat the shit out of me when I was a nestling for joking about his coming from Dracula country. He didn't like Dracula very much, said the bastard was a menace to vampires and would have been dead a lot sooner than he was if his nest leader back in the old country had his way. This is where you make some comment, like, 'Dracula's real?' "

"I've had that conversation already."

Larry looked curious but didn't inquire further. "We got to be friends, of sorts, when Peter discovered I was genuinely interested in history."

"You didn't resent him beating you up?"

"Of course I resented it, but that's how it is between older ones and younger ones. He got to show he was faster and stronger, I acknowledged his dominance. We got on fine after that."

"You didn't nurse any resentment and want to kill him?"

"Vampires can't kill each other."

"I've heard that."

"I nursed plenty of resentment when I was part of strigoi society. That's one of the reasons I got out." He gave her a hard look. "I don't play by the rules anymore, but I don't kill my own kind."

Selena gave the slightest of shrugs. "I have his tendency to treat everyone like a suspect, even when I know they're not."

"You should have heard her questioning her cousin about the honeymoon plans at her shower," Aunt Catie cut in.

"I was making polite conversation."

"You made it sound like they were heading for Ireland to avoid prosecution. Go, on, Lawrence. You can talk while she bristles with indignation."

"Sometimes I hate you, Aunt Catie. Tell me more about Pyotr, Larry."

"He liked power. Gravitated toward it, I mean. Liked to lord it over younger ones, but sucked up . . ." He gave a wince of irony, then went on. ". . . to older strigoi."

"Older than him?"

"Older and more conservative. Looked up to the ones he thought of as the elite and old school. Most of the old ones haven't immigrated, you know. Personally, I think the old school ones are the real troublemakers. No respect for mortals . . . or their own kind, for that matter. Power and dominance games are what matter to that bunch. They can make living in a nest pure hell."

"Peter made life hell for other vampires? Peter and this friend he sucked up to?"

Larry nodded. "Especially his friend. When Peter wasn't around Rosho, he was okay. Just barely. Sometimes he made the effort to relax a little, to hang with the homies. Then Rosho'd show up again and talk Peter into helping him take over another nest."

Selena sat up straight, warning bells going off in her head. "To do what? How?" *And why and where?* she thought, remembering Sandy's ravings. *Denver, maybe?* She didn't ask the leading questions that came to mind and carefully hid her thoughts and feelings behind her formidable mental shields. Best to objectively as possible let Lawrence tell her what he knew.

He leaned forward a little, obviously uncomfortable with the movement, but seeming to need to draw confidingly closer. "I hate this game. I've never been in a nest where it happened, but I know plenty of people who have. What happens usually is that some old vampire blows into town, looks around, and decides a local nest leader is vulnerable. They'll come up with some excuse for a challenge—lots of excuses built into the Laws—that way, the local enforcer can stand back and let it happen. Usually, the challenger will pick some nest leader the Enforcer of the City already has a grudge against or has had complaints against."

"Somebody the Hunter doesn't want dead but would like out of power?"

Larry nodded. "Like that. The outsider wins a fight

with the nest leader, and that gives the outsider control
of the nest leader and the nest. It can be rough for a
while after that. Eventually, the strigoi members of the
nest find excuses to drift away if things stay bad, but the
mortals are stuck, and the old ones take a literal defi-
nition of the term *slave*."

Selena's stomach churned at the images Larry conjured for her, but she didn't let any revulsion show.
"What about the companions?"

"They go with their vampires."

"What about companions that belonged to the defeated nest leader?"

He looked blank but not too successfully. "I don't
know."

"Could this new nest leader take the property of the
one who was beaten? Nestlings, slaves, and companions?"

He nodded slowly, reluctantly. "Winner's entitled.
Most strigoi won't touch anyone else's companion,
but—"

"But your friend Pyotr mentioned something about
this happening, didn't he?"

Larry looked disgusted. He looked away. It took him
quite a while before he said, "Yeah. Peter's buddy, Rosho the old-line asshole, he's got a thing about sharing
companion blood. Peter says he treated that kind of per-
version like it was no more than passing around a bottle
of somebody else's wine."

Gang banging, Selena thought. Psychic gang banging.
Sandy had been raped, mind, body, and soul, by who
knew how many vampires who'd waltzed into a nice
man's nest in Denver and—lawfully—taken over. She
wanted to throw up. She said calmly, "Please tell me

they don't make the companion they rape take their blood as well."

Larry looked about as sickened as she felt. It saved her from ripping his vampire heart out. "Peter never admitted to that."

No one mentioned the shattered wreck of china and spilled tea from Selena's having furiously swept everything off the low table between her and the couch. Aunt Catie kept quiet, expressionless, emotions surpressed, her neutral gaze fixed on Selena.

If Sandy Schwimmer had been forced to drink the blood of a vampire that wasn't her companion—? Selena couldn't imagine what that could do to a person. Except that she'd seen firsthand what it had done to Sandy Schwimmer. "They drove her mad." She stood up. "No wonder she's killing them. The bastards drove her insane."

Hell, who could blame her? The question for Selena now wasn't how to stop Sandy's vampire killing crusade, but how to save her. To save her, Selena had to find the poor madwoman first. She didn't think that was going to be hard, at least she had one place to look.

"Larry," she said softly to the wounded vampire she was very close to killing simply because he was a vampire and not because she didn't like him. "Larry, I want you to tell me the address of your safe house. You have one second, and no longer." She was fairly certain she could rip his heart out with her bare hands if he didn't comply in the given amount of time.

"In most cases," Selena recited quietly to herself as she approached the front of the dark building set squarely in the center of the block of brick row houses, "the cliché about killers returning to the scene of the crime is a crock of shit. But in the case of serial killers, returning to the scene to relive the thrill of the experience is frequently part of the killer's behavior." She was quoting from a seminar on criminal profiling she'd attended at the FBI training center in Quantico, Virginia, a few months before. She'd been thinking of Sandy as a serial killer until she learned the truth. *Maybe this time,* she thought, *the killer simply doesn't have anywhere else to go.*

There was a chance that Sandy had left town, but Selena didn't think so. Sandy had come to her, looking for help. Selena didn't think Sandy, disoriented as she was, would leave before making another stab at getting Selena to lead the revolution.

"Stab." She snorted. The shadowy image of some unknown, evil *he* bending over a victim flashed across her mind. "Yeah, I could see myself stabbing that."

The neighborhood was a low-crime, white-collar sort, and the hour was late. There was more than one building on the block where the lights were out and no signs of life stirred. Streetlights showed an empty sidewalk, cars were parked in a solid line on the curbs, and street traffic was at a minimum. The street was in the very heart of the busy city, but this section of town had settled down for the night. The building in the middle of the block exuded a different sort of quiet, one even hard for her to detect, and she was looking for it. Plus, she had the address. In all the other buildings, people were sleeping. In this one, someone very psychic was hiding, hoping those who lived by night and fed off mental energy would pass her by.

Selena shook her head sadly and took one more look up and down the street, all her senses searching the area. She wasn't a vampire—a dozen of them could have been lurking in the shadows and she *might* not have detected them—but she liked to think she had certain skills. Maybe it was a Roma thing, though mention of vampires had never come up in any family discussions she'd ever heard nor in any of Aunt Catie's training. Maybe it was the reluctant bond she shared with the badest ass of all badass Nighthawk Hunter Enforcer dudes. Maybe it was trust in her own abilities and a capacity to transfer law enforcement training, experience, and street smarts up to another level once she'd admitted that she could indeed function on a supernatural plane. It was probably all of the above, and there was no one in the street, she decided, and went up to the door.

Larry had given her not only the address but also the key.

For the most part, vampires didn't hang out in dark, musty basements during the daylight, and those who did were considered weird and socially unacceptable. Sunlight didn't turn them into overdone barbecue. "More's the pity," she muttered. All sunlight did was put them to sleep. This vulnerability could be dangerous, it could be fatal, but most vampires faced this crisis by sleeping in a nice, comfortable bed with the curtains drawn. Maybe in the past, they slunk off to heavily locked crypts with legions of Igors to guard them, but that sort of thing would be more conspicuous than practical these days. Of course, in theory, strigs needed to be a bit more cautious in their living arrangements than those who lived within the protection of strigoi society. But Chicago was a pretty quiet town as far as internecine vampire violence went. She and Ariel saw to that.

Larry's safe house was in the basement, but it was a studio apartment. He owned the building and was currently the only resident, part time at that. He was having it renovated and planned to rent it out to normal people through a management company. Vampires were big into real estate. Except her own dear Stevie. How typical that she'd end up with a male with no more use for money than spit—less probably. Then again, maybe he had a secret fortune stashed away and only lived out of a Suburban to be perverse. Did Enforcers actually get paid? Who knew?

"Who cares?" she whispered, pausing in the dark entrance foyer that smelled of fresh paint.

The fear and madness were there as well, tangible as the paint on the air but fainter and harder to trace; Selena didn't need to follow the trace; she knew where to look. Still, she moved carefully down the stairs, with her gun in her hands. Selena did not forget that not only was Sandy not in her right mind—or rather, that she had too many people in there with her—but that Sandy also had a chainsaw and wasn't afraid to use it.

When she reached the basement apartment door, Selena reconsidered and put her gun away. A chainsaw was not the quietest weapon of choice. She figured she'd hear Sandy coming in plenty of time to defend herself if necessary. Of course, Sandy might be armed with more than a power tool, but she didn't see Selena as the enemy. Sandy had come to her for help.

Fine.

So, instead of breaking down the door, something not all that easy to do anyway, Selena stepped up to it and knocked. "Sandy? Sandswimmer?" She stepped back to the opposite side of the dark hall and waited with as much patience as her nature allowed. She risked keeping her own mental defenses relatively open, not trying to project her sympathy and concern, but letting Sandy read for herself, at least as much as her twisted brain could interpret. The process probably didn't go on for very long, but long enough to make Selena disoriented, dizzy, and send a shiver of paranoid fear through her. Sandy's fear, she told herself, but still she looked around, trying to fight off the creepy feeling of the night closing in.

"He has a nice computer," Sandy said when she opened the door. "I noticed that when I was here before."

Before Selena could say anything, Sandy retreated back into the interior darkness. Selena waited a moment longer, found herself looking around carefully as a chill raced up her back, then went into Larry's place and closed the door behind her.

Selena was used to blood, more from the gruesome details of her profession than any association with strigoi. Vampires were careful about how they took blood; they had uses for it. Mortals simply liked to spill it. She supposed she could drown in all the blood she'd encountered at crime scenes over the years. She hadn't gagged at the sight or smell of blood for a long time. All the same, Selena had no interest in turning the lights on to have a look at this crime scene when she walked into the apartment. She was aware of the copper and iron smell, the sick, sweet reek of decay, and a lingering dampness in the carpet underfoot.

"Owls can fly," was the first thing Sandy said when the door closed.

"On United into O'Hare, probably," Selena replied, and wondered at her own words. The words came out of her like a subconscious answer to a riddle, or the response to some sort of code phrase. She shook her head. "Weird." Life with vampires was. "But vampires can't fly," Selena went on. Maybe Steve could, but . . . "It's against their silly laws, isn't it? To use airplanes."

"*He* does what he wants."

Ah, the mysterious *he*. Selena knew what Larry had told her about his friend Peter and Peter's nasty friend. Those things intersected quite neatly with Sandy's ravings. That was assumption on her part. "What's his name, darlin'?" she asked. "This *he* who took over your lover's nest?"

Sandy shook her head wildly. "You know how magic works. Say his name and he'll appear."

And we wouldn't want that, would we? Selena thought. She almost smiled, remembering how an anguished, silent cry from her had brought Steve to her bed a few nights before. Her slight amusement died, and she nodded acknowledgment of Sandy's words. Selena didn't tell the vampire's victim that she very much would like to meet the monster that had done this to Sandy. That sort of bravado was stupid when justice was what was required.

She gently took Sandy by the elbow. "Let's go back to my place. You can't stay here."

Sandy looked around and drew anxiously close to Selena. "It's not safe here," she whispered in Selena's ear. Selena led her out the door and up the short flight of steps to the building entrance. Sandy balked at the main door. "Maybe we should wait until the sun rises."

"It's not far to my car." Selena opened the door. Sandy's steps dragged, but Selena got her outside and down to the sidewalk, only to find herself standing before the building in the middle of a quiet block and wondering where the hell she was. And how had it gotten so dark?

The shadows moved.

"Oh, shit."

"*He's* here." Sandy's voice came from very far away.

"I believe you're right."

Selena swung her head from side to side. Shadows. Moving shadows. Everywhere.

Selena knew what they were like. She knew it was the wrong thing to do. She grabbed Sandy's wrist and said, "Run."

Chapter 14

IT WASN'T THAT long until dawn, maybe half an hour, forty-five minutes. Long enough for two mortals to die. The trick was to stay alive for the last half hour of this short summer night.

Live to fight another day?

Selena had the oddest thought, wondering if she'd ever get a decent night's sleep again as she dashed between a pair of parked cars, Sandy half a step behind her.

Her instinct was to call in for help, but to whom did she make the officer in need of assistance call? She didn't want to risk the lives of mortal cops, even for a half-hour distraction. Let's see, she didn't have Ariel's number on her speed dial; besides, he might have sanctioned this hunt. She didn't think so.

"Denver vampires?" Selena asked, as Sandy pulled her to a halt. They ducked down by a car door. Shadows swirled, figures darted, someone laughed softly nearby, but no one approached.

"Donavan's with them," Sandy said with a whimper. The longing came off her in a wave the vampires could pick up a mile away. "My Donavan."

"Your death, sweetheart. Get over it." That was the problem with being a companion. You couldn't dump the bastard and move on. They couldn't dump you, either, to be fair about it, which this was no time to be.

"*He's* here." Sandy clawed at her forehead and moaned. "Calling me." She swayed drunkenly. "*Wanting* me."

Selena caught her by the elbow to keep her from falling over.

They won't kill their lovers, Selena remembered. *Can't.*

That's a legend. How real was the legend? They'd messed up Sandy's head, more than messed it up. Did they want her back? To keep punishing her, or to kill her? She'd killed two of them. Would kill more if she got the chance.

The Denver nest was in Chicago. She bet Ariel didn't know there were strangers in town, hunting for meat on his streets. Speaking as the meat, she was not in favor of this. She knew about hunts. She'd been caught by vampires once before. She still had nightmares about it. She wasn't going to let it happen again. Maybe they could get to Ariel. Maybe they could survive this.

To be hunted down tomorrow night.

Now, there was a pleasant thought. It took Selena a moment to realize it wasn't hers.

He liked playing with heads, did this bad guy from Denver. "Yeah, me too," Selena whispered, easing her Glock from the holster at her waist. A head shot was about all that would slow the bastards down. She had to be able to see them first, if she was going to get a clear shot. Their presence pressed in against her senses, sending cold fear through her on a hot night. She was aware of darkness within darkness, but see them? No, she couldn't see them. Maybe they should have kept running instead of pausing to hide like this.

"Okay," she said to Sandy. "It's like this. We can stay here and die, or we can run and die. What do you think?"

Sandy clutched at her head. "I'm dead. In here."

"Yeah. Right. Let's run."

The point was to get their attention, to get them to circle closer. To get off a shot so that at least one went down, and they could go through the hole in the ranks. It was the best Selena could think of, and she knew it wasn't very good. It was a very long shot for mortals to win against vampires in a situation like this.

Selena didn't expect it to go her way, but it did. As soon as she and Sandy made for the other side of the street, a circle of shadows formed around them. The shadows were vaguely man-shaped, projecting hunger and evil glee. Laughter and whispered threats echoed in her ears. They were having a damned good time. A gleam of fang showed on one of them. Selena fired a trio of shots into that shadow, aiming high, hoping to hit the bastard in the face.

The sound of the gun was almost drowned out by the mixed roar of pain from the vampire and Sandy's scream of anguish. The vampire went down.

Sandy screamed, "Donavan!"

Sandy would have fallen to her knees beside her lover, but Selena pushed her forward, through the temporary gap in their attackers. Laughter followed them as they raced up the empty street, Rosho letting them get a head start, Selena decided. Fine with her.

They didn't run very fast, not with Selena having to haul the hysterical Sandy along behind her. The woman struggled, sobbing Donavan's name over and over. The vampires laughed and followed at a walk. Selena figured someone in the nearby buildings must have called the cops by now, and she listened anxiously for the unwanted sound of sirens. There was absolutely no traffic in the street. If a car were to pass by, she knew she'd somehow manage a carjack. She figured the hunting vampires projected enough mental warning to keep any nearby mortals away.

The hunters projected fear at her, they projected panic. Selena was pretty sure she could have managed these reactions to being hunted on her own, and sneered at the attempts to intrude on her thoughts. She hauled Sandy as far as the street corner before one of the vampires dropped the cloaking shadow and stepped in front of her.

"You should let her go," he told her. "You *might* have a chance on your own."

"Maybe." She shot him in the head.

When he reached for her as he went down on his knees, she fired again.

"Bitch!" the wounded vampire shouted.

"Yeah, she's kind of cute that way," Steve said, appearing out of a blur of movement. He pushed her hand down before she could fire again.

Selena screamed. So did several of the vampires. Her reaction was surprise, theirs was terror. They ran. The ones who stayed backed off into deep darkness. She could feel their gazes, heavy with menace, but ignored them. She put herself between the Enforcer and Sandy and stood her ground. "I thought," she said, "that you weren't coming back."

"I was talking about to your apartment, not about doing my job."

He was so smug she wanted to strike him. "You followed me." It was a fact, not an accusation. "You were sneaking around inside my head the whole time you were explaining about *dhampirs* inside your dreams." The notion was so complicated it made her head swim.

He nodded. "You tried to distract me from knowing you'd been sent the nest's coin by the murderer. It was easier to let you think the distraction worked."

"You knew all along I was looking for Sandy."

"Knew you'd find her. I followed you."

Which brought them back to here and now on a Chicago street where they were still being watched by several vampires. Despite Steve's presence, Selena in no way felt like they'd just been rescued. Sandy was still sobbing, though she'd stopped trying to get to Donavan and was curled up miserably on the ground. The vampire she'd shot crawled away on his hands and knees while she and Steve talked. Police sirens were now blaring in the distance, and it was still too far from dawn to do them any good, though it was only a few minutes away.

"We've actually got closer to an hour," Steve said. He took a step around her, not moving with impossible speed, but she was still powerless to keep him away from the hysterical woman.

Selena put a hand on his arm. "She has good reason."

He gave her a look, the sort of disgusted look one cop deserved from another for offering that sort of defense for a perp.

"She's been raped," Selena told him. "Mind, body, and soul raped. She deserves protection, not—"

"She deserves nothing," a new voice spoke out of the shadows.

The vampire that stepped forward wore his arrogance like an old-fashioned opera cloak. He was dressed all in black, slender and black-haired, his saturnine features enhanced by a widow's peak and a goatee. Selena practically expected him to say, "Good evening," and that he didn't drink . . . wine.

"Who's the stereotype?" she whispered to Steve.

"Rosho."

"Thought so."

It was only after a moment of deep, intense, suffocating silence that she heard the hatred Steve put into saying the name. Each letter had been etched in acid. She didn't think it had anything to do with Sandy Schwimmer.

She, Sandy, and all the other vampires might not have been there for all the notice the two older vampires took of them. The edgy silence drew out, and Selena noticed that the sound of sirens was no longer part of the background noise. There was no background noise. It was as if Chicago, with all its millions of lives, didn't exist. What did exist was the palpable awareness that these guys *really* didn't like each other and hadn't for a very long time. She watched them watching each other and wondered if they'd even bother with fangs and claws when it was obvious they wanted to feel their bare hands around each other's necks. Selena considered grabbing Sandy and making a run for it while the staring match went on, but it didn't go on long enough for her to make a move.

Rosho broke the silence with a soft, derisive laugh. "I heard you were slave to the Council." He waved his hand. "What a mistake she made in letting you live." He shrugged. "Go back to your mistress. You aren't needed here."

Selena didn't think she'd heard right for a moment. It sounded like Rosho was dismissing the Enforcer's Enforcer like he was a parking attendant who'd just brought around the Mercedes. After incredulity, her next reaction was indignation. How dare he talk to Steve like that! "Excuse me," she started. Not that either of them paid her any mind. Instead of bothering to answer Rosho, Steve bent down and drew Sandy to her feet. Selena took a step forward.

So did Rosho. "Get your hands off my property."

Selena fought down bitter anger at the vampire's words. "Let's get her out of here," she said to Steve. "Get her away from him."

The enforcer ignored her. He turned Sandy's face up to his. She whimpered, and he ran a hand gently through her hair.

"Give her to me," Rosho demanded.

"No."

Selena shivered at the blood-chilling finality of the word. There was nothing reassuring in Steve's refusal. He touched Sandy with a gentleness she might have envied, if his face had not been expressionless and his eyes hard as glass. When he asked, "Did you kill them?" Selena knew it was only a formality.

"You don't have to answer that," Selena heard herself say, like some parody of a police officer.

What was an Enforcer supposed to do, read a suspect their rights? Companions had none. Strigs had none. Even Law-abiding nest dwellers went in fear of the Council, and the Nighthawks who hunted the hunters. Enforcers were judge, jury, and executioner, answering to a secret, faceless cabal. As far as she knew, no one had elected this Council, but they ruled just the same. That stank. It was wrong.

"Get away from her," Selena said, echoing Rosho for entirely different reasons. "Or help me get her away from here until this can be settled."

"Settled how?" Steve wondered softly, sparing Selena a moment's glance. "In a civilized manner?"

"Why not?" Selena focused all her psychic energy on the bond between them, silently pleading for mercy, for time, for the vampires' worst nightmare to show a shred of humanity. She could feel all her emotions bouncing off a dark, blank wall. She said, "Whatever she did, there were extenuating circumstances."

"I don't do plea bargains, Selena." He turned away, totally dismissing her every word, thought, and gesture.

Rosho wasn't done yet. Donavan had recovered from the head wounds enough to come forward. Selena couldn't see the puppet strings, but the sense of Rosho pulling them was strong. The younger vampire moved reluctantly but inexorably at the other's command. When he spoke, the words might as well have come from Rosho's mouth.

"I belong to Rosho, Hunter. The woman belongs to me. Give her back to him. That is my wish."

"You can't give her back to them," Selena pleaded.

"I won't."

Steve's attention was focused on Sandy again. Her gaze was glued to his.

"She is our rightful prey," Rosho said. "You remember what it's like to be prey, don't you, boy? Her blood belongs to me . . . when I choose to take it. As yours belongs to me."

"The Law is with us, Hunter," Donavan said. "The nest leader decides—"

"Shut up." Steve turned a sneer on Donavan. "Weakling. Protect what's yours. *Never* give it away."

Donavan looked around in panic. "But he—"

"Donavan," Sandy whispered, pulling away from the Enforcer's influence at the sound of her lover's voice. She stirred in Steve's grasp, trying to get to the vampire who'd been her lover.

"She wants to go home," Rosho said. He glanced at the sky. "It grows late. Let her go."

"It grows late," Steve agreed. With no effort at all, he shifted his grip and broke Sandy's neck. He gently eased her to the street. "Take your companion," he said to Donavan.

Donavan didn't hear; he'd fallen to his knees with a howl of pain the instant Sandy died.

Rosho bellowed in outrage. The vampires in the shadows gasped, shouted, one let out an animal snarl of outrage.

Selena barely heard any of this over her own shout. "What the hell did you do?"

She was dead. Just like *that,* Cassandra Schwimmer was dead. Show's over, folks. Move along.

"No." Selena spoke to deaf ears. She might as well have been a ghost; no one took any notice of her. Selena looked down at the discarded rag doll's body; only Donavan's sobbing gave any recognition to the death, and even that was cut off by a cuff from Rosho. The rest of the nest members were more interested at looking up at the sky and checking their watches. Steve and Rosho had gone back to glaring at each other. Sandy was a broken toy, a lost plaything. Rosho was pouting. Steve was unapologetic at having taken it away from Rosho. A human was dead, and nobody gave a damn. What justice had been served?

How could Istvan the Enforcer do this? How could he be so unjust?

Why hadn't he listened? Why hadn't he cared? Why had he given her a moment's hope when he said he wouldn't give Sandy back to the creature who'd abused her?

"You didn't investigate. You didn't ask her why. You killed her because Rosho wanted her, didn't you?"

He didn't bother to answer, but she saw him give Rosho a thin, smug smile.

Justice had to be served. Justice was all that mattered. Somebody had to protect mortals when the Enforcers couldn't be bothered. Someone had to acknowledge the crime, and the gold coin was still in her possession.

Selena raised her gun. Futile as it was, she couldn't have stopped herself if she tried, and she didn't try. "Enforcer Istvan, you're under arrest for the murder of Cassandra Schwimmer."

He turned a look on her that was completely blank. If he recognized her, he gave no sign. He gave no heed to the gun aimed at his chest.

"You have the right to remain silent."

His eyes narrowed. "Not now."

"You have the right to an attorney. If you can not afford an attorney, one will be provided—"

"Be quiet." He turned away again.

She took this as proof of resisting arrest. The last time she'd shot him, it had been in the chest. She'd learned a lot since then. This time she went for the head shot. Her hands shook so hard she was barely able to squeeze the trigger.

The white-hot pain that followed filled her head and the world. The searing agony was nothing compared to the soul-devouring loss. The loss nothing compared to the guilt. The shame was worst of all. She'd struck her lover. She'd hurt her lover. Dear, God, what had she done? She'd hurt her lover. How could she have . . . how could she have . . . how could she have . . .

"Oh, for God's sake." Her words were a strangled gasp, but at least she'd forced more than a scream out of her lungs. There was asphalt beneath her knees, and her knees hurt almost as much as her head. She must have gone down hard. Her hands clutched at her head, she felt her nails digging into her temples. Where was she? What was that pain in her chest? Had she been shot?

Her gun? Where the hell was her gun? She needed her—

There was a roar. An awful, terrible, animal roar.

Selena looked up. She was surrounded by feral faces with pitiless, intelligent eyes. She was surrounded by vampires. She felt too bad to be afraid. She couldn't breathe. Fire exploded inside her. She'd been here before. That time Istvan had saved her. Istvan. Her Steve. A moment of joy intruded on the fearsome bleakness as she thought of Steve. He was here. He would—

She looked up, seeking, yearning. She saw him coming toward her, and held out her arms to him.

The last thing she saw before descending into dark hell were Steve's fangs striking down toward her throat.

Chapter 15

"DRINK THIS."

"It tastes like blood."

It is blood.

Damn, it tasted good! Lava hot, thick and rich as melted gold, it was like drinking stars. Or liquid crack.

That image almost made her stop, but a hand pressed her head closer to the wound, and she couldn't halt the sweet, orgasmic suckling. Why would she want to after having craved it for so long? She was enveloped by hard muscle and warm skin, and there was nothing in the world but this total closeness for a long time. Somehow, through all the heady, delicious, delight, Selena managed to form a thought directed at the source of all things. *What happened?*

I bit you on the neck.

You never bite me on the neck.

I had to this time.

Why?

To make it look like I ripped your throat out.

Oh. Of course. She should have known his sinking his fangs into the soft, pulsing flesh of her white throat wasn't because of some romantic vampire gesture. Only she couldn't remember what had happened or why.

"Just as well," she heard him say. The sound of his voice was sweet in her ears, caressing, though it seemed to come from miles and miles away. Selena was stretched out languidly, riding a warm, soothing river of bloodred, sparkling light. She never wanted it to end.

She managed to ask, *Why's it just as well?*

" 'Cause it's too late to have a fight." Though she whimpered in protest and clutched at it, Steve drew his wrist away from her mouth. He pulled her down beside him, holding her close. His hands stroked her, caressed, drew out the pleasure. Then he said, "It's dawn."

A moment later, he was inert and cold, and she was deeply aroused and caught in his marble embrace. His blood sang inside her. Her body sang with need, but her soul was content, sated. She was loved. Selena smiled as she went to sleep, cradled in a vampire's arms.

"Wait a minute. Okay. I think I remember what happened now."

Selena would have rubbed her aching temples, but Steve was heavy, and his body pretty much covered hers. She wasn't yet ready to make the effort to push her way out from underneath him. Vampires didn't snore, but they didn't roll over in their sleep, which made sharing a bed with one damn inconvenient.

Jesus, her head hurt!

But she was pretty much conscious and very nearly lucid, so she'd ignore the pain while she got her head completely together. She was aware that it was very late in the afternoon. She had vague memories of coming partially awake several times during the day when the ringing of the telephone filtered through heavy sleep. She was stiflingly hot, sweaty, her hands tingled from lack of circulation. And her head . . . oh, God, her head. She felt hungover, but this was more like a reaction to too much sex than if she'd been drinking—

She'd been drinking blood, hadn't she?

She'd done it before, but never so much. If you thought about it, it was really disgusting, drinking blood, at least from another sentient being. Okay, so there were whole tribes of people who lived on drinking the blood of cattle mixed with milk, and a rare steak was a joy to slice into, but there was a large degree of difference between enjoying the blood of cattle and the blood of humans. In fact, she knew that drinking human blood made humans sick. It was something you shot up rather than ingested, if you wanted to compare an intravenous transfusion to taking a drug. Transfusions saved your life, they didn't make you high. Ah, but the point was, vampire blood was a drug to humans, and humans were cattle to vampires, and maybe she wasn't as awake and lucid as she thought and had better start over.

"I'm going to open my eyes now."

When she opened them, the first thing she saw was Steve's ear. She studied it for a moment, fighting off the longing to kiss it and any other part of him she could reach. His ear was beautiful. His hair was beautiful. The way his head pressed into her chest was beautiful. A glow surrounded him; she worshiped his presence in her bed. She knew that was the blood talking, the fresh infusion making her want him more than ever. Just to prove that the blood wasn't going to get its way, she made an attempt at craning her head up to bite his ear, only she couldn't quite reach it.

"Bummer."

She closed her eyes again and wished she hadn't, as pain from her headache soared to migraine proportions. Lights danced behind her closed lids and turned into horrible, leaping satanic figures made of fire, rather like cartoon characters out of some rip-off of *Fantasia,* she made herself think, to prove that a hallucination wasn't going to get the better of her.

She concentrated on what was real and thought about the dreams. There'd been lots of dreams: good dreams, bad dreams, all of them real.

"Bastard."

It was the first word Istvan heard upon waking, and his first breath was a sigh. "Guns don't solve problems, you know."

"Neither does sex," she spat back.

"We didn't have sex. Not for lack of interest," he added. "But the time factor limited our options."

"You made me drink your blood."

"Don't go calling it rape, sweetheart."

"But you drank mine first, didn't you? A lot." After a rather satisfied pause, Selena said, "You have a headache, too."

"You shouldn't have shot at me."

"I do not shoot *at* a target that close to me."

He smiled at her indignation. "You didn't actually hit me."

She gave a short, caustic laugh. "At point-blank range?"

Her skepticism was refreshing. "Remember the scene in *Matrix* where Neo dodges the bullets? I can move faster than that." Before she could protest, he said, "You have the headache because you *thought* you'd shot me."

"Yeah, right," came the muffled voice from beneath him. "And why do *you* have a headache?"

"Because you thought you shot me. We're connected. The guilt reaction nearly killed you. There's a lot of magic flowing between us. Disturbing it takes a toll. Magic depends on psychic talent, will, and *belief* among all parties involved in the spell to really work."

"My aunt gave me magic lessons."

"Not vampire magic lessons. You don't know shit about vampires, sweetheart, no matter what you think you know."

"Whose fault is that?" She head-butted him on the shoulder. "And stop calling me sweetheart."

"Sorry."

"On which count?"

"Both."

"If magic requires belief, I'm going to stop believing in you right now."

"Good luck."

He didn't explain to her that because of the duration of their bond, a connection born of the strongest magic had been deeply disturbed by her actions. She'd already been in the throes of a massive coronary by the time he reached her. All he could do to save her life was strengthen the bond even more. If he'd been thinking clearly, been his usual pragmatic self, he would have seen that letting her die was the best thing he could do for her. But how could he have let her die? They were bonded. Besides, he liked her. Maybe her actions went against everything the strigoi declared allowable about companion behavior, but she'd been pushed beyond reason last night. He didn't blame her a bit for taking the shot. It was the sort of thing he would have done.

On a note that was at least a little pragmatic, her death would have sent him into shock. He didn't know how long it would have lasted, but Rosho would have eagerly taken advantage of it. No way he'd let Rosho win another round with him.

He vaguely wondered if Donavan would recover from his companion's death any time soon. Fool deserved a few months in a nightmare coma for what he'd let happen to the woman. Selena wouldn't appreciate hearing that he'd saved her life, not as furious as she was going to be over the woman's death as soon as the glow of greeting her awakened lover wore off. The sound of his voice wasn't enough to hold her for long.

Istvan considered rolling to the side of the bed, even getting up and leaving, but he enjoyed the feel of her too much to go yet. She was firm and warm against him, the perfect fit in every way. "The bond thing." It was an explanation for everything between them and a solution for nothing. That wasn't true, if he went against his own nature and decided to bring her to heel for the sake of the strigoi, then he could use the bond to make her his devoted property. With all the blood they'd shared last night, such enslavement would be relatively easy. "Can't do it," he muttered. Should, but couldn't. He didn't want a slave.

Maybe what I need is a wife.

Istvan sat bolt upright in shock. He didn't know where the thought came from, but he pushed it aside in sheer terror. And he didn't scare easy.

"It's the blood talking," he muttered.

"What is?"

He sat on the side of the bed and rubbed his face with his hands. "You don't want to know."

He heard her breath catch and felt the shift in her emotions. *Don't give in to this,* he thought, but he didn't stop Selena as she moved to kneel behind him. Her fingers began to massage the suddenly tense knots of his shoulders.

She said, "I don't need to know anything you don't want to tell me."

He put his hands on his knees and looked up, spotting the clock on the bedside table. "I've been awake a good ten minutes. Aren't you overdue to start yelling at me?"

She kissed his shoulder, then whispered in his ear, "Why would I want to yell at you?"

Her touch and seductive tone curdled his stomach, as well as sending a bolt of desire through him. He shifted his head to look at her. "Selena, snap out of it."

Selena looked into a pair of narrow blue eyes in a thin, long face, and for a moment she didn't recognize anything, not him, or herself, or the room where they were. Objectively, she was aware that the fantasy going on in her head had descended on her from one heartbeat to the next. She wanted, needed, desired, craved Istvan above all else, and whether it was false or real didn't matter. She didn't hurt when she gave in to it, not physically or psychically, and she didn't have to think or remember. It was lovely and soothing, this overlay of reality that consisted of the two of them closed within a perfumed paradise where they were meant to make love over and over and over and love was all—

"You need. No, it isn't."

Selena blinked, reality rushed in, and she pushed herself from his shoulders, disgust propelling her all the way off the opposite side of the bed. She wasn't sure if she was more disgusted with him or with herself. Istvan . . . she never thought of him as Istvan. She climbed unsteadily to her feet, shook hair out of her face, and said, "You're right; love isn't all you need."

He stood, and they looked at each other from across

the bed. "It almost had you there for a minute, didn't it?"

"Shut up."

"I'd love to, but you won't let me."

He looked like he'd tasted something sour, and a touch embarrassed at having spoken. She opened her mouth to ask him what he meant but understood before the question was voiced. Damned bond. She realized that he hadn't let himself talk to anyone for five hundred years, but when he was with her, the words came so easily that he could hardly make himself stop. He was lonely. Never mind his taciturn, badass reputation; he wasn't really like that at all. The gangsta attitude was simply for street cred.

"It is not," he complained, with an almost boyish pout. "You only think that because you're as badass as I am."

She supposed he meant that as a compliment. She chose to take it that way. She almost thanked him.

He walked gingerly around the bed. She watched as he moved, all long-limbed, economic grace. He looked dangerous even as he pointed past her shoulder toward the bathroom. "I'm going to take a shower." He held his hands up before him. "If you don't want to join me, at least try not to shoot me while waiting your turn."

Laughter bubbled up in Selena. "Okay, but I—"

Then memories of the events outside their personal soap opera rushed back in on her with the force of a hurricane, and fury blew away every shred of the affection the bond tried to make her feel for the monster. The headache that had been ignored but hadn't disappeared flared up to match the fury.

"You killed her." She couldn't take her gaze off his

hands, big, graceful, long-fingered hands. She remembered how her body sang when those hands touched her. She remembered the casual gesture that had ended Sandy Schwimmer's life. "You fucking killed her."

Chapter 16

"I CAN EXPLAIN that."

He didn't have to explain anything to anyone. He was Istvan the *dhamphir*. It occurred to Istvan that he could be as imperious as he wanted, blow her off, order her to be silent. He should have been tempted to behave like that, and not even because he was a vampire. He'd been born in a time and place and culture where men got to boss women around, and the women took it and pretended to be grateful for what little they got.

"I can explain," he said again.

"You took a life." He watched her angrily dash away a tear. "She didn't deserve to die like that."

"I notice you didn't say she didn't deserve to die."

"Don't you dare make light of it."

"I don't like killing mortals, Selena."

She laughed, and the sound plunged into him like a dagger. "I saw you do it. It was as easy as snapping a stalk of celery. She had reasons. You should have listened."

"I had no choice."

"You could have given her a trial. Weighed the evidence."

"I couldn't let her go free. I wasn't going to give her back to Rosho."

"You killed her because mortals are disposable, and killing is easier than finding solutions."

What she said had some truth in it, but it wasn't the only truth. "It was too late for her. If I tell you I did it to save her soul, would you understand? Could you, in this day and age?"

"You played God."

"I acted for God."

"Oh, please!"

He waved a hand at her. "Don't sound so righteous. You were the one putting bullets in vampires."

"I wasn't trying to kill them."

"You tried to kill me."

"That was different. You were resisting arrest."

"You were temporarily insane. I forgive you."

"I don't want your forgiveness. I was trying to get Sandy away from the hunters when I shot at them. We might have made it, if you hadn't shown up."

"You wouldn't have. Not with Rosho after you."

He sounded so certain, it sent a shiver of dread through Selena, along with a fresh jolt of pain to her head. As much as she hated the pain, awareness of it helped her to focus less on the indignant rage and more on the everyday world around her. Every-night world, she corrected. She balled her fists and closed her eyes and tried to get distance and perspective and professional detachment. About all she could summon up was a petulant thought that she'd never thought of herself as a night person. *You belong to the night now,* she told herself. *Live with it.* The night included far more than she had ever imagined, and an urban cop who worked homicide could imagine quite a lot of unpleasant things, having seen many of them.

I never wanted to belong to the night.

Steve's thought came to her softly, sadly, full of such open hurt and regret it brought the sting of tears behind her closed lids. She sensed the things he didn't want to think about, to remember, places he didn't want to go. But she felt the wounds, and how could she help but want to soothe them? She told herself she had more important issues to deal with.

"I don't want your sympathy," he told her.

Before she could reply that she had no intention of giving it, he turned and walked out of the room. Selena fumed for a moment that he'd walked out on a fight; then it occurred to her that he had *walked* when he could do any number of supernatural things to take the place of mere walking. Or could he? At least right now? Maybe he wanted to leave and couldn't summon the necessary energy. Maybe he wanted to leave but couldn't for emotional reasons. Maybe he didn't want to leave. And why did that set off little sparks of happiness all through her? How much blood had they shared? Maybe she should be the one to leave. The very thought set her heart racing with dread. Leave him? How? Besides, it was her place.

"Oh, dear." She hugged herself tight.

She heard the shower go on in the bathroom. The sound of running water reminded her that she was grimy, sweaty. Sore muscles began to make their presence felt as the ache in her head began to fade. She glanced at the bed. It barely looked slept in, though she knew they'd shared it through the day. And before that? She had no idea how he'd gotten her home. Everything that wasn't vivid and sensual or vivid and painful was an utter blank. The world boiled down to her and Istvan the Enforcer. Mostly it boiled down to her wanting Istvan.

"Steve," she made herself say, and her imagination supplied an image of him in the shower, steam boiling around him, long-muscled skin slick and shiny with hot, soapy water. "Oh, for God's sake."

She considered her options, and decided that shooting at him wasn't one of them. Why repeat herself? Maybe it was stupid of her to want explanations from him at this late date, but she did and he was hurting and she wanted and—

"Oh, hell," she said and decided she needed a shower as well.

"We're not having sex," she said when she climbed into the shower with him.

"Fine," Istvan answered and passed her the vanilla-scented shower gel. Her hand brushed against his thigh. His arm brushed against her breast. His senses were filled with the scent of soap on her skin a moment later.

She turned a little and had to lean back against him to tilt her face into the spray of water. "I mean it."

How could a man help but react when such a firm, round bottom made contact with his private parts? "Fine." His arms came around her; they didn't really have anywhere else to go. It wasn't as if she was some delicate, dainty creature that hardly took up any space.

She didn't want sex, he didn't want sex, but they were all over each other a few seconds later. At some point, he sighed while sucking a hard, pebbled nipple when a stray thought that guns weren't an answer and sex wasn't an answer and who the hell cared at this point crossed his mind. Her fingers were twisted in the wet tangles of his hair, pushing him away and pulling him close at once.

He wanted to bite her. He always wanted to sink his mating fangs deep into her lush, freckled flesh, but he resisted possessing her in anything but a physical way this time. The blood had already been shed. Too much blood, and not just what had been exchanged between them. This mating was necessary; it would finish what they started last night near dawn, that was all.

At some point before the water grew cold, Selena found the presence of mind to turn off the faucet. A moment later, he lifted her from the tub. As she pressed her face against his chest, breath ragged, voice muffled, she said, "We're not making love."

"We're having sex," he agreed.

"Fine."

He put her on her feet and let her slide, flesh smooth as vanilla satin, down the length of his body. Her hands caressed his thighs, her lips teased the tip of his penis but didn't take him completely into her mouth.

"Police harassment," he murmured after a few moments of this torture.

Her wicked laugh filled the small room, and she leaned back on her heels, her arms held out to him. He put a hand out, whether to pull her up or let her tug him down, he didn't get a chance to find out. Her face changed in that instant, a stab of alarm going through her. He understood her sudden concern instantly and just as swiftly acted on it. Memory led him to the right spot in the living room. By the time he returned with the condoms, Selena was on her feet. He grabbed her around the waist and took her back to the bed, muttering the whole time about the annoyance of a vampire having to use a rubber like some teenager scared of getting his prom date knocked up.

"Shut up," she said, and put the damn thing on him with a practiced skill that left him jealous of mortal lovers in her past. "Oh, good lord," she complained, picking up his reaction. Then she pushed him onto his back and had her way with him with a fierce aggressiveness that left him wrung out and murmuring weakly about having gotten himself attached to Xena Warrior Cop instead of a normal woman.

"You love it and you know it," she said, collapsing her hard-muscled length onto him.

She didn't fear him, would never let herself fear him. He did love that. She didn't worship him, but she did want him. It wasn't love, but it was something he hadn't let himself have for half a millennium.

"A connection to the mortal world." She said it for him. She propped her chin on his chest and asked, "What's so wrong with that?" Before he could so much as lift a sarcastic eyebrow at the obvious ridiculousness of this question, she said, "Even after what happened last night, I don't think all vampires are evil, damned creatures of the darkness. I don't know why you do."

"I've known more of them," he answered.

"Or why you're the most damned vampire of them all. It's not like you volunteered for the—Rosho!"

She jumped off him and to her feet even before he could stop her. Memories of the wild events of last night flooded her, not only the fear of being pursued by hunters or the angry futility of what had happened to Sandy but details of conversation, nuance, body language among the vampires. The sneering insults Rosho had heaped on Istvan came back to her.

"I heard you were slave to the Council. What a mis-

take she made in letting you live. Go back to your mistress. You remember what it's like to be prey, don't you, boy? Her blood belongs to me—when I choose to take it. As yours belongs to me."

"Rosho." She stared at Steve, wide-eyed. "Rosho made you a vampire."

"The hell he did." Steve sat up and swung his legs over the opposite side of the bed. He scratched his bare, flat stomach. "There anything to eat around here? Except you, that is."

She came around to stand in front of him. "Rosho made you," she confronted him. "And that's why you killed Sandy."

He smirked. "I'm not the jealous type. And Rosho had nothing to do with making me a vampire."

She knew that wasn't completely true; she felt it in the bond they shared as he shied away from painful memories. From what she'd heard and seen of Rosho, she was certain any memories Steve had concerning him were painful. That made her even more confused about what he'd done to Sandy. She knew that Steve liked to think of himself as a callous son of a bitch, but half the time she didn't believe that was true. "It was Rosho's fault Sandy did what she did."

"Rosho drove her mad," he conceded. "But she took it into her head to kill."

"She thought it would make her better. All of them shared blood with her. She hoped that eliminating them would literally get them out of her system. It was a crazy idea, but there was a certain logic to it."

"A madwoman's logic."

"Rosho drove her mad."

He nodded. "I know."

"Then why did you punish her and not him?"

"He never breaks the *letter* of the Law. Not yet."

"I know what the Laws say about companions killing vampires, but she was crazy."

"And would only have gotten worse if I let her live. There was no cure for her. I was inside her head, Selena. There was nothing in there that could be rescued except her immortal soul."

He really believed in immortal souls, she realized, believed with unshakable faith. What she thought of as murder, he thought of as mercy. "You really thought you did her a favor."

He put his hands on her shoulders. "I didn't execute her because she broke the Law. I killed the woman to keep Rosho from getting his hands on her again. If I'd strictly obeyed the Law, I would have had to give her up to him. He might have killed her, but he'd have done worse to her than he already had beforehand. And knowing Rosho, he might not have killed her. He would have changed her, turned a madwoman into a vampire."

Selena was so appalled by the notion she couldn't speak. In fact, the hideousness of such an action sent a wave of nausea through her. She was a Chicago homicide cop. She'd seen it all and had grown a cynical shell thick as plate armor, but this . . . this . . .

"I know," Steve said. "Rosho . . ." He chuckled. "I hate to say it, but Rosho makes most vampires seem genuinely nice." He eased her to sit on the side of the bed and turned to her closet after he put on his own clothes. He rummaged around in the depths for a few moments, then tossed a peacock-blue satin robe to her. "Pretty," he said, after she'd belted it on.

"It came in a Victoria's Secret box. From my mother."

"In the mistaken hope that you'd find a nice man to wear it for." He walked toward the bedroom door. "I'm not nice, but I have domestic skills. I'm going to go make breakfast now."

Selena stayed in the bedroom and told herself that he'd eat and leave and then she could think about something besides him again. There were ramifications in what had happened to Sandy Schwimmer that still needed to be dealt with. She carefully kept away from the computer. She wasn't even vaguely tempted to go on-line and share the news yet. She did check her answering machine. There were calls from her mom, her aunt, her partner Raleigh, and her watch commander. She needed to answer them all, but not with Steve in the house.

She wasn't going into the kitchen. She told herself that several times, though the longing to be with Steve was a fierce one. The smell of coffee tempted her, as well as the aromas of toast and frying meat. Her stomach announced that it wanted to go into the kitchen and told her she was being silly about not giving in to the whole companion's adoration of their vampire thing. She might not have given in to her stomach's wheedling if her memory hadn't once again circled to what had passed between the two vampires last night.

She was too curious not to go into the kitchen, and more hungry for information than for breakfast, though she was happy to have breakfast, too.

Chapter 17

"WHAT DID ALL that stuff mean? What he said."

Istvan looked over the rim of a coffee cup at Selena on the other side of the kitchen's narrow breakfast bar. He didn't pretend not to understand what she meant. He wasn't sure he wanted to go into it, but since she was willing to be diverted from the subject of the woman he'd had to kill, he answered, "It was a long time ago."

"In a galaxy far, far away?"

"A different world, certainly."

He should leave. He should finish his meal, finish his coffee, and leave—without bothering to help with the dishes or offering to take out the garbage. Domesticity was not seductive. The assignment was over, other duties called, but temptation lingered. He looked at the way the soft, slinky material covered Selena's breasts and gaped open just enough to give him a nice view of them, and he wanted to have sex again. He saw a couple of spots where he'd very much like to leave bite marks in tender flesh. The bond tried to create a stronger call than duty. That was one of the things that made having a companion so dangerous for him.

"I haven't had a vacation in five hundred years," he heard himself say. When had he gotten so tired? He leaned back in the chair. Selena poured him another cup of coffee. She'd defrosted some donuts. He put a third one on his plate and considered it. "Of course, we had no concept of vacations back then."

"Not gypsy peasant boys, at any rate," she agreed, picking up an orange to peel. "Bet even back then the noble oppressors found time to run off for weekends in Dubrovnik."

"They knew how to entertain themselves," he agreed. He ate the donut and drained the coffee cup.

She gave him a look so sharp it struck into his soul. "What?" The word wasn't a question but a demand.

He put down the cup. "What, what?"

"The bond works both ways, Stevie."

"Steve's bad enough. Don't call me—" She tossed the orange at him. He snagged it from the air, extended a claw, and finished peeling it for her.

She did not look impressed but said, "Thanks," when he handed it back. "You have this black haze around you," she told him, "and your mind's not quite in this century."

"Senility," he explained.

"I said something about rich folk in the past that reminded you of something you don't want to talk about, but I think you better talk about it, because whatever it is has bearing on what happened, and for some reason we both find confusing and annoying, you want me to forgive you for what you did last night."

While she took time to catch her breath, he glared at

her, narrow-eyed and suspicious. "You picked up all that from one sentence?"

She gave a smug nod. "I was watching—feeling—for it. You're not the only one who can play sneaky mind games, you know. You do do it better," she added.

"More practice."

"Rosho," she insisted. "What nasty memory did I stir up out of your murky depths just now that relates directly back to Rosho?" She leaned across the table. Her hand covered his, sealing the current between them. "What did he do to you that you've never told anybody about?"

The warmth of her skin seeped into him. He hadn't realized how cold he'd grown. "You're not my priest or my shrink."

"I'm your companion."

"And you want to make it better?"

She gave a snarling grin at his bitterness. "Maybe I want to rub salt on the wound. Would you prefer that?"

"Yes."

"In that case . . ." She fluttered her eyelashes at him and assumed a coyly sympathetic expression. "You poor baby, let me make it better."

He laughed. "You are such a bitch."

She took it as the compliment he intended. "Thank you." Her touch was comforting, but her next word was not a request. "Spill."

"Your interviewing technique could use some work, detective." She *looked* at him, an intense, serious expression this time, and thought curious thoughts loudly at him with demonic determination. It didn't take Istvan long to give in. "Where to start? With my father. My . . . fate . . . all goes back to my sire, and the boyar whore who made him."

"Is she the *she* Rosho mentioned?"

"No."

"Then who—"

"Do you want chronological order, or would you prefer to have a jealous fit?"

"Over you?"

"You can't help but be jealous over my other lovers. You can't help it, so don't get indignant. But rest easy, I have only one fond memory of the bitch who made my father, and that is of her death. Shall I tell you about it?"

"Is it relevant to Sandy or Rosho?"

The question took him by surprise, and to a connection he hadn't realized before. "Yes," he answered Selena. "Yes, it is relevant. You see, your friend was not the first companion to kill a vampire. I have that honor."

She was not skeptical, but she was shocked. "The Council let you live?"

"They weren't given a choice. Besides, the Council had less hold over the strigoi then. There were fewer Laws, fewer hunters to enforce them. And they weren't called Enforcers," he explained. "That is an American term from early in the twentieth century. It came about because of Al Capone and—"

"I don't want to know if Al Capone's a vampire. I want to hear about you."

Istvan shook his head in disgust at the realization that he was being as talkative as Char, the young Enforcer geek who researched strigoi history and culture for him. She was a nice girl, Char, too nice. Fortunately, she was involved with a mortal fully as mean and ruthless as his own dear Selena. Char would be okay, even if she did talk too much about vampire history, frequently at the wrong time, like he was doing now. Selena would probably like Char, and try to arrest the ex-con boyfriend.

"Well?" Selena persisted.

He could continue being evasive. He could order her to leave it alone. He could get up and leave. But despite the impatience in her bright eyes, her concern washed over him like a balm. "I'm not sure how old I was. Eleven, twelve?" He shrugged. "There is a strigoi Law now, forbidding the taking of children. It is a new Law by vampire standards, only a couple of centuries old. It is a Law I enforce rigorously. Taking children has always been considered stupid, dangerous, unethical by the ones who have ethics, but it wasn't against the Law in my mortal time."

Horror and distaste roiled around her. "Rosho bit you when you were a kid?"

"Yes." His simple answer caused her a great deal of pain for his sake. Her sympathy hurt him. "No, he did not make me his companion," he told her, not for the first time.

"But, how—"

He could not bear to tell it, yet he wanted *her* to know it. "As I started to say, when I was eleven or twelve, my father took me to the vampire who made him. He presented me to her as a gift."

"What?"

He held up a hand. "He did it for my sake, or so he tried to believe. He told me he wanted to give me a good life, that the lady would give me a warm bed, fine clothes, that I would never be hungry or cold. She gave me a warm bed, all right."

"Oh, dear."

Her understated consternation caused him to smirk. "My father also promised me that I would live forever. He didn't ask me if I wanted to live forever. And he didn't tell me the price. He was my father; I trusted him."

"Oh, dear," she said again.

"Being the victim of child abuse does not excuse most of the things I've done," he told her. "But as I said, I make very sure such things do not go unpunished these days."

"But nobody helped you."

He shrugged. "I helped myself."

Selena considered. "You killed her, didn't you?"

Technically, he should not admit to a companion that a companion once actually killed a vampire master. Companions weren't supposed to know that even thinking about such a thing was possible. It might make them uppity. But Selena was already uppity, having attempted to rid herself of him twice. Istvan admired her persistence but was certain she'd never succeed. On the other hand, it wasn't as if he'd been a normal companion, now was it? "The one my father gave me to had no idea what I was. She knew I was a son of her gypsy lover, but she never bothered to count up the years. What are a couple of decades to an immortal?"

"They added up to a fatal mistake?"

"Eventually." Memories he normally kept at bay vied for his attention. Too many of his kind got trapped in the past. They were always there, all those memories, crawling under the surface, building up behind the barriers built of magic and will. Some bad, some good, soft as down or sharp as blades, all memories were dangerous. You needed to live in the now, or immortality engulfed you. He concentrated on the here and now, on telling the story without getting caught up in it. "You see," he told her, "it took me a while to understand what I was, as well."

"Which is where Rosho comes in."

"You guessed it."

Selena watched him carefully, alive to the turmoil beneath his usual phlegmatic surface. She was more aware of him than ever before, wasn't she? Share the blood and you shared—

"Istvan," she said. How odd that she called him by that name.

He'd been looking at her all along, but when she spoke, he gave a gasping start, and their gazes met with dizzying impact.

Filthy hands, that's what he noticed about the strigoi first. The stranger's face and form were masked by a heavy, hooded cloak when he entered the castle hall, but he stripped off his riding gloves before throwing back his hood, and Istvan could not help but notice his hands. Caked with old blood, Istvan saw, crusted and well worn into the unwashed skin, with blackened blood under the long nails. The stranger was fine enough to look at when he finally revealed his face, but Istvan already held him in contempt because of his filth. It was an arrogant thing to stink so of the blood of mortals. The lady would not have approved, if the lady had been here.

When the stranger did take off his cloak and drop it carelessly to the floor, he looked around the hall as if he owned it. He gave orders, and the slaves cowered and rushed to do his bidding.

Istvan tugged at old Mathias's sleeve as the lady's eldest slave went past. "Who is he?" he asked.

"The sire of our mistress," Mathias told him. "Rosho. We have long-standing orders to obey him as we would her." The old man's eyes looked haunted. "He has not visited for a long time. I prayed I would die before he

came again." With that, the old man went about his
tasks.

Istvan might have followed Mathias toward the
kitchen, but Rosho called out, "Music. Where's the
Roma musician I've heard so much about?"

There was nothing Istvan could do but present himself
to this vampire lord.

Rosho grabbed him by the chin and turned Istvan's
face to the light. "You're not a pretty boy," Rosho declared. "You must have some other charms." He stroked
Istvan's cheek. "Play for me."

Istvan made music, and the whole time he played, he
felt the stranger's growing interest. The strigoi's gaze
slid over him, as intimate as a touch. Rosho's thoughts
battered for entrance to Istvan's mind. Istvan did not
falter once, did not miss a note, or let his voice show
any strain from fighting off Rosho's attempts at intrusion.

This quiet defiance only made Rosho laugh. "You do
have many charms, boy." He beckoned. "Come here."

The vampire was seated in the lady's carved chair at
the high table. Istvan stood before the great hearth, cold
despite the roaring fire at his back. He made no move
when he was summoned. "I belong to the lady," was all
he said. It was the only defense he had.

Rosho was surprised that he dared to make a defense
at all. Surprised and deeply amused. He was smiling
when he bared his claws. Within moments, Istvan understood why there was so much blood beneath the vampire's nails.

Istvan sobbed and clutched the ruin of his face with
his hands. Blood poured between his fingers. Rosho
laughed and batted his hands away, holding Istvan down
on the floor before the fire as he licked the blood from

the deep cuts. Istvan screamed at this violation. No one had tasted his blood but the lady.

The vampire only grew excited at the taste and at Istvan's protests. Eventually, he slung Istvan over his shoulder and called, "Show me to a bed!"

The slaves dared not protest. Istvan hung like meat over Rosho's shoulder as Mathias led the vampire to the lady's own chamber. The sheets were fresh, Istvan noted when he was flung down. He felt the calm of deep shock, almost as if he were without his own body, looking upon the scene and commenting. He could not escape the stink of Rosho, not of his body nor of his gleeful thoughts. Rosho battered at him with those thoughts, seeking entry into Istvan's mind. Istvan denied him that. He could deny him nothing else. Not his blood, nor his body. He could not even stop the reflex to swallow when Rosho tore open his own flesh, held Istvan's jaw open, and poured blood into his mouth.

As soon as the new magic of Rosho's blood mingled with the old spell cast on him by the lady's, all that was real shattered around Istvan like a mirror smashed to bits, and he was trapped inside each of a thousand pieces of broken glass. Rosho was with him, and so was the lady.

There was only a tiny, sane part of him left. That part told him to hang on, that the nightmare could not last forever. Eventually it would be dawn.

But until it was dawn—

Chapter 18

SELENA MANAGED TO make it to the sink before she threw up.

"I did not need to know that," she said when Steve came to hold her head. She really hadn't needed to go through the nightmare memory with him, but she had. His introduction to Rosho was burned into her now, as much a part of her being as it was his. "Thanks," she muttered, and not because he handed her a moistened dishtowel so she could wipe her face.

"I don't like him," she said after she wiped her face and thoroughly rinsed out her mouth. She didn't mind the taste of vomit as much as she did the memory of Rosho's blood. "I don't like him at all. It's a pity you weren't able to kill him then."

"Yes," Steve agreed.

She was still dizzy, and she could sense shadows and reflections of shadows moving just beyond the periphery of her vision. When she looked at his face, she expected to see the scars.

His smile was gentle, affectionate, hardly cynical at all. "The wounds healed by the next night. The pain was bad for a few hours, but as it faded, I began to finally realize what I was. That I was different, I knew. That I had power, I never guessed. The powers develop with puberty. I understand that now. And I think it helped that I learned how to hate. In a way, Rosho freed me. When the lady returned, I killed her and went home to my people."

Though Selena knew Steve wanted to let the subject go, curiosity drove her. "Then what happened?"

"Rosho and I didn't meet again until many years later."

"When you were a vampire?"

"No."

She looked at him sternly. "How'd a nice Roma boy like you get to be a vampire, anyway?"

"Rosho."

"Wait a minute. You said he didn't—"

Steve put a finger over her lips. "The way I met you," he said. "It was history repeating itself. Rosho set a trap for me. He meant to kill me, but it didn't work out that way. An Enforcer stopped him and claimed me as her companion. Her, I wanted."

She didn't mean to be jealous, she really didn't, but the emotion struck so hard Selena heard herself snarl. He chuckled and put his hands on her shoulders. His dark eyes glittered with wicked amusement. "I know," he said. "It's terrible to think you aren't the only one I've ever loved. I wonder what she'd think if she knew about you. After all, you're the first one in five hundred years I've wanted."

She couldn't help but be flattered, damn it! "You

didn't want me," she reminded him. "Any more than I wanted you."

"The bonding didn't give us a choice," he reminded her. "Any more than it gave the one who changed me a choice. She knew it was a mistake. I hated vampires. I killed vampires for my people and for the prince. We were enemies who were made to be lovers. It lasted only a few years; what we shared was too intense to last for very long. Only when she changed me did she learn what a great mistake making a *dhamphir* into one of them was. There was no changeling phase for me, and no need for a second rebirth into the Nighthawk line. I was reborn Nighthawk." He gave one of his depreciating, characteristic shrugs. "Well, there's a Law against it now."

"And just what was it that happened when she changed you?" Selena had her suspicions. He was so very different from the other vampires she'd met.

"I went mad for a while, for one thing," he answered. "Though maybe I was already mad and the magic only made it worse. My memories are vague . . . but my reputation lives on."

"You killed a lot of vampires?"

"So I've been told."

"By who?"

"By the one that finally volunteered to come after me. She came—"

"The Enforcer who made you came after you?"

"No. Do you want to hear this story or not?"

"Of course I want to hear it!"

"Then don't interrupt so much. I might not be so talkative ever again."

They were still standing by the kitchen sink. Domestic scene with vampire and girlfriend. Why was nothing weird to her anymore? "You want some more coffee?" she asked. "Want to move this into the living room and get comfortable?"

"Why not?" he agreed. He got the coffee, she put *Riding with the King* on the CD player. When they settled down next to each other on the couch, he went on. "The old one who found me, her name was Valentia then."

Selena was glad he abandoned the strigoi custom of ambiguity and concealment for the sake of pithiness. Besides, she was willing to bet this Valentia didn't call herself by that name these days, if she was still around. In five hundred years you could cover a lot of tracks.

"Valentia was small and delicate and . . ." He traced a curving form in the air. "*Voluptuous,* I think the term is. With a beautiful mouth, huge eyes, and thick black curls all down her back. The one who made me was a beauty of edges and angles, one who wore her danger with outward pride. Valentia was lovely, laughing, soft to the touch in mind and body. I did not see her strength, did not sense it. She let me taunt her, attack her." He threw back his head and laughed. "Then she knocked me on my ass and sat on me."

"What?" Selena had been leaning against him. Now she sat up straight and stared in disbelief. "How could she knock you on your ass? You're the meanest mother in the valley."

"The what?"

"*Lo, though I walk through valley of the shadow I will fear no evil, for I'm the meanest mother in the valley,*" she quoted. "Haven't you ever heard that? Where were you in the sixties?"

"On tour, mostly, with the Dead. Where were you in the sixties?"

"I wasn't born yet. It's a saying on a poster my dad had in the basement. So, pretty little Valentia whomped you, did she? Wow."

"I was certainly impressed. Of course, I've always had a weakness for strong women. She could have taken my heart, but she patted me on the cheek instead and told me I was really a good boy, and she was sorry for what they'd done to me."

"Well, there's a radical new approach to monster slaying."

"You're mocking me, aren't you?"

She settled back next to him, leaning in the crook of his arm. Clapton and B. B. King played on. "How can you tell?"

"I have superpowers. Though the night I met Valentia, I discovered that there was one stronger than I. She claimed to be the mother of all hunters, but she was retired except for special occasions."

"Were you flattered?"

"I wanted to fight like a demon, but she was so—"

"Masterful?"

"Sweet." He shuddered as he said it.

Selena found it very hard to think of a vampire as *sweet,* and had a feeling it was even more difficult for evil ol' Istvan to embrace the concept, considering his opinion of his species as a whole. She also wondered if he'd embraced this sweet little Valentia, him being so fond of strong women and all, but told herself to can the jealousy routine.

"We didn't have sex."

"I *wasn't* going to ask."

"But you wanted to. And did I *want* to have sex with Valentia? No. It would have been . . . sacrilegious."

She could tell he didn't like that any more than he liked

liking the old vampire who'd subdued him. He liked his opinion of vampires to remain low. "She was a goddess, was she?"

His response to that was an uncomfortable silence.

Selena ventured, "Was she the goddess they worship?"

"She said not," he answered grudgingly. "She called herself a servant of the goddess. Said she hadn't come to kill me or tame me, merely to talk some sense into me." He gave a faint, breathy laugh. "She gave me a lecture, all the while holding me down on the damp spring ground. To this day, I recall the feel of the cushion of pine needles under me and the smell of the earth waking from the cold. There were high clouds that night, driven across a half moon by a fast wind. I watched the shadows cross the light while she talked."

His memory was so vivid Selena was almost there. This time, though, she managed to avoid falling into him. She wasn't ready for another bout of shared consciousness after their flashing together on Rosho's rape, even if Steve's evening with Valentia sounded really interesting. "What did she say, this handmaiden of the goddess, to convince you to stop killing vampires?" He gave her a sardonic look, one that included a raised eyebrow. She'd always envied people who could manage that sneery single eyebrow tilt thing.

"She didn't try to change my habits, just to moderate them a bit. Her argument had nothing to do with the Laws, or duty to the Nighthawk line, or anything else I didn't give a damn about at the time. What she appealed to was self-interest on the most basic level. She pointed out that killing all the vampires in the world would seriously affect my own ability to survive."

"How'd it do that?"

"Nothing to eat."

Selena's stomach lurched. "Right." Enforcers were cops who got paid in corpses. She bet this aspect of the job had led to some interesting corruption cases among the Nighthawk constabulary over the centuries.

"The legend about vampires being unable to commit suicide is no legend. Valentia told me that it was part of the curse put on strigoi by the goddess they offended. I already knew that I couldn't die by my own hand. I'd tried a few times. Or, I tried to try."

"That must have been frustrating."

"Very. Valentia added the bad news that even if I destroyed every vampire in the world, I wouldn't have starved to death," Steve went on. "Though I would certainly have starved. A very unpleasant way to spend eternity. She convinced me that I'd go mad and take out the endless craving to hunt on all of humanity. Countless mortals would die in terror, and I'd get no satisfaction. The picture she painted terrified me."

"For which the mortal world is grateful."

"Except that vampires continue to hunt and enslave mortals. I sometimes wonder if the trade-off was worth it. Either way, monsters remain loose in the world."

"You would have been lonely," Selena pointed out, for some reason defending the strigoi lifestyle. "If nothing else, you wouldn't have had anyone to hate but yourself anymore."

"Valentia used similar arguments. She also claimed I'd eventually give in and make more vampires just so I'd have something to hunt. The prospect she painted of me devouring my own children was quite horrific, even though I vowed I would never give in to the temptation. She was quite a missionary," he said and sighed. "She stayed with me for a long time. Eventually, she got me

to respect and enforce the Laws. And, unfortunately,"
he added before she could ask, "Rosho is very good
about living to the letter of the Laws of the Blood. Pity
I didn't find him before Valentia found me."

"Bummer," she agreed.

They settled into a few minutes of companionable silence, letting guitar music be the only sound in the room.
Selena absorbed everything Steve had told her and took
a look at the information from her own perspective and
experiences. True, there were a lot of things about strigoi
history, society, customs, and culture of which she was
ignorant. She'd only heard about Blessing Day from one
of her on-line companion friends and about the lost vampire city and the origin of the nest coins from Steve.
There was much about the strigoi of which she was unaware. But this Valentia, this mother of hunters, servant
of the goddess chick . . . ! There might be a lot of things
Selena didn't know, but the child of an Irish Traveler
clan of charlatans and scam artists knew a fellow scam
artist when she heard of one. "And you call yourself a
Roma boy," she murmured low in Steve's ear, and patted him on the thigh.

"What?" he asked, suddenly wary and suspicious.

Selena shifted on the couch so she could look him in
the face. "Valentia pulled a *bujo* on you, my friend, a
con. Damn good one, too." Selena shrugged. "Maybe
she believed it herself."

He did not look pleased at her disparaging his Enforcer mentor. "I don't know what you mean. I don't
want to," he added warningly.

Selena wasn't likely to let a little thing like her lord
and master's displeasure stop her. "Valentia's interest
was in restoring the status quo and keeping things the
way they'd always been. By bringing you into the fold,

she used you to help reinforce the same old same old vampire class structure you were living with then and we're stuck with today." Selena took a deep breath. "Don't you see that?"

"No."

"Well . . ." She put her hands on her hips. "Why not?"

"I am *dhamphir*. I live outside vampire society." .

She sprang to her feet. "You *were* a *dhamphir*! You were turned into a vampire. You *are* a vampire. Get over it!" she added, realized she was shouting, and added with less stridency, "If you accept that you're a vampire, you'll have to stop hating them and then you can start fixing what's wrong with the whole bloody mess!"

He rose slowly to his feet, eyes narrowed very dangerously. "I don't know what you're talking about. I don't want to know. Even more importantly, I don't think you want to say another word."

"You could rule the vampires, you know."

"The Council rules."

"Only because *you* let them. You're not some ignorant peasant at the beck and call of the nobles anymore, you know."

"I'm aware of that."

"Are you? Deep down, don't you still see yourself that way? How many times do I have to tell you that you're in America now?"

"Land of the free?" he asked, with a very dangerous edge to his voice. His eyes looked like a pair of blue ice chips.

"Land of opportunity," she asserted. She knew preaching revolution at the Enforcer was a very dangerous thing, but if she could just get him thinking, the risk might pay off in the long run. "Land of possibilities. Oh, hell, Steve, never mind America. Everything is changing everywhere in the world."

"Not among the strigoi. Vampires do not change."

"Every society changes. Think about that, please. You pointed out a couple changes they've made to the Laws, yourself. Don't tell me there isn't room for change over time. You're the one to do it. You could even overthrow the Council if you wanted to."

"Don't be ridiculous."

"Or does this Valentia rule the Council?"

"She rejects the Council." His icy anger didn't hide his chagrin at revealing that tidbit to her.

"Can you do that?"

"Technically, no," he admitted. "But she is who she is."

"And you're the—"

"Meanest mother in the valley?" Pissed off as he was, he still smirked.

"Precisely."

"This conversation is over." He looked around the living room and sighed. Selena didn't like the sound of it. "It's all over." The lights in the room seemed to dim as though a chilling, dark fog swirled in from the night.

The phone rang before she could ask him what he meant by it. At first she glanced at the telephone on the end table as though it were an annoying bug she was ready to smash, but compulsion drove her to turn away from the Steve's sudden melancholy and pick up the handset on the second ring. "Aunt Catie, are you using magic?"

"It was the only way to get your attention. Are you all right? We've been trying to get hold of you all day. Where have you been?"

"I've been home." Selena spoke through gritted teeth.

This really was no time to get interrupted. "I've been busy."

"Are you sure you haven't been in trouble? Your cousin Paloma had an awful dream, and when I did a reading—"

"Aunt Catie . . . I have . . . company." Selena spoke slowly and distinctly.

There was a significant pause, and then she said, "Oh? Oh. Oh!" Followed swiftly by a brightly curious, "Really?"

The only response Selena could make to this was to hang up. She was half frustrated and half amused when she turned back around. "So I have an overprotective family. Be glad you don't—"

But Steve was gone. Vanished. Disappeared, and she hadn't felt him go. She felt it now, as the emptiness of being without his presence welled up in her companion's loving soul. Not that she was going to let a little thing like complete emotional devastation get the better of her. "Coward!" she yelled to the empty room. "Chicken! Come back here and fight like a vampire!"

Somewhere out of her sight, he might hear her taunts, but she knew he wouldn't come back. He was on his way out of Chicago, out of her life. It might be another two years before she saw him. She knew he'd try to make it forever. Did he care about how rough that was going to be on both of them? Some men really had a fear of commitment. They'd shared a brief interlude of bonded bliss, but he'd fought his way out of the shared addiction, thrown it off, and thrown himself out into the night to pursue that damned lone-wolf-against-the-world lifestyle he was bound and determined to wallow in. Maybe tomorrow she'd be glad he'd found the strength to go away.

"Fine," she grumbled and kicked the leg of the couch a few times. She wiped away the sudden flood of tears. She added, in a choked and sobbing whisper, "It's easier to run a revolution without you around, anyway. But I'll think about that tomorrow," she added and settled down for a good, long, heartbroken wail.

Chapter 19

"Because sometimes a guitar is just a guitar."

"That's not funny."

"It's a joke."

"No, it isn't"

"I thought you liked rock and roll."

"What does that have to do with that not being a joke?"

The band started playing the "Hokey Pokey" while Selena and Uncle Gary continued to argue over the nature of humor. The crowd shifted around them, and the scent of lilacs and gardenias filled the air. Someone handed her a silver cup of red punch. The bride danced by, dressed all in red, her arms around the shoulders of the Klingons dancing in the hokey pokey line on either side of her.

Strange dream, Selena thought, and took a sip of the blood. It was too cold. What idiot had put the blood on ice?

"We certainly don't do it that way at home."

"Then you, sir, come from a civilized—"

She turned around, and there was Rosho. Pale. Hand-some. Fanged. Wearing a tuxedo.

"Typical," she muttered.

He held out a pale, long-fingered hand. She noted the blood under his nails. "Shall we dance?"

Selena had never been happier to hear the alarm clock go off. Only through the dissipating fog of the dream she couldn't remember why she'd set an alarm for two-thirty in the morning. Where was she supposed to be? Midnight shift? Stakeout? Her mind was weighed down with despair, and her body felt as inert as lead. What difference did it make if she was anywhere or not? Everything was equally lifeless in her so-called life.

"Oh, puh-lease . . ."

She flopped on her back and stared at the ceiling and tried to figure out why she was awake at this ungodly hour. Whatever it was she was supposed to be getting up for, she was sure she hadn't penciled middle of the night mourning for good old gone Steve onto her cal-endar. Was she due at one of Aunt Catie's magic rituals? No, that ritual cleansing thing for Karen wasn't until later in the week, on Wednesday, and she was pretty sure this was Sunday. And it couldn't be police business, because she'd taken a leave of absence from work. Her excuse had been that she needed the time to take part in her cousin's wedding, but the truth was, she simply did not have any energy, any spirit, any hope, any Istv—

"Steve." She would not let herself call him by the name he preferred, even in the dark of night, alone in the bed they'd shared for so short a—"You're wallowing again," she told herself. "Which is disgusting."

All right, they'd had sex here a few nights back. Big

deal. Melodrama did not become her. The place was a bedroom, not a shrine. It wasn't as if she hadn't changed the sheets or anything.

She remembered studying the dullest of all Dickens's books back in junior high. . . . What was it called? The one they kept making movies of, which she couldn't imagine anyone wanting to see unless they got maybe Russell Crowe to play Pip, and even then, only if he spent the entire movie naked and they put in lots of explosions and John Woo directed. *Great Expectations*? Yeah, that one. The one with the weird little old lady who locked herself away when her fiancé didn't show for the wedding and pined for her lost love for the rest of the book. What had been the old biddy's name? Haversham? Faversham? Something with a sham in it, which was probably old Dickens's way of saying how *utterly stupid* it was to make your life come to a standstill just because some *male* walked out of your life.

"And why didn't I have insights like that back during the lit test in eighth grade?"

'Cause maybe you needed to be alone and lonely in the dead center of the night before your thoughts started circling around in endless, futile searches for anything to keep your mind off what really bothered you. And you always circled back to the center, anyway. Which could lead off on a quest for the romantic meaning of the *Inferno* if she'd ever gotten around to reading it. It had something about circles of hell, she knew that much.

Selena tried to channel her rambling thoughts into some coherent direction as she dragged out of bed. She didn't bother turning on any lights. A part of her thought her night vision was keener than it once had been, and another part of her thought she ought to know where everything in her apartment was by now, even in the dark. She always preferred the prosaic explanation to the mystical one; people with her background usually did, and she wasn't talking about being a graduate of the police academy. Witches were practical people, by and large. Even the ones who danced at the full moon naked once a month tended to do it indoors with the curtains closed. Speaking of naked, she distinctly remembered wearing a nightshirt to bed, but she wasn't wearing it now. Well, there had been lots of dreams, erotic dreams, weird dreams . . . one of them with Karen dancing with bikers, or something, at her wedding. Selena supposed she must have pulled the gown off in her sleep. Only . . .

She ran her hands over her body, and was left with the distinct, disturbing impression of someone else's touch on her skin. She sniffed. Was she imagining the faint scent of lilac and gardenia? She glanced out the bedroom window. Was it darker out there than night should be? Did the shadows move? This wasn't the first time she'd had a sense of something *lurking* outside.

"Steve?"

No answer, of course. "Nor should there be," she said out loud. She really wasn't awake yet, that was her problem. She'd been having nightmares ever since Steve left, but then, after all that had happened, nightmares really were a logical way of her subconscious dealing with the whole nasty mess. "Why am I out of bed?" Selena asked, and suddenly remembered. "Oh, yeah. West Coast time."

She found her abandoned nightshirt on the floor and pulled it back on before she went to the desk. The nasty mess had consequences she'd put off dealing with. She remembered now that she'd decided to finally go online. Tonight would be the night. Once she got to the computer, she hesitated, just as she had hesitated last night, the night before, and the night before that. *How do you run a revolution,* she wondered, *when you don't know how to tell the other revolutionaries about the first casualty?*

"Coward," she muttered, and turned on the computer.

Even after she had the computer on, she stared at the screen for a long time and thought of Steve before she went on-line. After she went on-line, she surfed search engines for a while looking for the name of the stupid character in the stupid Dickens book and tried not to think of Steve. That didn't take long. Nursing a headache, Selena yawned and finally made her way through the various security levels to the companions' chat room. Fyrstartr was there, along with DesertDog and Moscowknight.

Look who's here, DesertDog typed upon her entrance.

Been awhile, Layla, greeted Moscowknight.

You just missed Ghost, Fyrstartr told her.

She wanted to tell them, to explain it in all its gruesome detail. Selena wanted to foment rebellion, but she didn't know how to start. Even more appalling, it was so very hard not to be sapped of the will to do anything her own particular vampire wouldn't approve of. Pain stabbed through her head when she set her fingers to the keyboard.

I don't remember how long I've been off-line, Selena wrote. **A lot has happened. A lot I need to tell you. Can I ask some questions first?**

She had meant to jump right in and give a proper summary. She was very good at putting together evidence into a clear, concise case report. But the last several days had taken so much out of her Selena almost instinctively turned to the only support group she had for help. She needed to be strong, she would be strong, but she couldn't do anything for anyone until she got her head on at least a little bit straighter.

What kind of questions? DesertDog asked.

Companion stuff, Selena answered. Things I can't ask my friend. My friend skipped town again, she admitted. Left me strung out. Some bad things happened, too. We shared too much blood. And other things.

What things? Moscowknight asked.

Don't know how to explain the weirdest part. It was very intimate, but not in a physical way. Have any of you ever lived something your friend has done? Been caught in a flash from the past? Been so involved in one of their memories that it felt like it happened to you?

Yes, Moscowknight answered.

Really? Fyrstartr asked. I've been caught in visions of things happening in the present, and I'm always seeing the future. Did that before I met my friend. Never seen into the past. Never experienced that kind of closeness.

It is rare, Moscowknight wrote back.

Glad it's rare. Don't want to go through that again, Selena wrote. Lived it. Left me with a bad taste in my brain.

Nightmares? Moscowknight asked. Paranoia? Feel like the walls are closing in?

You've been where I am? Selena asked. This is a normal reaction? How long before I get over it? There's stuff I need to do. *So much I have to tell you,* she added to herself.

Your friend should be there for you when that sort of thing happens, Fyrstartr wrote.

He's not the supportive sort.

As you've said before, DesertDog reminded.

Unless you count being supportive as leaving me alone, Selena added. Which is fine with me, 'cause right now having him out of the way is good for what we have to do.

We? All three of the other companions typed.

I told you a lot has happened. I'm not sure how to explain it all to you. Sandswimmer, I need to tell you what happened to her. She came to me when she was in trouble. The bad guys found her.

Gender isn't discussed here, Fyrstartr reminded her again.

Let Layla talk, DesertDog wrote.

Sandswimmer was from Denver, Selena continued. **She is the one who killed the vampire found in the Denver park. An Enforcer then killed her.**

How do you know this? Fyrstartr asked.

I told you. I was there when it happened. I saw the Enforcer break her neck.

How could she have killed vampires? Why? Fyrstartr typed.

Why not? DesertDog asked.

She used a chainsaw, DesertDog. She said she got the idea from you.

Good for her.

Vampire society needs to be changed from within, Fyrstartr wrote. **But we don't have to kill vampires to do it. See what you started DD!**

The others had no idea how much effort it took Selena to write anything about what had happened. It needed to be told, companions needed to know what could happen to them. She was used to writing up concise, objective reports, to giving testimony, to making her cases. Right now, her hands shook as she tried to continue. She had to bring all her experience to bear, along with her considerable stubbornness, to fight the compulsion to keep whatever had happened concerning Istvan the Enforcer a closely guarded secret. Companions naturally tried to protect their vampire lovers. "Unnaturally," she muttered. Even among this core group of dissatisfied companions, she couldn't bring herself to repeat the details of what had made Sandy into a killer. Maybe talking to the others face to face, she could manage it, but not like this.

Her name was Cassandra Schwimmer, Selena told them. I'm sure her body has been disposed of. It will be seen to that her existence is forgotten. We're the only ones who can make her life and death count for anything. She did not kill her vampire lover, but he did nothing to help her when the others hurt her. Her crimes were committed in self-defense. Even the Enforcer agreed with that. The Enforcer obeyed the letter of the Law when he executed the person who killed the two strigoi. As far as the Enforcer is concerned, the case is cleared. The truth is, the vampire that drove Sandy to kill is still out there, still in charge of a nest full of vicious followers. He can and will mistreat companions and slaves to the point of driving them mad. He can abuse and kill nest property—that's us, guys—and as long as he stays within the Laws, he cannot be touched. Sandy fought back. I won't be a victim. Will you let yourselves be?

We know the Laws need to be changed, Fyrstartr wrote. There's nothing we can do while we are mortal.

Sandswimmer didn't think so, Moscowknight wrote. Patience isn't always a virtue when dealing with strigoi. I spent years being patient. It did me more harm than good.

Selena wondered about the details of Moscowknight's relationship problems but chose not to indulge her curiosity. She also didn't want to push them too far right now. They'd been obliquely airing their complaints for a long time, but getting them to step over the line into genuine rebellion wasn't going to be easy, especially after hearing that one of their number was already dead.

You all have your sources, she typed. Snoop around and find out about a vampire named Rosho. And watch your backs, she added. Then she logged off.

It was a little after three in the morning, and she was exhausted. She had nothing better to do than to go back to bed. Though she wished she hadn't brought up Rosho as soon as she closed her eyes. Sleep came quickly, but with it came the dreams.

The one that woke her up screaming started out with Karen complaining that Selena had no business bringing an Uzi to the wedding because it didn't match her bridesmaid's dress, and ended with a pack of wolves holding the crowd back while Rosho kissed the bride.

Chapter 20

"GOOD GODDESS, WHAT a rough night I had last night."

Selena looked Paloma over without any great sympathy. The pretty cousin behind the magic shop counter did indeed look like something the cat had dragged in. Since there were a couple of people in the store though it was nearly closing time, Selena kept her voice down when she asked, "You and the Tantric sex god have a little too much fun last night?"

"I wish. He's working nights in the ER this week. I tried calling you last night," Paloma added. "But your line was busy. Your phone's been busy all week."

"Been on-line a lot," Selena said, wincing under Paloma's accusing look.

"You couldn't call your family to share your troubles?"

"Who said I was having troubles? I was surfing and shopping."

She wasn't about to explain that she'd been having long, earnest conversations trying to convince a skittish

group of malcontents that meeting in Denver to do in a
nest of evil vampires was a good idea for an outing.
Some of the on-line companions refused to get involved.
Of the ones who continued the conversation, Fyrstartr
had argued the subjective nature of evil and the place of
law in civilization. Fyrstartr still leaned toward waiting
until they all became vampires and then changing the
Laws. Moscowknight's reply was that changing the
status quo could take hundreds of years. Hundreds of
years will give us plenty of time to get sucked into the
corrupt system, DesertDog said. How many people
would die or be unwillingly brought into the strigoi community in that time, Selena asked them. Moscowknight
agreed, and said that sometimes you had to take matters
into your own hands. That sometimes patience wasn't
possible, even for immortal beings. There was a moral
imperative, Selena told them, to wipe out monsters like
Rosho. Carmlaskid asked who they thought they were
to hand out the rough justice Selena wanted. Vigilantes,
DesertDog answered, and didn't that get everyone in an
uproar! They were all talking too much, and nothing was
getting done.

Her frustration wasn't helped by the continuing nightmares mixed with an unhealthy dose of paranoia. Selena
considered coming out of her apartment tonight something of a triumph. She'd been talking about Rosho so
much, all she could do was think about him. As it was,
she'd driven around until she was absolutely, positively
sure she wasn't being tailed by anyone, mortal or vampire. She'd really be glad when the reaction to Steve's
nasty memories wore off.

Selena came around to the back of the counter and
leaned against the wall to talk quietly with her cousin

until it was time to close the shop. "Sorry I've been incommunicado recently."

"Thought you were working on getting over that?"

"So, I backslid. Hey, I made it in time for tonight's party, didn't I? And why are you so wasted this evening?" Selena asked. Paloma did have dark circles beneath her eyes, barely hidden by an expert makeup job, and there was a certain haunted look in those big baby blues as well.

Paloma made a dismissive gesture, but her eyes stayed serious. "I think I'm nervous about the wedding."

"Me, too," Selena admitted. "Don't know how I let myself get talked into being a bridesmaid. I keep dreaming something awful will happen, and it's all going to be my fault."

"Hey, at least you aren't stuck with dreams that tend to come true. It's both a gift and a curse, you know."

"That's what they tell me. Most of your dreams don't come true, as I recall. And before you remind me that you are trying to enter the family business, remember that I have friends who work bunco, you gypsy witch, you."

"All Baileys are genuine psychics. Except for the ones that aren't," Paloma answered. "And very few of us work the *bujo* anymore. I think Great Aunt Bridget retired recently. Apparently, she started channeling Carl Sagan, and they were both so embarrassed about it she decided it was time to quit. In a way, it's a shame family traditions have changed with the times."

"You're proud of our long history of scams and cons? I can still remember how upset my dad was when he discovered great grandma's priors."

"Eight arrests, no convictions." Paloma spoke with pride at this record. "Woman had a way of turning the evil eye on anyone likely to testify against her."

"It was three arrests," Selena corrected the family legend. She checked her watch as the last two customers came to the counter with their choices. She'd noticed over the years that very few people left the shop without making at least a small purchase, and she wondered if Aunt Catie had put some sort of spell on her merchandise. Then again, Catie wasn't likely to resort to practicing that sort of magic, even on tourists, in an establishment frequented by some of the whitest white witches in the country, who would be bound to notice. She had her reputation to maintain. Selena supposed that those who found their way in here were seriously looking for something, even if they weren't consciously aware of it when they walked in.

She checked her watch while Paloma made change and put things in bags. "Am I the first one here?"

"The last. Cecile and Sara are downstairs setting up. Karen's upstairs with Aunt Catie. Came in for a reading before the ceremony. Girl's getting nervous."

"Is she thinking of backing out with only two days left until the wedding?" At least Karen had the option of walking away from a commitment to her partner. Some people got choices of the person they spent their lives with. *Pout, pout,* Selena thought, and fought down the sigh of longing to be with Steve. *We didn't choose each other,* she reminded herself. *It's not love, it's matching blood types.*

"She better not be thinking about canceling the wedding. I've spent too much money on an emerald green satin dress and pumps dyed to match to let her get out of it now."

"Hear, hear," Selena seconded. "And I've lost and kept off ten pounds for the sake of that dress."

"We will be beautiful."

"And no one will look at us."

"Which is as it should be," Paloma conceded. She began closing up the register while Selena brought out the ritual tools for warding the store. "What I'm not at all happy about is that Karen's big day has invaded *my* subconscious. It's not like this is the first time a Crawford's married a Bailey."

"But it's the first time Aunt Catie's gotten involved in the festivities. Mom didn't have the full ceremonial treatment. She was such a rebel," Selena added.

"Aunt Catie says it's too bad we can't do tonight's cleansing properly."

"Why not?"

Paloma gave her an arch look. "No virgins."

"Oh, right." Tonight's rite involved a ceremonial bathing of the bride and various other rituals meant to ensure a happy, prosperous future for the *maiden* about to embark on her first sexual experience with her new husband. Tradition called for all unwed young women of her family to assist in the ceremony. In the good old days, it was just naturally assumed that all the active participants were pure as the driven snow.

"Chicago snow doesn't stay pure very long," Paloma said, picking up Selena's thought. "Aunt Catie says the best we can hope for is that the old gods appreciate that the ceremony is intended as a sign of respect, and no ancient power decides to hit the wedding cake with lightning come Saturday night."

"You've had that dream, too?"

Paloma turned a shocked look on Selena. "Yeah. So's Aunt Catie."

Selena dropped the stick of incense she'd just lit. It rolled under the counter, and she and Paloma dived after it. By the time they retrieved the smoldering stick and were back on their feet, Aunt Catie was coming down the stairs, a tense and sober Karen following closely after her.

"Good, you're here," Aunt Catie said when she caught sight of Selena. "Change of plans," she added coming up to the counter.

"Aunt Catie, the dreams—" Paloma began.

"I know," Catie Bailey interrupted. "You and Karen go on downstairs. Tell Sara to start without us." Selena couldn't help but notice the pleading look Karen gave her before she disappeared down the basement stairway. Aunt Catie crooked a finger at Selena when Selena would have followed them. "The change of plans is for us, dear."

Before she could ask a question, Selena's attention was drawn to the stairs to second floor. For an instant she picked up a wavering movement of shadow, and the next instant, Lawrence was standing beside her aunt. He looked healthier and wore a long-sleeved shirt on this warm summer night that covered up whether or not his severed arm was regenerating. Selena wanted a peek or at least to ask.

Once again, her aunt spoke before Selena could. "You and Lawrence and I are going for a ride." It was not a suggestion or a request.

Selena cocked her head to one side and waited for an explanation. She didn't get one. Lawrence gestured toward the door, and Aunt Catie moved toward it with the imperiousness of a dowager empress. The effect was annoying but effective. Selena frowned but followed, and Lawrence brought up the rear.

"What about warding the building?" Selena asked when they were outside.

"Sara and Paloma will take care of it. Where's your car?"

Selena led them half a block up the street to where she'd found a parking space. When she unlocked the car, Catie got in the backseat, and Larry slid into the front passenger seat. "Where to?" Selena asked as she started the engine.

"You're a detective," Larry said. "You investigate things."

"What things, Aunt Catie?" She pulled out into the evening traffic. Selena's guts clenched with fear, even before she caught sight of the worried expression on her aunt's face when she glanced at her in the rearview mirror. She knew where they were heading without asking, but she asked anyway. "This is something to do with Karen, isn't it?"

"The first thing we're going to do is cruise around Karen's neighborhood," Catie answered. "If there's anything to find, we'll find it. Then we'll talk."

"Find what?" Selena asked.

"Drive now," Catie commanded.

"But—"

"She doesn't want to prejudice our perceptions," Larry said. "Magic stuff."

"I *know* about magic stuff, fangboy."

Aunt Catie reached around the front seat to pat Selena on the shoulder. "Snapping Lawrence's head off won't make you feel any better."

"I really wish you wouldn't put it that way, Caetlyn," Larry said.

Selena almost laughed. Larry and her aunt exchanged an amused look. And it occurred to her that the two of them made a cute couple. Okay, Larry looked younger than Aunt Catie, but he probably wasn't. Steve didn't look any older than her. Selena gritted her teeth. Why couldn't she stop thinking about Steve?

"Because you love him," Aunt Catie answered.

"Will you stop that!" It was families that drove you crazy, and psychic families could *really* get on each other's nerves. "It's not love. It's—"

"Love at first bite," Larry said. It was a wonder the look Selena gave him didn't stake him through the heart, but it bounced right off, and he kept on talking. "You can go for hundreds of years taking lovers and being content with those relationships, but there's nothing any-one involved can do to stop that soul mate connection of equals when it finally hits. Don't know if I'd ever want that kind of instant love-sex-completion-acceptance lightning bolt to hit me, I like to get to know somebody before I make a commitment." He glanced over his shoulder at her aunt. "But seeing it happen to you and *him* gave me faith that at least some of the legends are true."

"Some things are inevitable," Catie said.

"Like my stopping this car and kicking you both out if you don't change the subject," Selena informed them.

She noticed that her teeth were still gritted, and made an effort to relax her jaw. Soul mate her ass! What kind of romantic bullshit did vampires believe in? Okay, maybe sometimes she had certain kinds of syrupy warm romantic nest-building *urges* concerning the meanest mother in the valley, but that was just . . . the . . . bond—

"Shit."

"I think she finally figured it out."

"Shut up, Aunt Catie."

Selena stared straight ahead as she drove. The streets seemed full of light, streetlights and headlights, she told herself, but for some reason she imagined fireworks. Her life was tragic, right? Her situation was hopeless, at best. Well, at least *fraught* with weirdness, violence, and a very uncertain future. Why was it that all of a sudden life didn't seem so bad? Because a *vampire* told her he'd witnessed her finding her soul mate? Okay, she'd always known what happened between her and Steve was rare and special, but this was the first time it occurred to her that the connection might be a good thing.

Fortunately, before this reverie could go any further, Larry reclaimed her attention. "You have anything to eat? Healing takes a lot of energy," he added when Selena glanced his way. "I'm really hungry all the time."

If he was *really* hungry, it meant he was fighting hard against the urge to hunt down and feast on the flesh of mortals. "There's some protein bars in the glove compartment, I think," Selena told him.

"Thanks."

Getting anything out of Selena's glove compartment was not necessarily a safe experience. There was a whole lot of stuff in there besides emergency rations for times when she worked stakeouts using her own vehicle. There were maps and a flashlight, a can of pepper spray, a makeup bag, and lots of other things she couldn't remember. She should have warned Larry before he stuck his hand in, and half the contents escaped into his lap.

"Is this a bra?" he asked as he started to awkwardly return items to the glove compartment.

"Yes. Do you have to paw through everything?"

"Haven't you ever read that vampires are curious? We have a compulsion to count things."

"I remember learning that on *Sesame Street*."

"That's where I found out about it, too. What's this?"

"I have no idea."

"Looks like a computer disk."

Selena took the time while waiting at a stoplight to look at the pink plastic diskette Larry held up. "I know it's a computer disk, but I've never seen it before." Something nagged worriedly at the back of her mind, but the information skittered out of her reach when she tried to grasp it. Was this some piece of evidence she'd collected for a case and forgotten to turn in? She had no idea. "Slip it into my purse, okay? I'll have a look at it later." The light changed, and she drove on in silence while Larry ate all five of the Power Bars he'd found.

After another ten minutes, a creepy feeling replaced her attempts to remember where the diskette came from. The night grew progressively darker, and not at all nice. Selena said, "Okay, Karen's building is on the next block. What do we do, Aunt Catie?"

"Be very, very quiet, Selena," Catie answered. "Drive around the block a couple of times, then find a place to park."

Chapter 21

"I don't see them, but I know they're there."

"Definitely more than one," Selena agreed with Larry. She didn't see anyone, either, but, like the vampire beside her, she *knew*. There was a sort of icy tingling in her veins that was as accurate as radar for picking up the presence of other vampires in the shadows surrounding the old brick apartment building. Of vampires. Not *other* vampires, she corrected her screwed-up perceptions. This acute awareness was a new wrinkle in her psychic development. The street, the buildings, the bushes, the trees, the traffic, she was aware of her surroundings, but only as a hazy backdrop to the lines and pulses of energy emanating from the other psychic beings in the area. She didn't know if she was more annoyed or pleased at the extra oomph she'd received as a bonus of her most recent interlude with Steve.

Larry sniffed. "Not all of them are vampires." He licked his lips. "Warm-blooded creatures out there."

Oh, dear. He *really* was hungry. She wasn't sure she'd

be able to stop him if he decided to step out for a bite, or even if she wanted to.

"Slaves?" Aunt Catie asked.

"Probably."

"Watching Karen's apartment?" Her voice was low, but her indignation was fierce. "How dare they?"

"Obviously strangers in town," Larry said.

"Obviously?" Selena asked.

"No local vampire's that stupid. None of the established nests would dare mess with the Baileys," Larry told her. "There's been an unspoken understanding among the local witch families and the strigoi for decades."

Selena scratched her cheek. "Really?" She gave her aunt an annoyed look. "They messed with me. Maria Ventanova—"

"Paid for it, dear."

"I wish you'd told me you knew about vampires *before* I had an encounter with them."

"That was two years ago. Get over it. It's worked out fine for you." Selena sputtered while her aunt went on. "They are a private people. We respect their ways, as long as they respect ours." Catie sighed. "But there's no Law stating they have to leave us alone."

"It's just the opposite, really," Larry said. "The Law says we have the right to take anyone we want who has psychic gifts, to use as slave or companion, depending on the degree of their talent. The religious strigoi see it as an obligation to bring the gifted into the life. You can't become a vampire without that certain psychic something that you Baileys have in spades. Of course we're attracted to your family."

"But acting upon that attraction is frowned upon," Catie added.

"By who?" Selena asked. "Ariel?"

"By me."

"Ariel would be better. He's the Enforcer of the City."

After a stubborn pause, Catie finally said, "Yes, that would be better." She sighed. "Ariel is new to Chicago. He's quite the conservative and well aware that there's no official treaty between our kind and his. He is aware of me, but not too impressed. You, on the other hand, Selena, impress him."

Selena shook her head. "No, I don't. Steve made him forget about my existence."

"How inconvenient. At least for the moment."

Not necessarily, Selena thought. Drawing an Enforcer's attention while she was busy rousing the rabble wasn't a very good idea. Steve's not wanting anyone to know about her wasn't only good for his loner reputation, it gave her cover as well.

"Ariel couldn't legally tell these jokers to back off, could he?" Selena asked Lawrence, who shook his head in response. "Doesn't sound like he'd want to, either. Why Karen?" she wondered. "Why now?"

"Another old tradition," Lawrence said. "Claiming a mortal bride or a groom as a companion on their wedding day goes way, way back. You bite the mortal, and the mortal instantly dumps the person they're marrying to become your devoted love slave. Kind of tasteless, if you ask me . . . you know what I mean."

"You mean it's a cruel, vicious, heartless way vampires have of thumbing their noses at the mortal world?"

"Those are the sorts of dreams that have been terrifying Karen for the last few nights," Catie said. "Of having a dark-haired stranger forcing himself on her at her own wedding. And she's felt like she was being watched."

"Looks like she has been," Selena said. Selena cursed herself for thinking for even one minute that the warnings from her subconscious had been anything but true. She'd been lulled into thinking it was a trauma-induced reaction. That almost comforting explanation had done nothing but waste precious time. Damn it. She'd really believed Rosho and his crew had gone back to Denver. Instead, he'd had days to make his plans for her cousin. "Damn vampires."

"Listen, Selena, we aren't all like that. Most of us aren't like that anymore."

She patted Larry's shoulder. "I know." But the ones who were still operating under the old rules had to go.

"Do you think we should have a talk with this bunch?" Aunt Catie asked. "Warn them off?"

"Am I supposed to show them my badge and tell them to move along?" Selena asked. "You going to get out of the car and throw a curse at them?"

Aunt Catie nodded emphatically. "We could do exactly that."

Lawrence flashed a bit of fang. "Want me to make an example out of one of the slaves?" he suggested.

Catie did not look shocked, which did surprise Selena a little. "I think you should find out who they are before you have a nosh," Catie told Larry. "Find out everything the worm knows about his master's plans before you take his life."

It was a warm summer night, but they had the windows rolled up, and they spoke in whispers. Warm night or not, Selena felt a cold chill at her aunt's comment. She also realized she couldn't let Larry loose right now.

"He can't kill any of them, Aunt Catie. Not if he wants to survive as a strig in this town. The vampires out there know we're here as much as we know they're there. They're watching us, waiting for any move from Lawrence. They'd let him make the kill and then report what he'd done, with a couple of witch women egging him on. Ariel would come after Larry for hunting some one else's slave. He'd probably then sanction what their nest leader already plans to do. Besides, I know who they are. So does Larry," Selena said. "Their singling us out is more than psychic lines of probability coming together. I'm not sure if it's my fault or Larry's, though."

"Fault?" Catie asked.

"Me?" Larry protested.

"You know who they are. And how they know about us. Don't you, Lawrence?"

"Well—"

"You're still staying with my aunt aren't you? Why haven't you gone home?"

"I enjoy your aunt's company."

"You're a strig. So, when the new players took over your apartment building, there was no one you could complain to. What did they do, take over everything you own? Go through all your papers? Find your address book? The wedding invitation?"

"You're making this up as you go along, aren't you?"

"That doesn't mean it isn't the truth."

Aunt Catie tapped Larry on the shoulder. "What is she talking about?" she asked when he turned to look at her.

It amused Selena that Lawrence didn't try to evade her aunt's question. "Oh, hell, Catie. I'm a one-armed strig who's sworn off doing all the bad shit my people get into. I don't even have a companion to back me up. Everything Selena said is true. They moved in and took over while I was gone. When I went back to my apartment a couple days ago, I barely got away before the old bastard got his hands on me. I'm not getting into dominance games, and I don't mind being broke, but I never thought your family would get hurt. They must have found out about the Baileys through what they found among my possessions."

"And what you told Pyotr."

He shook his head. "I *never* mentioned any of you to him. I swear. If Rosho's looking for a new companion, taking your cousin's exactly the sort of thing he'd do."

"What do they know about me?" Selena asked before Catie could make a comment.

"It's not you they're interested in," Catie reminded her. "It's Karen."

Of course, Aunt Catie didn't know about the night Sandy Schwimmer died, that Selena had put up a fight against the vampires from Denver. She'd talked to them, been seen by them, attacked them before Steve intervened. Steve had made it look like he'd killed her. That was what he'd told her, wasn't it? She had some vague memory of his mentioning that. Problem was, she had too many vague memories from the whole affair, and those memories were mixed up with his memories, and a lot of hard-to-sort-out dream imagery. The one thing she was sure of was that Steve was good at covering his tracks. He'd have made sure to cover hers, wouldn't he? He was her soul mate, right?

And the thought occurred to her that even though he couldn't kill her himself, that didn't mean Istvan the Enforcer wouldn't let somebody else do the job in order to get a Roma woman he could get pregnant out of his life. Even as she thought it, she forcefully pushed the notion away. In fact, she shook her head hard as though that would get the thought out of her mind. He wasn't that cruel or cynical. Maybe he was a five-hundred-year-old creature of the night, a ruthless hunter and Enforcer of the Laws, but didn't mean he wasn't a nice Roma boy at heart.

"Yeah, right."

"What are you muttering about, Selena?"

Selena started the car. "I'm taking you two home," she told them.

"But—"

"Don't worry," she cut her aunt off. "And *don't* do anything until you hear from me."

Selena went back to her apartment and paced. It was all she could think of to do for a while, because she was too frantic to do anything but burn off some energy. What the hell were they going to do? What kind of resources did she have? How did a few psychically gifted mortals and one lame vampire fight off a nest led by an ancient strigoi that got his kicks from sadistic games? Sandy Schwimmer had tried to escape Rosho's clutches, and she'd died. Selena knew she and Sandy had been defeated even before Steve showed up to interrupt the hunt.

"Okay," she muttered after a while. "Maybe all we have to do is cancel the reception. The reception's the only thing scheduled for the evening. If the plan is to grab Karen at the reception, we can eliminate the opportunity."

We can eliminate that particular opportunity, she thought, but if Rosho wants Karen, he'll find a way to get to her. If she changes her pattern of behavior at all, that'll tip him off, and he'll attack sooner. Hell, he knows we're onto him or at least suspect him. Of course, he's been broadcasting his intentions to every member of the family with the talent to hear him. The arrogant

bastard wants a fight. Or maybe he just wants to let us
know there's nothing we can do to stop him. This vampire thinks like a serial killer. He wants the attention, he
wants to show that he's smarter than the cops, he doesn't
think he'll ever get caught.

"Maybe he won't. He's been at this for hundreds of
years."

*Don't think like that, you idiot! Don't let him box you
into playing the game his way. You don't catch the bad
guy by following his scenario.*

"Right. Glad we got that straightened out."

She was still prowling the living room. Selena wondered when she was going to start wearing a hole in the
floor. To try for a change of pace, she put on a CD,
Santana rather than Clapton just to break her own usual
pattern. Point was, vampire Law couldn't touch him. He
wasn't breaking vampire Laws. Steve said Rosho was
very careful not to break the Laws of the Blood. So, she
was going to keep a lid on the urge to send out a psychic
scream for help to Steve. The last time she'd asked Steve
to rescue someone from Rosho, the rescuee had died.
This time, Steve would probably offer to give away the
bride.

Selena had to fight down a bad bout of nausea at that
image. "Okay," she said. "What do we do?"

Hit them when they're vulnerable, of course. She sat
down on the couch and tapped a finger on her chin while
she thought. *The night belongs to them, and they can
monitor thoughts in the daylight.* They keep mortals to
protect them in the daylight, but mortals could be gotten
past, and monitoring thoughts didn't mean you could
completely protect yourself from the people thinking
them by shouting mental orders at them. Sandy Schwimmer had gotten past guards and telepathic commands.

She'd killed two of the bastards, and she was one small woman. "Who had the strength and single-mindedness of the totally insane."

Selena had a flash of memory of the crazed look in Sandy's eyes when they'd talked in the Navy Pier parking garage. The woman had been mad, but she'd had the right idea. Sometimes insanity could work to your advantage, Selena supposed. She really wished she'd been able to help the woman who'd declared that Selena was the companions' Enforcer. She still had the coin Sandy had given her.

"What I do not need is a bunch of white witches to help with this. What I need are people used to dealing with vampires on a daily basis. People with experience." Like her little cadre of disgruntled companions. "Fearless vampire killers unite," she muttered. "If you can stop talking long enough to get anything done." What was she supposed to do, jump into the chat room and invite everyone there to attend her cousin's wedding reception? "Where stake will be on the menu."

She didn't think she could do this in a live chat. There was no guarantee who would be there, and the ones who were on-line would go off on chattering tangents and she'd never hammer home the point that this was something nasty happening in real time to them. She needed one-on-one, face-to-face confrontation with the only people who could possibly help her. The secure chat room ensured a bit too much anonymity for the participants. For all she knew, every one of the companions was too far away from Chicago to arrive in time to help. Or they could all be in Wauconda or Schiller Park or out in DeKalb. "Having a few phone numbers and E-mail addresses wouldn't hurt." Sandy had found her, if only she had access to Sandy's—

Sandy took a pink plastic diskette out of her purse.
"For you."

"What is that?"

"Everything I could find." Sandy opened the glove
compartment and tucked the diskette inside.

The memory came back in a flash of blinding pain.
As the pain cleared, Selena remembered that Sandy had
told her she worked in computer security. Selena had
done a bit of that herself. She knew there were ways to
track down the not-as-anonymous-as-they-thought users
of the web. Sandy had given her the information. It was
the only legacy the poor woman had left. Selena hurried
to dig the diskette out of her purse and put it into the
computer's A drive.

A few minutes later, she knew at least a little bit about
most of the people who shared the companions' chat
room. Carmlaskid lived in Scotland. Other than an E-
mail address, there was no information on Ghost.
DesertDog was in Arizona, Canuk in Alaska. She'd been
right about Fyrstartr living in California but was surprised to discover that Moscowknight did as well. She'd
made the assumption that Moscowknight was indeed
Russian. More important than whereabouts and superflu-
ous credit information and web surfing histories, she had
some of their names, bits of biographical information,
some of their phone numbers, and all of their E-mail
addresses. She started with an E-mail message.

My name, she began the message to them, **is Selena**
Crawford. I live in Chicago, and I need your help.

She went on to explain about Rosho not returning to
Denver, about her family, her cousin, the wedding, and
everything else she could think of. Except Steve. She
didn't mention she was Istvan's companion. She didn't
figure that would win friends and influence people, con-

sidering how unpopular Istvan the Enforcer was in the vampire community. She told them when she needed them in Chicago and gave them her address and phone number.

After that, she sent the message and hoped to several gods and a few goddesses that the cavalry would deign to show up in time for the battle.

Chapter 22

THE FIRST THING Selena did when she opened the door and saw the man in the hallway was wonder how many outstanding warrants were out for him. The second was to notice the large canvas bag he carried. The third was to come to a startling revelation. He wasn't a companion. She knew who he was, who he had to be. She'd been expecting him since he called from Saint Louis on his way from Arizona, but—

"DesertDog?"

"Haven," he said, and pushed past her into the living room, contemptuously adding, "Don't start on me, cop," as he went by.

Well, wasn't he just going to be a joy to work with? At least he had made it on time, if just barely. He looked competent, even though she knew he'd driven the whole way from Tucson with no sleep. Her other guest, on the other hand, had not arrived looking scruffy. Selena sighed, closed the door, and turned back to the living room. She glanced at the clock on the stereo system, fought down the rising sense of panic, and concentrated on the two other people in the room. The small woman who'd been perched on the edge of her couch was now on her feet, looking over the newcomer with a combination of appalled distaste and female interest.

Selena knew exactly how the other woman felt. Even with the sneer, the cold expression in his dark eyes, the tattoos, and the stubbled chin, Haven was a hard-muscled, handsome man who reeked of danger and testosterone. He had that tall, dark, and dangerous certain something that sensible women ran from but that the sort of women who ended up becoming vampire companions found practically irresistible.

"Jebel Haven, meet Martha Siriaco. DesertDog, this is Fyrstartr."

Fyrstartr gave Selena a blistering look. "Siri," she said, holding a hand out tentatively to Haven. Her left hand sported a large diamond ring. Her long nails were painted pearly lavender. "Call me Siri."

Haven dropped the bag. It landed on the floor with a heavy, metallic clatter. He ignored Siri's offer of a handshake. He looked around the room. Selena went into the kitchen and returned with some beers before he had the chance to ask. She even brought a glass for Siri. Then she stood back and surveyed her merry band. She didn't know what she'd get, if anything, when she sent out her call for help. Siri had arrived first, on a plane from Los Angeles yesterday afternoon. Siri was short, starlet slender, with beautiful, delicate features, a designer label wardrobe, great makeup, and no weapons training to speak of. She wore her short auburn hair in a tousled style that shrieked to Selena that the haircut alone cost more than she made in a month. Siri did not strike Selena as a rebel organizer type, but Siri told Selena she had her reasons. And at least she was a companion.

Haven, on the other hand, was more of the sort of help Selena'd hoped for in this time of crisis. A moment in his presence convinced her he was tough, capable, ruthless, and meaner than a snake. She didn't mind that; she was used to dealing with hardass felons, which was something else she was certain he was. She also knew instantly what he wasn't. Once you'd been bitten, you always recognized your own.

It was Siri who said it. "You aren't a companion."

Haven tilted his head to one side. "Yeah?" His voice was deep, slightly rough, indifferent. "So?"

"But—" Siri took a step back. Her mouth thinned to a disapproving line, and she glared. Selena hid a pleased smirk as she realized that delicate little Siri wasn't in the least bit intimidated by the glowering Haven. "I started the support group for companions," Siri said to Haven. "Who the hell are you? How did you find us?"

Haven turned to Selena. "You want a vampire killer or not?"

"I'd kind of like you to answer Siri's question, actually," she told him. She put herself between him and the door. She saw his annoyance, but no matter what, he wasn't leaving just yet.

"You're the one who talked poor Sandswimmer into killing vampires, and you're not even one of us," Siri accused Haven.

"I told her how I'd do it. I didn't talk her into anything." He jerked a thumb at Selena. "Unless Xena here's been lying to us."

"You're the one who's been lying, Mr. Haven."

"I'm a companion, I just ain't been bit yet. I left Little Mary Sunshine at home, but if you want to give her a call," he checked his watch, "in about six hours, she'd be happy to explain our dating situation to you. She likes explaining things," he added with an amused affection that made Selena wonder what sort of nice vampire girl this bad man hung with. She was obviously someone like Lawrence, who didn't believe in biting someone before knowing them very well. In Haven's case, that was probably quite wise.

"He's one of us," Selena told Siri.

"You have been with the group since nearly the beginning, Haven," Siri conceded. "That counts for something."

"The fact that he showed up counts for a lot," Selena said. She checked the clock again and swore under her breath.

"Bein' a virgin also makes it easier for me to kill the bastards," Haven said. He riveted his attention on Selena. "Sorry I'm late. When and where's the show?"

He was indeed late, at least a day later than she'd asked the companions to show up in Chicago. She was relieved that anyone had answered her SOS at all. Siri had arrived on time, but the sight of the Californian at her door had been more depressing than heartening for Selena. The last day and a half had been difficult on so many levels. There'd been magic involved, and favors called in, and family discussions and turmoil, as well as Selena having to make a choice between mortal ethics and supernatural danger. Siri's only contribution so far was to describe a graphic vision she'd had on the plane of a wolf leaping through a stained-glass window, though she and Siri both thought this might be more of a memory of an old Dracula movie than a genuine view of the future.

"Have a seat, Haven, and I'll fill you in."

He sat, but before Selena could begin, Siri crossed her

arms under her breasts and said nervously, "I really don't know how useful I'm going to be tonight. I've never actually hurt anyone, except for the time I hit somebody with a chair. I think I kicked him a few times, too. But it was under extraordinary circumstances, and I—"

"These are extraordinary circumstances, remember, Siri? It's okay to be scared," Selena added. "I'm scared."

"You don't look it."

Selena shrugged. "Practice. Haven's scared under the macho posing. Right, Haven?"

"Damned scared," Haven bluntly replied and gave a wicked grin. "Scared every time I go into a firefight. Adds to the rush."

"I'm not a danger junkie!" Siri insisted.

"You hang with a vampire, don't you?" Haven asked her. "You risk getting caught every time you log online. You showed up here."

"I don't know what I'm doing here! I thought I had a responsibility . . . because of what happened to Sandswimmer. Because I started the chat room, and I thought I'd be a coward if I didn't take some responsibility for what happened. But I am a coward, and—"

"Rosho's responsible for Sandy's death," Selena reminded the nervous woman. "As far as I'm concerned, you can be in this because of guilt or because you want justice for what happened to her or because you want to change the underneath world or because you're an adrenaline junkie," Selena added, with a glance to Haven. "Why you came doesn't matter, as long as you're at my cousin's wedding reception tonight and contribute something to keeping the vampires away from her."

Selena checked the clock again. She had to change clothes in a minute. She had to get to the church. She was suffering a huge bout of guilt for having used her own psychic abilities to help Aunt Catie persuade Karen that she'd only been suffering from a bad case of pre-wedding jitters so that Karen wouldn't cancel the wedding. And that wasn't the only thing she had to feel guilty about.

"Okay," she said to Haven, "here's what's happened. Yesterday morning there was a police raid on the house Rosho's nest lives in. The Chicago police were not looking for vampires," she added at Haven's curious look. "What they discovered was a group of homeless crack-heads that had moved into a temporarily abandoned renovation project."

Haven did not look surprised or appalled, he merely nodded his understanding. He said, "Drugs and paraphernalia were found on site. Everyone in the house was arrested, and no one has made bail yet."

This cynical acceptance of police corruption broke Selena's heart. She had called in favors, planted evidence at the scene, messed up a few minds, and everything Haven had said had come to pass, especially the part about all of Rosho's helpers still being in jail. She couldn't very well have arrested the mortal members of Rosho's nest because they were aiding and abetting vampires, but she had still arranged to get them out of the way. At least nobody had gotten killed. It wasn't the slaves' and companions' fault that they were attached to a particularly bad nest of strigoi. Maybe after Rosho and his fang gang were eliminated, the mortals would have some chance of recovery.

"Rosho's an old-fashioned boy," she went on. "No lawyer on staff to get his people out. Problem is, the mortals were there, five of them, but the vampires weren't in the building. I went through the place thoroughly. Found nothing. Rosho knows my family's aware of him. Probably expected we'd raid the place and left his mortals there to fight the witches, except it wasn't the Bailey coven that showed up but the Crawford side of the family, and we showed with guns, badges, and warrants."

"Very nice," Haven said. "But you still have the vampires to deal with." He glanced out the living room window. "What time's sunset?"

"Whatever time it is, we don't have time to find the vampires. Every white witch and strig on the light side in the state's been looking for them, and all anyone's found is big psychic black holes all over town. We haven't got the time to investigate all the places they could be hiding. They're going to have to come to us. That's why there's going to be a wedding today, and my poor cousin's going to be bait at her own wedding reception."

"She should elope," Haven commented.

"If Rosho wants her, he'll track her wherever she goes," Siri said. "You know what strigois are like when they're stalking a new lover."

"I can guess," Haven said. "They like to play with their prey. He'll only make it worse for the girl if she runs."

"I think there's at least five, maybe eight vampires," Selena went on. "I didn't get a chance to count when they were chasing me and Sandy. What I do know is that he and some of his Euro-trash pals took over the nest Sandy lived with in Denver. Sandy killed two of the vampires who raped her. I know at least one of them was from Rosho's original gang. I'm hoping both of them were."

"Why?" Siri asked.

"Because the Denver vampires aren't involved in this voluntarily. Their nest leader was under Rosho's thumb. That was Donavan, Sandy's lover. He lost it when Sandy was killed, so he's not part of the equation. We need to take out Rosho and however many of his friends are left; then the Denver vampires won't be a problem."

"They'll be released from his mastery," Siri said with a nod. "Grateful for their liberation rather than enemies of the cause."

"Viva la revolución," Haven muttered. "Couldn't we just kill them, too? They *let* the bastards do their nest leader's companion. Why do they deserve to live?"

"Because we need all the allies we can get," Selena answered. "If we really are going to have a revolution, having vampires on our side will help."

Besides, taking out one very old vampire in the middle of the night might be more than a trio of mortal hunters could manage, and taking out a whole nest of them was going to be impossible. She didn't underestimate that she and Haven were dangerous, and that Siri might come through in a pinch, but the odds were not in their favor. What Selena did have in her favor was the knowledge that she had killed a vampire once, but, like Siri said, it had been under extraordinary circumstances. She couldn't very well repeat that performance. She could see the headlines if she did. *"Off-Duty Cop Sprays Bullets into Crowd at Wedding Reception!" "She snapped,"* a bystander reported. *"Shouted something about vampires and brought out an Uzi. I think having to wear a bridesmaid's dress sent her over the edge."*

"Selena?"

"What?" Selena blinked, and Siri's worried face came into focus. "Sorry. I was thinking that I ought to be at the church by now. I better go change clothes."

"But what's the plan?" Haven insisted. "What do I do?"

Selena looked at Haven's bag. "You have weapons in there?"

"That's why I drove. There's more stuff out in the Jeep. Couldn't bring the arsenal on a plane."

"Good." Selena jerked a thumb at Siri. "Show her how to use them."

"What do I do?" Siri asked.

Selena looked Haven over critically. "Get him shaved and into a suit. He is not coming to my cousin's reception looking like that."

Chapter 23

EXCEPT FOR THE threat of vampires, Selena thought, it was a perfectly normal summer Saturday evening at Navy Pier. Which meant that it was crowded and happily noisy, full of kids on the carousel, long lines waiting for the short ride on the huge Ferris wheel and the short movies in the IMAX theater, not a table was empty at any of the restaurants, either inside or out. She swept the crowds with not only her extra senses but also her policeman's eye for trouble. What she saw were families on a night out and dating couples everywhere, hand in hand, enjoying the bright lights and cooler air of the early evening. If there were vampires in the area, their presence was well masked by psychic white noise from thousands of minds.

No one paid any special attention to her, a tall woman made taller by a pair of painfully tight high-heeled pumps, dressed in a long green satin dress with a matching lace bolero jacket. There were wedding parties on the pier all the time, her outfit made it obvious what she was doing here. Selena made her way carefully up the length of the pier. She came back past the children's museum, where a young audience was enthralled by the boundless energy of a group of dogs in an obedience competition, and the brightly lit windows of the stained-glass exhibit, and finally found her way back to the sculpture garden near the entrance. The air was full of music, and people danced with mosh pit togetherness below the outdoor stages. The air was also perfumed with the aromas of fried food and whiffs of diesel fuel from the big yellow speedboats that whizzed passengers on lakefront tours. The renovated pier reached out a long neon-lit arm into the calm waters of Lake Michigan, and boats of all shapes and sizes filled the water and the docking slips. Some of the larger ships berthed at the pier were close to the size of small passenger liners; they offered dinner cruises and hosted parties of all sorts, including wedding receptions. The wedding guests were boarding the *Queen Eleanor* while Selena did her reconnaissance. She was supposed to already be on the boat with the wedding party, smiling and posing on command for yet another photo session. The photographer and videographer would be furious at her holding up their show, but she didn't much care.

Selena had told her fellow crusaders to meet by the shoe statue out front, which seemed a fitting rendezvous point. Siri and Haven were there when she arrived. Her first comment upon approaching the pair was to Siri. "He cleans up well, I see." Then she looked at Haven and asked, "What's that?"

"Flame thrower."

"Goes well with your tie." The canister he carried didn't outwardly look like a weapon. It might have been mistaken for a fire extinguisher, and possibly might have started life with such a benign purpose. Haven struck her as the sort who excelled at improvising weapons from household devices. *Bet he was a treat in the prison machine shop,* she thought. "I'm not sure that thing is such a good idea in a crowd."

He gave her a look that clearly asked if she wanted his help or not. "I have a very accurate aim."

"Okay." She wasn't going to argue about it.

Siri was dressed in a short ice-blue dress of shiny doupioni silk, with a matching shawl. The ensemble made Selena envious, but she smiled when Siri shifted the shawl to give her a quick glimpse of another home-made looking weapon slung on a shoulder strap. Siri gave a nervous smile. "He says it fires incendiary rounds."

"And a charming accessory it makes," said a man, stepping out from the shadow of the big silver shoe.

Not a man, Selena realized as Siri whirled furiously on the newcomer. Not a mortal, at any rate, but the new-comer was the blondest, tannest vampire Selena had ever seen. He was big, too, topping her six-foot height by several inches, with broad shoulders and a deep chest.

"You!"

It was a hard word to hiss, but Siri gave it her furious best. Selena noted the instant recognition and hate in the California companion's expression. The newcomer gave a depreciating smile and shrug.

"Old friend?" Haven asked. He shifted the flame-thrower a fraction; his thumb hovered over a switch at the top of the apparatus. "Siri?"

The tan vampire ignored the others for the moment and spoke to Selena. "You know me as Moscowknight, Layla. Good evening, DesertDog."

"His name's Yevgeny," Siri snarled. "Why aren't you

dead?" she demanded of the newcomer. "I thought you were dead."

"I don't think she likes him very much," Haven said to Selena.

"She has good reason," Yevgeny said. "Selim never told you what happened to me?"

"Leave Selim out of this. I don't care if you did change your mind at the end. What you were going to do was awful. You have no business being alive. And what are you doing here?"

Selena recalled the conversation back at her apartment and asked Siri, "He the one you hit with the chair?"

"Yes."

Pale brows lowered over extremely blue eyes. "You hit me with a chair? I have no memory of that. I was attempting to commit suicide at the time," he told Selena and Haven. "I wasn't a vampire then."

"What are you doing here?" Siri repeated.

"It's not all that safe for a vampire to travel on a commercial airplane, you know," Yevgeny told them. "There was a flight delay at the airport that had me worried. I managed to reach O'Hare before dawn, but I couldn't find my way to Layla's right away. I went to sleep on a warehouse roof. Passed out before I could get to shelter, and the sunburn is still fading. I followed some of your actions in my dreams, but I had to wait until sunset before I could join the hunting party."

"I didn't ask you how you got here. I want to know what you think you're doing trying to be a hero?"

"Perhaps it's part of my community service."

"Moscowknight," Haven interrupted Siri and Yevgeny's conversation. "You're one of our crew? You're not a companion."

"Pot calling the kettle black," Selena murmured.

"I used to be a companion," Yevgeny said. "That should count for something. "Believe me," he continued. "No one has a stronger reason to fight for companions' rights than I do. I've known you were our leader for some time, Siri," he added. "But I haven't told on you to the Enforcer of the City, have I? I have a great deal to make up for. I'd like to start by offering my help tonight."

Selena put herself between Siri and the vampire. "This is all very interesting, but we don't have time to explore personal histories or guilt trips. Welcome to the crew, Yevgeny. Happy to have your help."

"But—" Siri sputtered.

"Get over it," Haven advised.

Siri gave them a dirty look. "I was going to say, but he can't kill vampires."

"No, but he can beat the shit out of them," said Larry, materializing out of the shadows. Selena frowned; the way they could appear like that was so annoying. The dark-haired vampire exchanged a nod with the blond one. Then Larry touched the dangling sleeve of his suit coat. "And I'm not completely helpless. Catie's coven has finished warding the *Queen Eleanor*," he told Selena. "Those protection spells might slow some of the bad guys down, if they get that far."

If they get that far. Now there was a thought. Selena's plan had been to use the companion group as body-guards on board the cruise boat. That wasn't a good plan, she realized now. It was a defensive maneuver that would leave Karen vulnerable if Rosho made it onto the boat. Why let him get onto the boat? It was far better to go on the offensive, wasn't it? Selena winced at the thought of putting bystanders at risk, and weighed it against the prospect of leaving Rosho on the loose. It wasn't only for Karen's sake that the old vampire needed to be disposed of. The world in general would be a better place without him in it.

"Selena," Lawrence said. "You're wanted on the boat. What do you want us to do?"

"Siri, you and I are on the *Queen Eleanor.* You three do what you do. Hunt." The two vampires and the mortal grinned. She gave Haven points for having the most dangerous smile. "Be careful," she instructed. The trio of males had a moment to look pleased at her concern before she added, "I don't want any civilian casualties. And don't let anyone see you."

The two vampires and the mortal vampire hunter suddenly wore identical smirks. Okay, so vampires could teach classes in being discreet, but she had her doubts about Haven's ability to be subtle. There was nothing more she could do but turn and walk away from the amused males, with Siri hurrying after. Heading for her assigned post, Selena prayed that she hadn't unleashed hell on the city.

"Because sometimes a guitar is just a guitar."

Selena shook off the sense of déjà vu and blinked at her Uncle Gary. "That's supposed to be a joke, right?" She looked around to see if there were any wolves in the area, but the only canines nearby were the ones in the obedience trials. The view of the stage with the canine obstacle course was pretty good from the top deck of the cruise boat. The dogs looked like they were having a great time.

The grizzled retired beat cop was not pleased with her lack of enthusiasm. "What's wrong with you tonight, girl? You're standing around stiff as a board. Let's dance."

The band was playing a medley of disco hits from the seventies that Selena wouldn't have danced to even if she hadn't been on duty. The bride and groom and lots of middle-aged guests were slipping and sliding on the dance floor, which had somehow gotten covered in pastel confetti. They all seemed to be having a wonderful time. Even Aunt Catie was out on the dance floor, laughing and shaking her bootie, and staying close to Karen.

"No, thanks," Selena told her uncle.

"You keep staring out at the pier and at the water like you were expecting the boat to be boarded from land *and* sea."

He'd been a Navy SEAL before he became a cop, and he was one sharp old dude. Selena glanced at the sky. Vampires couldn't fly, but they could jump pretty high and far. "And air," she told her uncle. "Actually," she added. "I'm just looking for escape routes."

"For what?"

"I don't want to be around when Karen tosses her bouquet. I'd probably catch it, and you don't want to know what I'd end up bringing to the altar."

"Long as you marry a cop, I wouldn't care." He gave a disgusted snort, and finished off the glass of champagne in his hand. "You're not funny tonight, kid. Stop acting like you're walking a beat. The buffet's not worth crashing the party for," he told her. "What happened to proper sit-down dinners at weddings?"

"Dinner comes later, Uncle Gary, after the boat leaves the dock." Which she hoped would be soon. Not that vampires couldn't swim, or wouldn't still be there when the *Queen Eleanor* returned to the pier, but the cruise might give the swat team on the ground a few more hours to hunt. And she and Siri a few more hours to fret. She forced herself to smile. "I think I'll go ask when we set to sea." It was as good an excuse as any to work her way through the crowd.

She didn't go far before she spotted Siri, elegantly leaning against the ship's rail, gaze fixed on the shore. Selena was stopped for brief conversations with a great aunt and a cousin from each side of the family before she made it to Siri's side.

"You're supposed to be watching Karen," she reminded the Californian. The Californian, she noticed, wore a vacant expression, and her pupils were huge. Siri's hands were wrapped around the rail in a death grip. Selena passed her hand in front of Siri's face. "Hello? Where are you?"

"I smell smoke," Siri answered. She uncurled a hand from the railing, and grabbed Selena's wrist. "Smell smoke."

Yevgeny whirled away, barely dodging the burning vampire when it sprang up from the floor. Larry kicked it, and it went back down, hitting a pool of spilled oil. The oil caught fire, and flames raced across the garage floor, sending up stinking dark smoke. The vampire's face was a mask of pain, her hair was a torch, but she tried to rise again. Haven stepped forward and shot a jet of flames straight into her screaming mouth. Larry beat out the fire that had started on his trouser leg. While he bent over, a vampire jumped on his back. Larry flipped the attacker over his head. The vampire landed on his back in the puddle of burning oil, and Larry didn't let it get up. On the other side of the garage, Yevgeny was laughing and pounding the head of a third vampire to a pulp against a thick concrete pillar. Sprinklers rained water down from the ceiling, but water wouldn't work against the chemical mixture Haven sprayed on the next vampire that rushed at him from the shadows.

When Siri let her go, Selena didn't know where or who she was for a few seconds. When she realized she was on her knees and probably ruining her dress, she grabbed the rail and pulled herself to her feet. Reality didn't seem very real to her for a few more moments. Then noise, sight, and color penetrated her awareness. The band was playing "I Only Have Eyes For You." She felt the evening breeze on her face and caught a whiff of fried food from somewhere on the pier. The thought of fried meat made her gorge rise, but she swallowed hard and looked at Siri.

"You do that often?"

"All the time," Siri answered. She was pale beneath the perfect makeup but quite composed. "I told you I had visions."

"That's happening right now?"

Siri nodded. "The boys seem to be having a good time."

Selena wiped sweat off her brow. Well, that shot her makeup job to hell. "That's a very useful talent. Can you turn it on and off?"

"No. Sometimes I can focus it. I was trying to find out what the others are doing right now." She glanced toward the bride. "That's what I got."

Selena didn't doubt Siri's vision was completely true. "I only saw four vampires. I know there's more than that."

"Was Rosho in the garage?"

"No." Selena was certain that if the old vampire were there, the good guys would be getting their asses whipped. "Try to concentrate on where he is," she told

Siri. Siri touched her again, and Selena did her best to project all of her impressions of Rosho to the other woman.

Siri absorbed what Selena sent but shook her head after a few seconds. "I get darkness. Pools of reflected color on the floor. No. Just darkness. I think it's my imagination. Give it a minute. I have to get some distance from the last one."

That made sense. Selena looked around, her sense of urgency growing. She had no doubt Rosho was nearby. Her aunt's coven had put up a spell wall, but that wouldn't stop him. Lawrence, Haven, and Yevgeny could take out Rosho's nest, and that wouldn't stop him. She had the distinct impression he was out in the shadows, watching every move they made, laughing at them, and wanting Karen.

"He can't have her," she murmured. "He isn't going to have her."

"Over your dead body?" Siri asked quietly.

"Probably," Selena answered. "But I'll do what I have to. Not because Karen's family," she added. "But because it isn't right."

Siri nodded. "My lover didn't give me a choice. I know I would have loved him anyway, if he'd only walked up to me and introduced himself. He should have given me the choice. They have to learn to give mortals choices. You're willing to kill for the right to have a choice."

"Or be killed," Selena reminded her. Siri was looking at her like she was some kind of hero. "Let's not forget the downside to opposing evil. Evil frequently wins."

On the pier, a dog began to bark, its deep voice carrying over the cacophony all around. Selena began to turn her head toward the sound, but the band finished the current song, and the *Queen Eleanor*'s cruise director stepped up to the microphone. "Ladies and gentlemen, thank you for your patience. We're finally about to set sail for the evening. We'll be pulling away from the dock in just—"

Whatever else he might have said was lost when Siri touched her, and the world shattered into a million fragmented shards. Selena fell forward, through a kaleidoscope, into darkness. Then—

He was nearly out of fuel, and two of them had Haven backed against the garage wall. He choked on the smoke, fought to see through the blinding fumes. Larry was facedown in the shallow lake formed by the sprinklers, his back a mass of oozing claw marks. Yevgeny was nowhere in sight. Another vampire stepped out of the shadows, slender, handsome, cold, and deadly. "Help!" Haven shouted. "Somebody fucking help!"

"Rosho! Holy shit, that's Rosho!" Selena didn't have time to be disoriented. She fought it off with all the will she could muster. She was left dizzy but in control of her faculties. "They're in trouble!" She discovered that she was holding Siri by the shoulders. "I have to get to them. They're in trouble."

"I know," Siri said. "It was my vision."

"Right. I know where they are." Haven's cry for help echoed in her head. The need to respond was as strong in Selena as any officer-in-need-of-assistance call. "I have to help them."

"But . . . ! The boat's leaving!" Siri pointed wildly. "Your cousin!"

"Stay with her." Selena ran for the gangway. The sense of urgency clawed at her like a wild animal under her skin. She shoved people aside, and shouted at those who didn't move fast enough.

"Me?" Siri stuck with her. "What do I do?"

"You've got a weapon." Selena glared at the crew members that were beginning to detach the stairway connecting the *Queen Eleanor* to the pier from the side of the boat. They halted what they were doing without asking any questions. Selena paused for one last instant before hurtling down the stairs. "Anyone with fangs comes near my cousin," she told Siri, "shoot him in the head."

"But . . ."

Selena didn't wait to hear any more.

Chapter 24

SELENA COULD BARELY see once she reached the ground. Okay, it was night out, but the place was lit up like daylight. There was neon everywhere, and streetlights and lights poured out of the long row of buildings that lined the pier. The nightly fireworks blossomed overhead to the accompaniment of oohs and aahhs from thousands of voices. Everything was bright, sharply lit. She knew it for a fact, but her eyes and all her extra senses didn't perceive the surroundings that way. She didn't get it, she sure as hell didn't like it, but she struggled forward into the growing shadows. She had to get to the parking garage. She didn't have time for the fear that crawled up her spine and weighed down her limbs. She moved into the crowd, and it was like swimming against a relentless outgoing tide. Someone accidentally hit her in the face with a huge cloud of cotton candy and she tasted spiderwebs instead of sugar.

In the growing darkness, a shadow moved on the edge of her vision. Selena spun to the left and looked up to see a wolf looking down at her from the top of a long staircase. Her muscles tensed and she bit off a cry as she waited for it to leap at her throat, but all it did was sit on its haunches and tilt its head curiously to one side.

Some of the encroaching darkness cleared from Selena's head, and she gave a faint, nervous laugh. It was a big black dog, some sort of sheepdog, maybe. Probably one of the animals from the dog show. She really was seeing evil everywhere, wasn't she? Her face was sticky from a combination of cotton candy and tears. Crying? What on earth was the matter with her? Her head hurt, and she suddenly couldn't remember where the parking garages were.

Of course she knew where they were. She'd been in one only a few days ago. With . . . with . . . Selena scrubbed her hands over her face. Why was it so bloody noisy? And why were all these people here? The deep rumble of artillery explosions behind her drew her to slowly turn around. Her gaze was drawn to the sky where great, multicolored chrysanthemums bloomed and vanished one after the other, leaving dissipating puffs of smoke in their wake. "Ooh," she said. "Aahh." She reached out a hand. "Pretty."

What the hell was the matter with her? One glass of champagne and she was acting like an idiot. But when had she had the champagne? Why? She was on duty, right? She didn't drink on duty. She must be working undercover, because she couldn't think of any other explanation for the outfit she was wearing. How was a person supposed to run in high heels? She was in pursuit of a bad guy, she was pretty sure of that, but—

Selena gave a sharp shake of her head, and tried to regain her focus. On one side of her was a long row of buildings. Some sort of shopping mall? On her other side the hull of a large boat blocked the view. Where was she and what was she supposed to do?

"Someone," she said, "is messing with my mind."

She did not like people messing with her in any way; it annoyed her. Annoyance helped her remember that she was standing around like an idiot when she had people to rescue. She firmly believed that temper and stubbornness went a long way in keeping Selena Crawford free of psychic influence. Once more she began to make her way through the crowd, muttering, "Some vampire thinks he can just waltz in and take over my head, does he? Who does he think he is, Steve the Enforcer? What's some little fangboy think he is compared to the meanest mother in the—"

Darkness came up and hit her in the face with the force of a tornado. When the light came back, Rosho was standing in it. "I think I have had quite enough of this game."

"Oh, shit." It was not a particularly clever or heroic thing to say, but the words summed up a great deal of shock, terror, and anger. Besides, it wouldn't have been at all in character with her tough persona to squeak "Mommy!" which was exactly what Selena wanted to do. Besides, her mommy might show up, and then they'd both be dead. She didn't suppose running away was an option. Fear, at least, drove away all the sticky mental cobwebs and traps.

Rosho stepped very close to her. He put a hand under her elbow and drew her even closer, another couple in the happy crowd. "You have no options," he whispered in her ear. "You never did."

Okay, she was scared. Definitely. No doubt about it. She turned, very quickly, and head-butted him. "Oh, yeah?" He only blinked in response, while her forehead hurt like hell, but she gave herself points for making a point.

He changed simply holding her into an embrace, with one hand still grasping her arm, the other pressed into the small of her back. "I think you know I always break my toys before I throw them away." His voice and smile were equally silky. "Hello, Toy."

He was a beautiful creature, and he knew it. He took great pleasure in Selena's looking at him, seeing only himself reflected in her eyes. She stared, throat dry with fear, very aware of his thigh touching hers as she took in the sharp lines of his high cheekbones and the jaw that narrowed to the sharp point of his bearded chin. His wide mouth quirked in a preening, pleased smile. "Does it bother you," she inquired after a few seconds, "that I'm taller than you are?" His grip turned very painful. Claws bit deeply into her skin. She'd expected it, and she didn't allow him the satisfaction of a physical or mental flinch. She was a daughter of the Bailey *familia*. They did not spoil demons. "If you think I mind having bloodstains on this dress, you know very little about modern wedding customs."

"I think we will go somewhere very private," he said. "No one is looking at us, Toy. Even if they were, calling for help would only result in many deaths."

She didn't doubt it. They were standing in front of the children's museum. Of course he would attack children first. The Enforcer of the City would be very annoyed with Rosho, but that would be later, after the children were dead. "You're betting on my cooperation," she told him. "And my coming along quietly will keep you from breaking any laws."

He didn't bother to answer, and she didn't bother to struggle as he put his arm around her waist and took her along the promenade. It surprised her that he headed them toward one of the doors leading to the indoor shopping arcade rather than toward the entrance. How could he expect to find privacy inside, she wondered. The place was open until midnight on weekends.

But there was indeed one deserted spot in the long hallway full of bustling shops. He took her around a corner, and suddenly they were alone. The sign outside the entrance said Closed. The door was not locked. "I asked everyone to go away," he told her. "I was very polite about it. Most of the staff went voluntarily."

She knew for a fact that magic did not work on everybody. Anyone who used magic had to be really, really good to get the sort of cooperation Rosho was talking about.

"I'm really, really good," he said.

"You probably just bribed the ones you couldn't control or scare."

"Whatever works. Privacy is what matters."

"Why don't we go back to my place?" Selena offered. "I'll put on some Clapton. We can have some wine—"

"Later. I plan to drink quite a bit at your cousin's party."

Rosho pushed her inside ahead of him, into a room full of glass. He pushed hard enough that she ran into a solid glass pedestal with enough strength to knock her to the floor. She rose to her knees on smooth tiles, fighting for breath from the force of the impact. The lights were off, but huge stained-glass windows facing the pier filtered through faint colored light from the world outside. Selena told herself that the rainbow lights in front of her eyes came from the reflections. She was not surprised to look up and find Rosho standing over her.

"I know who you belong to," he told her. "The boy

tried to cover the truth that night when he broke my last toy. But I saw the thread between you long before he put on a flimsy show of taking your life. Pathetic of him, really, trying to protect you from me. I take who I want."

His last words brought the complete situation clearly back to Selena. "I won't let you take my cousin."

"I never wanted her." He laughed softly. He brushed fingers through Selena's hair. His claws left bloody trails in her scalp. "Playing with you was pleasant. I've always enjoyed creating diversions to mask my true purpose. I sent you the dreams while I watched you at night and dreamed about you during the days. It's another way of playing with shadows."

And why didn't I figure this out? she wondered as he spoke.

"Because you're as stupid as the boy who owns you."

Selena surged to her feet. "Don't you call him stupid!" It was a ridiculous reaction, considering the trouble she was in, but she preferred the adrenaline rush of indignation to the terror that was trying to claw its way to the front of her mind. "And don't call me stupid, either," she added. "Because I will kill you."

He was neither amused nor angry at her words. He didn't even look bored, though she half expected him to yawn. She looked around for a weapon or an escape route. There was glass everywhere, beautiful, sparkling hanging and mounted panels that had once been windows in fine old buildings. There were Tiffany and Frank Lloyd Wright designs among the collection, and many modern stained-glass panels as well, plus sinuous glass sculptures in rich colors mounted on marble, glass, and metal plinths. The place must be gloriously colorful with the sunlight shining in, but it was dark here now.

Darkness could be a fugitive's friend, but not when you ran from a vampire.

Despite the futility of it, Selena took a chance and ran. It was the expected move, of course, only another game for Rosho, but Selena figured you never knew when you might catch a break. You try, or you give up, she thought. If she gave up, she knew she would end up worse off than Sandy Schwimmer by the time Rosho was through with her. Maybe the smart thing to do was simply to kill herself and get it over with. Damn it, why wasn't she carrying a weapon? Or at least a cell phone?

"Glass," she said, and ducked around a huge sculpture shaped like a half-opened seashell. Glass could be used as a weapon. As far as Selena could tell, Rosho wasn't bothering to chase her. He was between her and the main entrance, she was sure of that. He could move fast enough to be between her and any possible exit as soon as she headed for one. She needed to break some glass.

The seashell was too big to do her any good. Everything nearby was too big. She raced around frantically looking for something breakable in a room full of glass. The irony nearly choked her. Or perhaps the choking sensation came from fear, fear he projected at her. "That's cheating, you bastard!" His laughter rang through the gallery and in her head, followed closely by images of things he had done to Sandy, to Steve, and what he was going to do to her.

"I'm not impressed," she shouted. He appeared in front of her a second later and pushed her against a wall beneath one of the huge colored glass windows. The pain of the impact nearly made her pass out. She might have welcomed the sanctuary of unconsciousness if she wasn't certain Rosho would follow her and make her nightmares very real. "This time I'm impressed," she said, rather than let the pain get to her.

He held her in place with one hand, and slowly ran his other hand over her breasts and belly and thighs. "I haven't begun to impress you."

"You don't know how to get a real date, do you? Rapists have very inadequate personalities."

"Rape is about power."

That, too. She could grit her teeth and cope with his touching her. Rape she could survive, it was his teeth she worried about.

He sensed her thoughts and reminded her, "You're a companion. Having anyone but your master inside you will be unbearable torture."

She fought hard to do it, and knew her expression came out more as a grimace than the dangerous smile she tried for, but she did bare her teeth. "You'll be surprised at what I can bear. Whatever you do, I will kill you."

He ignored her bravado. He kept on groping her as he put his lips to her ear and said, "I can only play for a little while, Toy, but I wanted you as an appetizer. When I'm through here, I have to join your friends. I can feel the strigs and the mortal killing my servants one by one, foolishly unaware that they are about to take my creatures' places. Then I'm going to gather a new group of slaves. Your witch family will belong to me. I'll start with your mother, your aunt, pretty Paloma. But I won't touch silly Karen. I already told you I didn't want her. Siri has possibilities."

Selena realized that she'd let a shopaholic with a platinum card loose in a mall. Here were all these gifted people gathered together in one place, and he was going to collect them as prizes and property, and no one could

stop him. Siri has a vampire lover, she thought. So does
Haven. Wouldn't they protest? Did Rosho plan to fight
every vampire out there and become king of the world?
Then she remembered what Lawrence had said about
Enforcers allowing the dominance games to get rid of
troublemakers. A bunch of rebellious companions would
definitely be judged troublemakers. And she'd brought
them all together in one place.

"Yes," Rosho said. "It's all your fault."

He kissed her then, a long, slow crushing of his mouth
against hers. She wasn't sure what he got out of it, but
she was left with the sensation that he'd forced her to
swallow acid. She supposed the expected response was
for her to spit on him, but, while it was tempting, she
kneed him in the groin instead. The idiot actually didn't
see it coming. The brief look of surprise on his face was
priceless, except that when he hit her he had his claws
out and tore a line of deep cuts from her right shoulder
down across her left breast. When she screamed, he let
her fall to the floor.

Glass, she thought, searching around blindly. *I need
some broken glass.*

As if in answer to a prayer, sharp fragments of glass
began to rain down on her out of the sky, like a shower
of lethal confetti. The sound of the overhead window
breaking as something heavy hurtled through it reached
Selena as an aftershock. Rosho whirled away from her,
but it was the growling that got Selena onto her feet.
She stared past Rosho's shoulder, and what she saw in
the center of the light pouring in through the broken
window was a snarling black wolf.

A–Big–Bad–Wolf.

Chapter 25

SELENA BEGAN TO laugh. It was not at all the sort of thing a sane person should do when faced with a pair of monsters, but laugh she did. Rosho turned around and slapped her, which certainly killed any impending hysteria before it had a good chance to get started.

She didn't think Rosho'd broken her jaw, but she opened and closed her mouth a few times to make sure as she glanced between the hole in the window, the wolf, and vampire. She put her hands on her hips. Then she said, "I suppose you were waiting for the perfect entrance line before you bothered to show up."

Steve morphed from wolf shape to take the form a tall, naked man. Watching the transformation was a dizzying experience. He looked at her and shrugged. "I was waiting for the dog show to be over. I didn't make best in show, so I ate the Border collie that did."

"Bad dog."

Sarcasm was her way of showing relief and joy at her own true love having bothered to show up in the nick of time. Her heart hammered wildly in her chest, and the pain was almost forgotten in the flood of delight spreading through her at Steve's appearing like an avenging demon out of the night. He'd come to rescue her! He did care! Wasn't he wonderful?

She did not bother masking her annoyance and suspicion. "Why are you really here? And what took you so long? Do you know what he was going to do to me?"

Istvan basked in the flood of anger his darling Selena unleashed on him. He saw her gaze shift worriedly to the broken window. "Don't worry, hon," he told his cop girlfriend. "The alarms are all off, and the crowd's thin on this end of the pier."

"Magic." She spat the word out. "I am so sick of magic."

"It's forensics that pisses me off. We'll just have to make sure your fingerprints aren't on anything before we leave."

While he spoke to Selena, most of Istvan's attention was on Rosho. The old vampire had frozen at the sight of his shifting shapes, and he continued to stare at him, mouth working like a landed fish's.

"Idiot," Istvan said. "What do you think happens when a *dhamphir* becomes a vampire?"

Rosho got his flapping jaw under control to say, "Myths . . . the legends . . ."

"All true."

Rosho shook his head. He took a belligerent step forward. "You are nothing . . . a gypsy peasant. You tasted like mud."

Istvan didn't blame Rosho for not wanting to believe, even with the evidence before him. "You never were very bright. You've heard the whispers about me for centuries, but unless someone is saying your name, you don't hear their voice."

"He really can do all that movie vampire crap, you know," Selena said. She had a way of sticking large pins into any attempt at pomposity. "I used to think it was smoke and mirrors. It's not, is it, Steve?"

Selena had a grudging understanding of magic, but what he did—what he was—went far beyond the scope of any other magic that had ever appeared in the world. Or as close as made no never mind when Lady Valentia wasn't around to make him look like a rank amateur. Selena would know in her soul it was true, but it came as no surprise to Istvan that it had taken her outer senses a while to acclimate to the notion of being the chosen bride of the real Count Dracula. What nice girl would want that in her bed? Selena, of course, was not a nice girl. Being good didn't mean you had to be nice, he thought fondly. It was one of the things they had in common.

"I'm sorry I had to let the old fool hurt you." Rosho was going to pay heavily for every drop of Selena's blood he had shed. Companions healed quickly, and he was tempted to kiss it and make it all better.

"Can you do bats?" Selena asked conversationally. "I've never seen you turn into a bat."

"We'll talk about it later, hon. I have to work now."

"And why did you let him hurt me? You've been here the whole time . . . waiting."

"I used you as bait."

"I figured that out. You set this up the night he killed Sandy."

"Yes."

"Bastard. You were running a sting operation on this jerk, weren't you? Letting him stalk me while you stalked him? You might have mentioned it to me."

"I couldn't risk tipping him off, could I? I serve the Laws. He had to break the Law before I could do what I've wanted to do to him for centuries."

"That's called entrapment," she said. "A good lawyer could get him off."

Rosho shifted his gaze back and forth during this interplay, panic creeping deep into his bones. "What Law? I have never broken the Laws of the Blood!"

"Really?" Istvan asked. "The Law states you must defeat a vampire in combat before claiming his property."

Rosho tried to sneer. He laughed, but the sound was shaky. "I have not yet taken your property."

"True." Istvan nodded. He looked at Selena. "I couldn't let him go that far."

She touched the row of cuts on her chest. "Thanks."

"You look delicious, by the way." The flash of anger in her eyes told him that was not the right thing to say. "Sorry." He looked back at the old vampire. "I guess you haven't quite broken any Laws, Rosho. You want to fight?"

Rosho's confidence suddenly returned in a blast of psychic power. His laugh this time was very real. "It would be pleasant to have you in my power again, boy."

He still didn't believe. Rosho the noble boyar warrior couldn't let himself believe in defeat. Good. Istvan prepared to take a step forward.

"Broken glass," Selena said before he moved. "You're naked."

"I have very tough skin," he said. "But since you mention it . . ." Istvan bent, selected a long, sharp shard of red glass, and flicked it through the air. "Peasant boys don't use swords," Istvan said over Rosho's hiss of pain.

The glass dagger was buried in Rosho's chest. "But we're pretty good with knives."

Rosho's features changed into a fanged hunting mask, and he leapt.

Selena watched them, and in some ways was able to sense what was going on, but her eyes only caught blurs and flashes, evidence and residue of violence filled the room as the vampires struggled. Glass flew, blood sprayed, she heard the snapping of fangs and the scrabbling of claws on tiles, the meaty rending of tough flesh. She pressed herself against the wall, stayed very still, and hoped to not be noticed. She was glad to stay out of the line of fire for once. Mortals needed to know when to keep their heads down when the immortals played their games with each other.

While they fought, she worked on trying not to be resentful that Steve had used her. She saw his point in not tipping his hand to Rosho. She worked even harder on not resenting having to be rescued. It wasn't because she was a *girl* in a green satin dress. She was tough, but she was mortal. She was not in their league without a great deal of firepower once the sun had set. She considered edging toward the door, maybe making a run for it, maybe continuing her initial goal of helping Haven, Larry, and Yevgeny, but staying still was probably safer. Besides, she was too curious to see the end of the game to leave now, even if she didn't have any doubt of the outcome. And Steve was here. For once she gave in to the stupid companion compulsion to be near her lover.

A moment later she was a little too close as a blow from Rosho sent Steve hurtling backward into her. "Nice butt," she observed, squeezing it before she pushed him back into the fray. He gave her a dirty look, and stopped a handful of claws aimed for his throat with a flick of his hand. She noticed that Steve hadn't bothered sprouting fangs or claws for this bout with his old enemy, and all the blood was Rosho's. "You're showing off," she called after him.

Steve turned his back on the wounded vampire to talk to her. She couldn't help but notice his erection. "I have been waiting for this for a long time."

"Yes, well . . . if you two would rather be alone . . ."

Rosho jumped on Steve's back. Steve plucked him off and slammed Rosho onto the floor at her feet. "I think I'll kill him now," he said to Selena. "Should I make it quick and merciful, or take my time about it?"

Selena considered the line of destroyed lives this stupid, selfish creature had caused going back hundreds and hundreds of years. It didn't take her long to make her choice. "Take your time, dear," she told Steve. "I'm not in any hurry."

She didn't look though; she closed her eyes and wimped out on watching Rosho get what he had coming to him. What she heard was bad enough, and it would be the background music for nightmares to come. She eventually put her fingers in her ears, but that didn't help.

First he dumped Rosho's remains in the lake. Then Istvan pulled some silk scarves out of a display case in the gift shop and cleaned off much of the blood before returning to Selena. She was still standing hunched over beneath the broken window, eyes scrunched tightly closed, her hands covering her ears. The drying blood from her own wounds was a rich perfume to him, but this wasn't the time or place to indulge in tasting it. Magic or no magic, people would notice the damage to the place soon.

"Come on," he said and lifted her gently in his arms.

He thought she kept her eyes closed because, though she could feel the rush of air on her skin, she didn't want to know they were flying.

Selena opened her eyes when she was sure she was standing on a firm surface. Even then, she waited a while before she looked around. They were in a parking garage. Steve leaned against the door of his black Suburban, wearing jeans and a black T-shirt. She wasn't sure when he'd had time to put on clothes, but he could move fast. She smelled smoke.

"Oh, my god, the boys!"

He put a hand out to stop her before she could run off. "Show's already over. I checked in on them before I rescued you. Haven's currently helping the other two dispose of the bodies of the ones who didn't run away."

"Oh. Good." Selena swiped hair out of her face. She was so tired and so glad this was over. She only relaxed for a moment though. "Shit. That means you know about us."

"The companions support group? Yes."

Was that an evil twinkle in his narrow blue eyes? "What?" she demanded.

"I go by the screen name Ghost." She hit him on the shoulder. "You did call for help from the group. I came, didn't I?"

"You knew about us all along!"

Istvan put his hands on Selena's lovely, sturdy waist and drew her close, savoring her warmth as much as her indignation. He really was going to lick all the blood off her soon, and the scent left by Rosho's touch. "Shh. You don't want anyone to notice us, do you?"

"Ghost. You're Ghost."

He smirked. "On the Internet no one knows you're a vampire."

Her fury singed him. "You spied on us."

"I participated." He saw her mentally flipping through every chat room conversation she'd had with the group. "You're more worried about what you said when you were bitching about your 'friend' than you are about incriminating the revolutionaries, aren't you?"

"Damn right. It only fed your ego. I remember Ghost encouraging me to bitch a few times." She shook off indignant embarrassment and got back to business. "What are you going to do to us?"

"I'm a ghost in the machine," he said. "What can a ghost do?"

She was wary yet hopeful as she tried to read his intentions. "You'll let us have a revolution?"

"No." He put a finger over her lips before she could protest. "But I'll help you pursue justice. Within the Laws," he added sternly. "You're very tired," he added, cradling her face between his hands. He held her gaze with his. "You don't want to talk anymore right now."

She slapped at his hands. "You really think that's going to work?"

"It's worth a shot." He took a step back, but he still held her. "How about, I'm really tired and I don't want to talk anymore."

"Okay," Selena agreed. Some of the tenseness left her, but an emotion he read as honest affection remained. For him? She said, "I need to let Aunt Catie and Siri know about—"

"Haven and the strig can fill them in."

"I don't suppose I should go back to the reception looking like this. Unless you'd like to meet my relatives."

"No."

"Fine. You want to go back to my place?"

He thought of her warm bed and her soft breasts and her affection. Sex with affection sounded nice. Later. He needed fierceness first.

"I know what you need," Selena said. "I want to fuck your brains out, too."

They were so very alike. Soul mates, like her aunt and Lawrence had explained in one of the conversations he'd overheard. He wondered if he should tell Selena that he'd never been far from her side while she was under threat from Rosho. He protected what was his.

"I'd love to stay the night," he told her. "But I won't stay longer than that," he warned. Why did she keep smiling at him? "I'm not the settling down type."

"I know."

She wasn't buying his lone wolf line anymore, was she? Istvan barely believed it himself. He'd always said he'd never have another relationship, but she was a Roma girl and so strong and beautiful and determined and—

He tried, "You won't want me to stay. I'd get in the way of your trying to sneak around me to continue the revolution."

She put her hands on his shoulders and drew him closer, the superior smile turning seductive. Her gaze was the one burning into his, and it was full of the irresistible promise of sensual delights. His senses reeled. It didn't help that he was already horny from the fight with Rosho. He wanted her, and she knew he wanted her, and she projected her desire for him for all she was worth. Okay, so she'd learned that there were ways a companion could influence a vampire. "Get in the car," he ordered roughly. Selena sent tingling heat through him as she stroked his cheek, then hurried to obey. She was lucky he didn't drag her in the back and have her right now, but his own true love deserved better than that after what she'd been through.

As she settled into the passenger seat, she said, "You really have got to get a different car."

"Yes, dear," he answered meekly. He quirked an eyebrow at her. "I suppose you'll tell me to take out the garbage next."

"Oh, no," she said sweetly. Her lips curved into the most captivating of smiles, and she had the audacity to pat the Enforcer of Enforcers on the arm. "You already do a pretty good job of that on your own."